THE SILENT YIELD

A Novel

Dido G. Kotile

ISBN: 978-1-7347364-5-8 (Paperback)

ISBN: 978-1-7347364-4-1 (E-book)

Library of Congress Control Number: 2025900606

Printed in the United States of America.

The Silent Yield is a work of fiction. All the characters, incidents, organizations, and places portrayed in the novel are either the product of the author's imagination or are used fictitiously. Any resemblance to actual people, living or dead, events or location is entirely coincidental.

Acknowledgements

To my family for their unwavering support and patience. Special thanks to Guyo for reviewing the draft and Lokho for designing the book cover. To my editorial team (Blessing Michael & Fay). Your feedback has made "The Silent Yield" better. I am deeply grateful.

<u>Other Books By Dido G. Kotile</u>

❖ *The Lonely Path,*
❖ *The Unfortunate Event & Other Stories.*

Chapter 1

William Stanley and Jerry Smith, the two top executives of Dare Seed Company, stayed behind late in a luxurious Des Moines office headquarters in Iowa-USA. Everyone had gone home for the day. The last building janitor had just turned off the light in the hallways and headed towards the exit door. The two initiated their small talk, sipping a Colombian brand coffee. Occasionally, they discussed the prospects of the company and individual employees. That Wednesday evening, Dr. John Blake, the scientist based in Monge-Africa, was on their radar.

"What did you find out?" Jerry asked.

William took time before answering. After a pause, he slurped the last drop of coffee in the cup and sat back. Euphoria and pleasant feelings emerged as he finished the first cup and stretched before retaking his seat.

"I think the plan will work. He suspects some mysterious activities by the Monge Seed & Fertilizer Company."

William hesitated and then continued.

"He thought some metamorphosis took place in the seed when released to the outside world."

"What do you mean?"

"Jerry, didn't you get it? He didn't know what we planned with the on-farm project." William emphasized. Jerry kept quiet.

"What's wrong, Jerry? You don't seem excited."

"I was just wondering. Maybe we should pause the advertisement for the new sweetcorn variety for breakfast. I'm not too fond of the strong criticisms we are getting. The media think we have exaggerated the health benefits of this breakfast miracle."

"We dominate the market. The feedback was phenomenal. The taste was addictive. What do you expect?"

"The competitors can still tear us down. We have to be ready."

"Don't worry, everything is under control. The health benefits are the game changer."

Jerry resumed. "I think we are underestimating John's potential. He lived in Africa long enough and might have connections. Don't you remember the CIA report? His dirty little side income we ignored. We can use that against him if things turn out sour."

"Not yet. First, we must ensure that information doesn't get to the media. We have averted the scandal in the past and can keep him under the radar."

"I am glad we settled that scandal out of court. No need to worry unless something else comes up on him."

Jerry reached for his cup and realized that he had emptied it already, allowing a moment of pause as if directing subtle flavors and aromas to the surroundings.

William let a minute pass. "There is something serious we overlooked."

Jerry stooped forward. "What is it?"

"I checked his background. The records of twenty-five years ago when he was in the Peace Corps in Kenya."

He looked at some handwritten notes. "Oh, it may not mean much, but another thing surfaced recently, and I don't like it and don't know whether it was a compliment or a concern."

"What?" Jerry intercepted.

"It may not mean much. The information suggests that John may have participated in some dubious activities during his Peace Corps years. It didn't explain what he did, but his name came up. The local source mentioned an incident at the school where he taught. A scandal or something students got involved in."

"What kind? How did we miss that?"

"Who cares about the foolish things he might have done twenty-five years ago in that part of the forgotten world? He probably smoked Marijuana."

"No way. Are you serious? That's illegal. It's a narcotic case in Kenya, and its use is a criminal offense under the Penal Code, and if convicted, one can be behind bars for 10-20 years," Jerry stressed, making a whistling sound.

"Not like what we have here. A joke, where even with the subsequent offense with a penalty for misdemeanor or felony, one can only get 90 days to three years maximum."

"Hold on. It's not like a crime of murder in the village. If there were anything of major value, we would have known it. Michael, our regional office in Monge, had launched an investigation. John's Peace Corps experience will likely surface, and we don't want this to become an albatross on our back amid genetic upheavals."

"I wonder how we missed that, Stan?"

"Relax, Jerry. How come you know Kenyan law regarding Marijuana?"

"I visited the country as a tourist and learned some dos and don'ts."

William smiled. "The world was different twenty-five years ago. John might have fooled around with native girls and those kinds of things, smoked pots, and did some foolish things. The things young people do when they don't know what to do with their time. What else do we expect him to do in the boring African jungle."

"Is that supposed to be a compliment?" Jerry laughed.

"Remember, Katherine mentioned several things he told her, and we thought she inflated her story."

"She did. Why would John tell her that he coerced his girlfriend into aborting a pregnancy?"

Do you mean they were so close to sharing that kind of information?"

"I think so at that time before she accused him of harassment. His contact with Katherine could be mutual, and I don't think he forced her. Jerry resumed discussions.

"Don't bring that up again. We were through with it. After nine years, it's history now."

"Let's focus on his positive, impeccable records. He might be bluffing, or the girl lured him. Those natives adore Westerners, and one can easily get away with anything."

Jerry jerked his head. He did not expect a comment like that from his boss.

"I am joking, of course," William realized his racist remark.

What do you think of him now?" Jerry switched the topic.

"There was nothing else we had on him besides the dark activities from the CIA report.

"He had a stain. Those little things can break the reputation."

"He's on the watch list for sure." Jerry cocked his head.

"What if they found something new? God forbid. I hope it's not a drug."

William continued. "Hold on." He checked his notes. "Oh, here, something else. Our contact thinks that he has participated in some business. Mineral transactions and those things for personal gain that we knew from the CIA report but not connected with any drug or support for rebel groups."

"No wonder he had frequent trips to the neighboring countries," Jerry said.

"Don't worry. We will conduct another background check before initiating John's transfer to Kenya."

Jerry waited. "Our earlier investigation came up with nothing. A new round of investigation is in progress?"

"Let the process take its course. I won't expect anything significant unless it sheds light on some hard facts or something that gives us a lead.

"I hope we didn't miss anything. And what about the pot-smoking incident?" Jerry jumped in.

William laughed. Jerry turned around with an insinuating gaze.

"You did the same in college, smoked pot, and caused trouble in the 70s."

"How do you know?" Jerry asked.

William kept silent for a while and then replied. "Your eyes gave you away. Ralph Waldo Emerson was right when he said the eyes can speak."

"We all have our dirty secret, I guess," Jerry mumbled. "And you knew this before you hired me?" William nodded. Jerry felt a little embarrassed and tried to get out of it.

"Let's look at the serious issue in our hands now. We both disagreed with John's decision to withdraw the seed we recommended. Things are not going well, and there might be some genetic mix-up. Angry and disappointed farmers are waiting to explode." He cleared his throat and continued. "I won't be worried about the farmers. The Monge government will deal with them." William replied.

Jerry jerked his head and turned to face him. "We no longer have any vital cards we can use when the time is right." He shifted his seating position and leaned back on his rocking chair. William nodded. "We have to discontinue the on-farm experiments. I fear this will bring us down, and I won't allow it. As I said earlier, we must act following expediency."

"What else do we need to know?" Jerry sighed.

"He is secretive and better off there in the African jungle than in the USA. He had a smooth transition and had already put his genius mind to work. We will keep him there in Monge, and when the right time comes, have him coordinate the research project in Kenya as well." William paused. "Regarding the previous incident during the Peace Corps years. Our source reported one thorny issue that our regional office has not yet fully confirmed. All these are speculative, and I don't want to go into it until we have a clear picture." Jerry stared at him.

"How's your trust level with him?"

William rolled his lower lips and crushed his upper teeth as he considered the response. "He set experiments in farmers' fields without our approval and played a humanitarian role. We have enough land in Monge, and he did not need to go that route. Monge has not officially accepted GMO crops, and we were allowed to do experiments in the fields acquired by our company. It would be bad publicity if this information got out. We cannot afford negative publicity about GMOs in the African jungle. It will blow our big plans."

William checked his notes and continued. "With all the information we have gathered on him and still waiting for more, I think we can make him do anything we want. His hands are tied. He cannot afford harmful exposure, and we have this troubling evidence close to our chest." He sipped a glass of water. "Do you remember those women who came forward with allegations after Katherine before he left for Monge? They can tarnish his reputation here in the USA. He will have no chance in the "Me Too" era. We can dig deeper and look for unpleasant episodes during his Peace Corps days, but I think there may be little left to discover after all these years. The investigation has not concluded, and you never know. They might dig up something. We must get this information before assigning him any new research role in the upcoming Kenya project."

Jerry nodded in agreement.

"The current events in Monge with farmers are problematic and can be damning evidence to ignore. Our company's reputation is at stake. He cannot allow contradictions. Bringing public attention to the miracle seed project could backfire and interfere with our collaborations with the government of Monge on the other project." Jerry said.

"Maybe it's a good idea to see how the seed behaves in a wild environment."

"No, this was not necessary. We are there to make money. In any case, you know our secret endeavor. We have to work behind the scenes. Let the local group work for us. No need to worry, although John had plunged us into unnecessary publicity." After a brief pause, he continued. "I have reassigned one of our scientists to verify his work. The local scientist is very loyal and competent. We must know everything John does, including what gene he's transferring and the sources from where the genes came from. Our secret financier will donate millions to make this project work." Jerry's face sparkled. He remembered the philanthropist behind the five-million-dollar project to help the developing world curb its population explosion.

"I have instructed that any sample we received from John undergo further testing here at our Des Moines lab. We have to be proud of our state and give this honor to our Midwest. I have Arjun Raja and Allen Taylor, two brilliant minds who can do a thorough job. And I need to assign one of them to work on gene splicing. Who do you pick?"

"If we need total loyalty, I could pick Raja; besides, he has more to gain by working for us. We can keep renewing his contract, and we can also send him to the field." Jerry suggested.

"I agree," William waited a few seconds and continued. "We must keep the information about this work completely secret, and I think Raja could do it. My hunch is telling me that John has changed and will not budge. After withdrawing the seed from further research, I suggested that he take a break and return to it. He's vacationing in Kenya as we speak." William paused. "It bothers me that he was less interested in visiting the USA and never communicated with his mother. She tells me that her only son sends colorful Safari postcards, one or two at most, and does not even use emails to communicate with her. They were not close. She blamed herself for not disclosing to him about his father, a product of sperm donation. The donor ended up in jail, and she didn't want him to know about that. I know he is a loner, but I worry about the information he holds.

As long as he doesn't publish as we agreed, things will be fine." He concluded.

"For sure, we will keep an eye on him. Our competitors have tried to lure him." Jerry nodded.

"What is the name of John's field assistant?" William asked.

"Tongo. John spoke highly of him. I gathered he could handle his research work with farmers, and John relied on him heavily for the on-farm activities."

"Did our contact talk with him about the problem in the village?"

"Yes, we had a lengthy discussion, and I think he was ambitious. John might have noticed and instructed him to withdraw all the experiments in the farmer's field and confine them to the lab as we earlier wanted."

"With all these people involved, I am afraid this project will get out of hand."

"No, Monge is the best place I could think of using the philanthropist's million-dollar project. We can keep things tight under control in Monge." William shifted his position again.

"Do you believe the story of the gene mix-up or the widely circulated notion about wandering genes, pandemic allergies, weedy corn plants, or even the bizarre notion of mass miscarriages and induced infertility propaganda we heard?"

"We will wait and see. I am getting mixed messages. It's getting late. We can call it off. By the way," He turned around. "The CIA report about the rebel leader and the area is alarming."

"What's his name again? Amos Juju?" Jerry appeared hesitant about the name.

"Amos Jaja, a charismatic, fearless man, bordering a psychopath. They credited him for exceptional organization and tactics. His band of degenerate outlaws had caused havoc in the land, and the Monge army feared them. I am afraid this lunatic might succeed."

"What's your point? Are you suspecting that he might go after our company?"

"Didn't you read his rhetoric? He vowed to rid Monge of all foreigners. Our company is on his target list, so I am concerned about John's involvement in the on-farm experiments." William jerked his head as if he remembered something else. "Are you thinking what I am thinking?" He leaned forward. "What if our seed caused all these problems in the village? At least the allergy. Any other complications cited are still unsubstantiated. The substantial evidence suggests that the chemicals they used earlier might be the fault.

Jerry narrowed his eyes and leaned forward slightly. "As long as we drive the narrative of the gene factor."

"Yes, we do." William jumped in. "Other than the two of us at the headquarters, only Michael at the regional office in Monge and John knew the component of the genes involved.

"Anything else?" William asked.

"I think we need a second opinion on the genetic analysis of the seed. I would suggest our scientists at the headquarters conduct a comprehensive analysis."

William agreed. "We have to be careful, though. We don't want too many hands in the pot. Raja had confirmed the health benefits of the sweetcorn variety for breakfast. We will do a comprehensive analysis later."

William stretched and looked at the clock on the wall. "I am not concerned that things might get out of control. He had perfected the seasonal sweetcorn for breakfast. He tried to contact me about the gene factor in the sweetcorn for breakfast, and I expected a full report. Our focus should be on the field corn variety. Monge Seed and Fertilizer Company had agreed to shield us. With our close ties with General Bukasa, things will be fine for now, but when push comes to shove, we are on our own." He stood up.

"On another note." Jerry switched the topic. "I am more worried about the rebel activities and their maniac leader. From what I heard, he had no mercy left in his heart."

"You're right, after reading all the destruction he caused. There is no good left in him."

"The CIA is watching the insurrections closely. Regardless, I believe General Bukasa will rule Monge forever. There is a plan to bring a peace-keeping force to restore stability, and you know what that means." William winked.

Jerry held onto the edge of the table and tilted forward. "Are you sure they did not implicate this thug in any wrongdoing?"

William continued. "Listen, the journalists love to cover his story. They kept adding juicy stuff to sell their papers. Look at what they wrote in the cover story about him here."

...The sources confirmed that Amos Jaja was sentenced to life imprisonment with hard labor in Kenya prison and staged a heroic escape fifteen years ago. An innocent refugee boy they accused falsely and unjustly imprisoned for a crime he did not commit. He then returned to his country and staged a guerrilla war against the government of Monge. "You see how they glorified him.?"

"Sure. This language bolstered the rebel leader's ego and turned him into a revolutionary hero.

"How can we emulate a terrorist?" William stressed. "We may need to take heed. Please read the report thoroughly; it would help us clarify the pros and cons of our African projects and understand the issue we face."

"Aren't we solid in Monge?" Jerry jerked his head.

William did not respond. He switched off the light and came out of the room. Jerry followed shortly. He then turned. "Yes, we are solid for now, as long as the General is there."

Chapter 2

illiam Stanley hurried and grabbed the receiver's handle and boomed into the distance phone call. "John! John! Do you hear me? What's the progress of the seed in the field?" He said after a long intermission, ostensibly expecting another unavoidable interruption to continue.

"I can't hear you well, John!" William threw up his hands in frustrations, and the phone fell to the floor. He picked up the phone and waited.

The faint voice from Africa faded and flickered on and off, barely audible. Not sure about the reaction he would get, Dr. John Blake came on the line and hallowed to the silent phone. "There is more to this gene than I previously thought." He tried to emphasize.

"It's the gene." John attempted to speak.

"I can't hear you properly." William cursed the poor transmission. The line got disconnected.

He walked back and forth around the kitchen table, expecting John to call. His wife prepared herself a cup of coffee and joined him.

"Is everything okay, honey?"

"No need to worry. It is about miracle seeds. If you only know its potential. I don't want to give it away yet." He squeezed her hand. She glanced with a skeptical smile on her face. William understood that glance from his sweetheart of fifteen years. "Trust me on this, honey." He planted a light kiss on her chick and patted her back. "I am expecting an update from John." William gulped a glass of juice and stretched his hands over his head. The phone buzzed. They looked at each other. He winked at his wife, and Helen sensed an irritation in his facial expressions and understood the efforts he put in.

"Take it easy." She encouraged him and picked up the phone. "It's for you from Michael—the African Regional Office in Monge.

"It's Michael. John had trouble connecting with you earlier and asked me to reach you." Michael apologized for the phone problem.

William signaled silence.

"It's something about the gene, and John will provide the details when the connections become clearer."

He stood transfixed, his slow breath coming out at intervals.

"That's the most I can say over the phone now."

The phone went dead. Mike felt somewhat relieved and did not need to talk about it. He won't even know with certainty what happened and can't trust his voice to deliver it. He clenched his teeth and let the matter rest for now.

Chapter 3

 John mailed a colorful postcard of a wildlife safari in East Africa to his mother. She was an avid collector of postcards. He scribbled a short message, letting her know that he was on his honeymoon vacation. He then noticed his vibrating phone call and quickly picked it up.

"No problem, Lucy, you know I love Kenya and feel comfortable here. I can't wait to see you, darling. Text the itinerary if there is any change in the schedule."

He pushed away any work-related thoughts from his mind for now and shifted his mind to the exotic places where he would like to spend his honeymoon vacation with Lucy, either in Kenya's coastal resort or to the Caribbean, Antigua & Barbuda. His thoughts lingered as he stood and let his mind dream and reflect.

***

"Welcome, babe. How's the trip?"

"Great, just a three-hour flight, and I am still fresh."

He gave her a big kiss and hugged her. With an arm around her waist, they walked to the waiting taxi.

The driver navigated through the maze of Nairobi traffic and got on Kenyatta Avenue, towards Serena Hotel. It was the worst time of the day, and he dreaded the peak hours of traffic jams. With Lucy by his side in the back seat, John sat and basked in the ambiance of her sweet aroma. He could sense Lucy was tense as he held her close.

"This is the part I hate about Nairobi traffic, with all the numerous potholes and crumbling asphalt."

The driver avoided it and swerved slightly left and right.

"The city has neglected and poorly maintained the roads," John murmured.

There was no traffic light to control the movement; instead, traffic police handled the busy lines. John remained amazed that there was hardly any accident with all these monstrous slow motions and maneuvering.

"Relax," he held her tightly. She turned to look at him in disbelief as the reality of Nairobi traffic sank in.

The driver remained calm and turned sharply to avoid an oncoming car. A matatu driver cut in. The conductor, barely a teen, held on to the side sliding door with one hand and howled for passengers. With one hand holding the door frame, he swung back and forth, following the rhythm of loud Lingala music. The taxi screeched to a halt, and Lucy clung to John for a heart-stopping moment. She covered her mouth in shock. It appeared as if time stood still. John wrapped his arm around her waist and cuddled her.

"Did you say something?" He asked.

"No, I was praying." Lucy glanced.

John cracked a smile.

Lucy turned and looked at him. "We were almost dead."

Her blinking eyes sent him a signal, and he quickly apologized.

"We will be fine, honey." He squeezed her. "The first time on the street in Nairobi during rush hour, everyone will feel the same way. At one time, I wanted to walk, but in the end, we will all get used to it."

After a few stretches of zigzag winding road, the traffic cleared. She leaned towards him and whispered.

"Tongo seemed worried. Did you talk with him?"

"Yes, we talked about the allergy outbreak, and he confirmed that many people had typical symptoms, including sneezing with itchy, runny, watery eyes and a blocked nose. Did you hear about this?" John asked.

"Yes, I am surprised the government didn't declare it a pandemic. Instead, they blocked off the area with military barricades, and as usual, we expected them to cover up and pretend nothing happened. The hospital and clinics were filled up and overwhelmed, and no regular allergy medicine was available," she paused.

"The worst-hit area was the village beyond the valley. I grew up there, and my aunt, who brought me up, still lives there. She started sneezing last week. I hope she gets better."

Lucy turned to look John in the eyes.

"Is this caused by the seed you introduced?" Their eyes met and held, and she sensed uncertainty in his gaze but couldn't interpret the message. She looked at him again in the eyes and smiled.

"What is it, Lucy?"

"It's the color of your eyes. It looks like the color of a bird's eye."

John laughed and stroked her cheek.

"It's hazel, and you have brown. This eye color is common in North Africa, the Middle East, Brazil, and people of Spanish heritage."

He leaned and whispered, "I don't think I have any connections from that part of the world."

She tilted her head and leaned on his shoulder. "How did you get it then?"

"I don't know, it's the miracle of the gene, probably one of my ancestors."

She kept quiet for a while and turned.

"Is there anything else about the seed beyond the allergies?"

He wrapped his arm around her waist. "May be, but the allergy always happens. I never thought it would be life-threatening. However, in severe cases, it can cause low blood pressure, breathing trouble, asthma attack, and even death if not treated." He squeezed her hand. "Some people have died according to Tongo's note and the news clip he sent me. The cause of death is not fully confirmed. Tongo thought it was due to allergies. The pollen from the field crops."

Lucy shook her head. "I heard many strange things, too; they believed it was serious. Tongo said the allergy progressed into severe symptoms, including wheezing, coughing, chest tightness, shortness of breath, swollen lips, tongue, and eyes, as well as vomiting and diarrhea. The victims needed an emergency room immediately, and no hospital space was available. She glanced and added. "The area already had some political issues, you know."

"All these upheavals and insurgents had intensified their rebellious activities," John reassured her once again that everything would be fine.

He rubbed her earlobe with a gentle stroke of the tips of his fingers.

"I don't know how it will turn out. Many unknown factors can complicate the situation."

They watched the traffic through the window for a moment and remained silent. Lucy readjusted her position and craned her neck to get a glimpse of a hawker selling fruits to the passing drivers. John whispered to her ears.

"We are here to have fun, don't worry. I will deal with all those issues when I return."

He winked and held her hand in an affectionate clasp.

"We will visit some exciting sites, such as Nairobi National Park, Giraffe Center, Kenya National Museum, Bomas of Kenya, Uhuru Garden, and many other places in Nairobi within the next two days before we fly to Mombasa."

They drove by Nairobi National Museum, "Look at the sign; we are close to our hotel, and we can even walk to the Museum and Nairobi Arboretum."

John sensed the amazement in her eyes when they arrived at the hotel. He gave the taxi driver a generous tip and asked him to return the next day at 8:00 am.

At the lavish hotel, Lucy remained mesmerized by the luxury hotel with all the amenities she could imagine, a spa with an indoor pool, sauna, and hot tub. She couldn't decide which one to start with and followed John's recommendations. At twenty-eight, Lucy had a brief taste of adventure in the real world. She grew up in a rural area, brought up by her uncle when her parents died in a car accident.

A divorced woman with two boys, Lucy had accepted her fate. Her friend connected her to get a job at Dare Seed Company. She would tease her that the best thing that ever happened to her was her work at Dare Seed Company, where she met John. At first, he only met with her a few times a week until one of her colleagues nudged her why she wouldn't get married and rebuked her for living in a state of unholy matrimony, spending a life with a person who would never marry her. John understood the African cultural norms, did not rush her, and gave her enough time. She remembered how it all happened and was reluctant to meet someone from a different culture. Lucy started questioning her role and wanted to end the relationship. However, as she got to know John, Lucy accepted and returned his love. John picked up the cue and told her to take a two-week vacation with him and visit Kenya. She suspected he might have some special announcement to make.

They spent the rest of the evening at the hotel and had dinner. It was the moment John had been waiting for, and while his initial introduction to her was a coincidence, he looked forward to this day. He felt like a different person after she joined his team at work. His colleagues even tried to trap him and lure him into a match-making connection.

After he met Lucy, John's worldly perspectives and family life began to make sense. Something in him got ignited. He observed her work ethic. She's efficient, organized, reliable, and trustworthy. She handled a difficult situation with a calm attitude and consistency, a perfect match for all he needed in a woman.

***

The next day, after breakfast, the taxi driver arrived on time and took them to various sites. They had to tread through the hassle of traffic again. Lucy took it with stride and optimism. Her excitement and laughter had already rubbed off and became contiguous. As he promised, John showed her some shopping areas in Nairobi. They started at Masai Market and visited Kariokor, Gikomba, and Majengo. Lucy was overwhelmed and mesmerized by rich cultural artifacts, handcrafts, trinkets, Kiondos-woven carryall colorful bags, various artworks, and wooden carvings. At the Gikomba market, John impressed her with his Swahili and bargaining skills, and he got better deals. A street seller accosted them to try roasted maize sprinkled with salt, chili, and lime. Lucy looked at John. "Do you want to try?" She nodded.

"You would love the taste; yummy!" John commented. With a full mouth, Lucy could only nod in agreement. "Do you roast them in the US?"

John smiled. "No, we don't roast like you do here. We do eat corn on the cob. We can boil and eat a specific variety of sweetcorn during breakfast."

He gave her a side glance and continued.

"We eat fresh, frozen, or canned sweetcorn, and field corn is mainly for corn meal or livestock feed. Let's return to the taxi, check other markets, and then head back to the hotel to rest. We still have three hours before dinner."

They arrived at Mawimbi Seafood Restaurant and got seated for dinner. John read the menu: grilled salmon, cooked to perfection, plated on top of a bed of wok sautéed veggies, sprinkled with orange zest and salt, and glazed with succulent sweet and sour sauce. He immediately placed an order for two.

The blurred image of the dish heightened their appetite. Soft music played as a band performed in the background while they ate. The air was pleasantly temperate, with a cool breeze drifting through. From the window, they could see stars peeking through the scattered clouds on the horizon, beckoning in the night. They were mesmerized by the deep blue shade of the sky's nocturnal embrace.

***

John reviewed their to-do list at the hotel, which included everything they needed to do in Nairobi and Mombasa. He then handed it to Lucy.

"Is there anything we need to add to the list?" She looked through and smiled."

That was a long list," she said with admiration. She could only imagine tourists visiting Mombasa and staying at Diani Reef Beach Resort and Spa.

"I don't have anything to add." She paused and then said. "Tomorrow is Sunday, and we have All Saints

Cathedral nearby." John hesitated; he did not expect this diversion.

"No problem. It's your trip, and we can be flexible. After that, we will go to the shopping mall and the bank. We will open a joint account and continue our other activities on the to-do list."

He kept quiet, placed his hand over her shoulder, touched her soothingly, and caressed her neck gently.

By the way," he turned around to face her. She looked up. As he held her closer, their eyes locked and lingered. "I think it's time."

He knelt and asked for her hand in marriage, "Lucy, will you marry me?"

He pulled out a ring he got earlier before she arrived from his pocket and handed it to her. This sudden, unexpected event jolted her. Word failed to come out. She got a little choked on her words and responded softly with teary eyes. He lifted her tiny size 110 pounds in the heat of the joyous moment. Like the cover of the night, a moment of silence eclipsed and engulfed them. John noticed his phone's vibration and ignored it.

"What is it?" Lucy cooed in a soft, melodic voice.

"It was from Tongo. I will get back to him later."

"Do you trust Tongo with your data? I heard that you don't like to share information."

John beamed. "It depends. Trust is a slippery word in my work and can be deadly in the wrong hands. I used encrypted code and was not worried." He patted her hair with a gentle, affectionate gesture.

"I appreciate his dedication and can trust him to some extent. Sometimes, he wanted to know more than he needed. I don't know whether this was cultural, but I noticed that most people here like to ask personal questions."

"Is what I heard about the gene true?" he didn't respond immediately; instead, he gently stroked her cheek.

"Most probably not. Are you taking me back to work again?"

Her face broke into a grin. "You're right. I was curious. You didn't even ask about what I had in mind."

"I thought it was the same thing people have talked about in the village. We kept hearing scary stories about what the seed caused, right? All that and many more spooky things."

John came closer to her. She held onto his arm. It's strange how our world revolves around our daily activities. What else is there to talk about? Besides, this is what everyone was expecting. He held her hand and massaged her palm.

"It's okay. I am fine talking about work. You can ask me anything."

"What's that noise?" She strained her neck to see. "It's

Hadada ibis, one of the noisiest birds in the city. It's flying by and very common around here."

"That was noisy."

"Anyway, back to your question about the seed. There is little I could share at this point, not more than what you already know."

He came closer. "I would call it the wandering gene. When the right time comes, you will know and witness the silent yield." He winked. Lucy looked with a surprised facial expression.

"Relax. Remember, it's our honeymoon vacation. I will have plenty of time to discuss and deal with everything that happened with the seed and the gene factor."

He cupped her mouth with a soft touch before she attempted to speak.

"Let's enjoy ourselves."

Chapter 4

John picked up the telephone and tiptoed to the next room. He didn't want to disturb Lucy, who was asleep, exhausted after the honeymoon trip. John cautiously approached the sofa seat in the living room and sat down.

"Oh, it is you! You sounded different."

"Are you still up?"

"Yeah. We had a late dinner with some community members after we returned from the trip, and I just got back. We had great discussions. A lot of companies are preparing to participate in the upcoming state fair."

John scratched his head. He had been looking for an opportunity to tell Stanley about his concerns about the sweetcorn for breakfast.

"Did you conclude the lab analysis you mentioned?"

"Yes, I did." John took a long pause. "Just before the planting season here in Monge, I ran one more analysis."

"What did you find?"

"Not good. The deletions of Y chromosomes in the cell."

"What do you mean?" John paused to regain his posture.

"I am sure you know Chromosomal abnormalities and gene mutation can cause genetic disorders. It impacts the Y chromosome severely, jeopardizing its important role in sex determination and male fertility. A catastrophe for the health and survival of male species."

"Are you out of your mind? How could this happen?"

John expected this question and had prepared his response.

"Stan, I have no idea. Probably a mix-up." He hesitated. "My suspicion was that the pollen from the ES variety must have been fertilized, which resulted in the following outcome: I did not analyze before we dispatched the seed for multiplication. The lab experiments on rats and chickens feeding on ES seed have all come out as expected and Positive. I have proved this beyond a reasonable doubt. This variety is a miracle we anticipated. I needed one more trial to dispel this rumor about the deadly allergies, as well as the weedy traits and the effect of all these on the XY Chromosomes."

"Did you analyze the same sweetcorn variety that you sent us?"

"Yes, we got negative results. The seed can induce undesirable traits."

Stanley took a while before he responded. His palpating breathing intensified. "You better have an explanation for this."

John kept silent until William repeatedly asked him how such a mistake could happen. What's this undesirable characteristic? Does it have a name?" He snapped.

John took a while and responded. "My experiment was highly confined, and I never shared it as we discussed. However, Monge Seed and Fertilizer company had an experimental site close to our experiment, and I suspect there could be some cross-pollination."

William looked up and wondered where the discussion was leading.

"Is the seed you sent us from the on-farm trial?"

"Yes."

"What!" William cut him short.

"Monge Seed Company had an experimental variety around the area?" William interrupted him again.

"Let's address the issue with what you encountered. I need an answer. You seemed to justify that the seeds acquire undesirable traits. Frankly, you were careless with this part of the experiment by taking it to the farmers' field."

"Stan, as I told you, what happened had happened, and I am investigating. We are collecting samples from all over and will find out."

"Are you suspecting the Monge Seed and Fertilizer Company?"

"I understand they have a new variety similar to ours out. Frankly, I am concerned that when our company got into a secret partnership with Monge Seed and Fertilizer Company, it undermined my work. I felt sidelined, and yet you entrusted me with this project." He kept his voice steady. "I believe someone has misinformed you about the work I do." He added.

William ignored the first part of his comment. "If I take the case as a mix-up. How did it happen? Why didn't you verify before you dispatched the seed to the headquarters?"

John grits his teeth, not wanting to show irritation, but he tries calming down.

"Our final report is still inconclusive," he wrinkled up. "I must say this, though: we won't know the details until we collect samples and complete the analysis. Besides, the variety in question is not in circulation anymore. Monge Seed and Fertilizer Company had withdrawn the seed."

He took a deep breath and concluded. "Our two varieties at Dare Seed Company site were in isolation, separated by barriers of sorghum plants. There was no way that a mix-up could occur."

John continued. "The miracle seed was the best that ever happened. We had abundance and surpluses, and plenty of people needed food." John attempted to say it before William jumped in.

"We are not in that kind of business. Follow the guidelines from the headquarters office. It was clear." William growled.

"Okay, we can halt any further experiments with these seeds."

The phone vibrated, and William's voice rose, tightened, and deafening. John held it away from his ear.

"I am hearing that you have started playing the humanitarian role. Did you donate seeds? What are you up to? Don't you know the kind of publicity this could generate?"

William let out a guttural howl tainted with despise. "Besides," He fumed. "What would people think about our company when they learned that we were experimenting with unproven remedies in the backyard of an African village? Common, John. You should know better than this primitive approach. You had no explanation for what happened. You didn't explain to me what the gene does."

"It suppresses the expression of the Y chromosome." He hesitated and continued when he noticed William's silence. "The reduction of fertility and impact on the health and survival of male species."

William stopped. Rhythmic breathing intensified the extreme agitation of the moment. John could only hear his forceful breathing sound to the point of pulsating fury. John waited. He took a deep breath and added. "The gene could alter the way we think about population. It could make people impotent."

Stanley choked. A grimace of disappointment crossed his face. He broke into hysterical laughter tainted with a vengeance, "Don't be silly. Cause impotence? What do you mean?

"It destroys the Y chromosome in the sex cells. The end of male species." He emphasized.

"Are you sure of what you are saying? God knows how many people have already fed on this product. A recall is impossible. Our company is doomed if anybody mentions this." He slumped the phone down and quickly picked it up. "We need to meet somewhere together alone.

Keep your mouth shut for good, and consider this discussion never happened."

"Somebody somewhere would find out, Stan. It is in the gene, and anybody can do testing." John said rather meekly.

"Nobody would find out unless you opened your mouth. We will exhaust this product in the market and stop further production. Only you and Raja at the headquarters should know right now. We need to keep it that way."

"I think you're forgetting the issue we discussed here in Monge. What about all those people? They experienced and knew what had happened. They were eager for solutions."

William exploded. "You inserted the gene. What do you expect? I don't buy the idea of mixed-up. Could it be something inherent in the gene?"

"It's possible. My emphasis was on the health benefits. Any unintended consequences could happen during gene editing, including losing other traits."

The phone conversation went silent.

John had nothing to add. He realized the angry tone and didn't want to prolong the discussions, but William kept talking. The hoarse tone of his voice, characterized by an acrimonious, angry overtone, made him remain silent. "Are you sure about this?"

"Yes."

"In that case, we have to destroy this gene. We cannot face our Western customers with this news." Stanley repeated.

"We are still at the experimental stage and will need more time to understand how the gene behaves."

John tried to come up with a reasonable answer. "There is a possibility that the news we got from the remote part of the villages could be the impact of the chemicals they used earlier. I have heard strange stories about deformed plants in the area, and some of them were sent to our lab in Monge for analysis. I am not overruling the possibility of a mix-up, and I need to confirm the analysis of the seeds from Monge Seed and Fertilizer Company."

I need answers. I can't believe you're taking this devastating impact so lightly! All our customers, including my family used the product for breakfast daily. This is an act of sabotage.! Has the dark African jungle turned you into a moron? Why didn't you tell me before this all happened?"

There was no answer. John was probably shocked to hear this vulgarity and William's vicious anger. He knew the released gene would be challenging to recall, and the gene was already loose in the wild, and there was nothing anyone could do to bring it back to the laboratory or the field. He bit his lips and wondered whether William was fully informed about the decaying political situation in Monge.

John cleared his throat. "Yes, I can destroy this variety, and there will be no more seed from it, but…"

"What?" William roared.

"There is a problem. We've lost control. The genie is out of the bottle as we speak."

William sighed. "John, are you admitting that all these problems we were hearing came from this seed? The allergies, the complications of pregnancies, and all the multitudes of various catastrophic events they rumored?"

"We don't have any evidence of those tied to the seed. I am afraid there is no way of assessing the extent of the damage or the presence of the gene in the environment. It might have spread fast." John hinted.

William took a deep breath.

"There is only one way. We must destroy all the corn plants in the country."

"What, Stan. That's impossible and an unrealistic approach. You don't want that to happen. We are already worried about the loss of the exotic variety. You know the hybrid has already replaced them. There is no trace of exotic varieties in the country anymore; destroying all their native plants would be the last thing we can think of. It's a genetic genocide."

"So be it. The plan is already in progress. It's a done deal, Monge government is on our side. We can reassure the country, provide them with food, and take over the supply chain. We can curve off this region and use it exclusively for seed multiplication to supply the whole world. Our plan had to shift."

***

John laughed aloud.

William's mind raced ahead. A triumphant smile appeared on his face. It became clear. He had a perfect solution for the world's pathetic overpopulation problem. "We can turn this adversity into a golden opportunity. The third world will need this miracle. The uncertainty of the scientific world had given us a gift on a silver platter."

"Ya, but..."

"What's wrong?" He cut him in. "You don't sound optimistic?" William pressed.

"I do. I have seen that potential already." John sounded apologetic.

"I realized what it does and wanted to stop it. My moral obligation wouldn't let me continue the experiment—especially with its ferocious attack attributes and suppression of reproductive cells. As for the popular sweetcorn, we can't take it off the market. We've proven its nutritional value, health benefits, and success with diabetes patients. How can we deny people this easy cure?"

John called twice. After a long silence, he continued, "Stan, this variety has incredible benefits—you know that. What are you going to tell the board and investors?"

The phone remained silent before William came on the line. His voice was sharp. "You'd better watch out and follow protocol, or else." A pause. Then, coldly: "You made a terrible mistake. The seed should have stayed in the lab."

John glanced at the mirror on the wall, catching a glimpse of his exposed teeth. The message was clear. He could only imagine William puckering and twisting as if ready to swallow him whole.

"We have to meet face to face and talk about this. I will come to Monge." William announced and hung up.

John attempted to speak to the dead silence of the phone. He wanted to give him more information.

The level of resentment towards the presence of foreign companies in the country had reached an all-time high, and the ruling clique of the government could no longer hold the center.

The underground movement had gained the upper hand in some areas of the country and successfully portrayed Dare Seed Company as a vermin and fountain of global greed.

Chapter 5

amuel Barasa, a research scientist at Dare Seed Company, entered the rectangular-shaped greenhouse building through the rear door. He turned when he heard a musical sound coming from John's experiment section and walked toward the plants in the pots. He looked at the leaves and wrinkled his face. Samuel surveyed the machine at the corner of the room. DNA synthesizers, sequencers, and some other automated devices, as well as equipment used, to engineer microorganisms genetically. Well, anything is possible. He thought. Samuel then walked across the first row of potted plants near the entrance and abruptly stopped when he saw a cage at the end of the row in the corner. In the next row, he noticed some tropical plants, including bananas, the leaves of which obstructed his views as he tried to confirm the source of the humming sound. Tongo came down the steps of the ladder with a hose in hand. Samuel stepped back and looked up.

"Dr. Blake instructed me not to let anybody get closer to the cage. They get scared easily."

"What?" Samuel looked at him, still not fully recovered from what he saw. He focused his attention on the movements in the cages. "What are those creatures doing here?"

Samuel did not hide his repulsive attitude towards Tongo, who played multiple roles. He knew Tongo had a similar attitude towards him and had complained to John. "You know the natives rule the country now, and you don't have to run to John for everything." Samuel used to tout him repeatedly with habitual remarks.

Tongo recalled all his discussions with Samuel over several issues and had contemplated getting even for his uncouth behavior and condescending attitude.

"Rats. Don't you see?" Tongo started watering the plants and pointed towards the farthest side of the row.

"I see them. When did the project start?"

"More than two seasons ago. They fed regularly, and I just gave them their evening meal." Samuel didn't like how Tongo sprinkled the water and tried to move aside.

Samuel looked at the powder in the packet on the bench. "Do they feed on this?" He observed the corn and sorghum grain crushed into powder and the coded label on the envelope. It must be a genetic code. He thought.

"They also take some vitamins." Samuel raised his eyebrows with heightened curiosity and laughed at how Tongo emphasized it.

"Dr. Blake's pets."

"I see, and you believed him."

"Yeah."

"What a...dumbass!!"

Samuel dodged a stream of water, but not fast enough. He rushed and stepped out of the section, soaked and dripping wet from top to bottom. Tongo laughed in his head and couldn't wait for another opportunity. He followed him with his eyes until Samuel stalked off the building. Samuel turned and pointed his middle finger at him with a vengeful scowl. He could not return to the office with wet clothes, so he visited his small experimental plot within walking distance of the office's main building, near the buffer zone, and towards the village. He strolled along the beaten path used by laborers from the surrounding areas. This path will lead to the workers' residential area. Most of the company laborers lived in cluster houses not far from the experimental station. Still further, adjacent to these houses, the workers maintained small pockets of farms scattered all over and extended to the edge of the forest. Some of the employees of Dare Seed Company came from these settlements. Some workers also came from nearby villages, using all means of transportation to work. Samuel entered the experimental field of corn.

The partially dry leaves of the weeds crunched under his feet. He tried to unbutton his shirt to allow a breeze of soothing air. He scanned his eyes over the surface of the field. The clods of blocks of the soil already crushed into soft particles after weeding were still visible. He softly strolled along the tread of the tire mark between the rows of plants. A distinctive, earthy odor hit his nostrils pleasantly mixed with breezy vibration. The deep and well-drained soil remained firm and compelling. Each step he took bounced back, crunching sound under his leather boot. He bent and scooped a handful and let it trickle through his fingers with admiration.

***

After observing the plants for a few minutes, Samuel returned to the office before it got too dark. The open air and the sun had dried his clothes. He took slow steps, walked along the demarcated fence and slowed down when he reached the millet field at the corner of the buffer zone near the junction of the pathways and stopped. He came to an open space where they erected a pit latrine and benches. The farm laborers used the space frequently. They assembled in this open space during their short breaks to socialize and smoke. Samuel needed to use the toilet. After a few minutes, he heard people talking and recognized the voices of Joseph and Tongo coming from the direction of the office building. He waited in the toilet. Joseph and Tongo came closer to the open space and stopped. Samuel listened. He could hear everything they said.

"Any progress?" Joseph asked.

"I could not break the code. The access required a finger touch screen and facial recognition. I will figure something out, though."

Joseph lit a cigar, puffed, and slowly let a stream of smoke into the air. He passed it on to Tongo. Their silent smoking session lasted a few minutes without interruptions. They took turns. "What do you think about the news in the village?" Tongo took a long puff at the cigar and began his narrative. "I know what you might be thinking. We never planted any seed in the area where they encountered the problems. My uncle's farm was the only farm where we planted the seed. I sneaked in the miracle seeds, and after the harvest, we stored the seeds. Dr. Blake was very particular about how we should handle it and wanted to account for everything. I suspected something in the gene caused all these problems." He puckered his lips in bewilderment.

"I don't get it," Joseph interjected. "Are you sure about the seeds you planted on your uncle's farm?"

"Yes, I told you. Dr. Blake called it the miracle seeds."

"Do you know what the seed does?"

"There is a rumor that it enhances procreation."

"What's this talk about weird experiments with rats? Do you know what genes he inserted into them?"

Tongo shook his head. "No clue. I don't know the composition of the gene. Dr. Blake doesn't share that kind of information.

I know for a fact, though. We did not plant our seeds in those areas where they encountered problems."

"Do we know where the farmers got the seeds?" Joseph realized the futility of his question since Monge Fertilizer and Seed Company was the country's sole supplier of seeds and fertilizers.

"Some farmers saved their seeds, you know," Tongo hinted.

"As for the rat experiments." Tongo continued. "Those rats looked scary. They exhibited strange phenomena with extreme fecundity and aggressiveness. I have been observing them closely. Some had opposite traits and were almost extinct with no offspring."

Tongo stretched his hand, checked the time, and then added. "As I visited farmers, I got their feedback and heard their concerns. They believed it was during that season that they noticed some strange deformation around the village.

They blamed the effect of the donated pesticides that caused the damage from the previous season."

"Common, Tongo, this story kept coming back, and life had remained the same in the village. Oh, I forgot to ask. Did your uncle distribute the same seed to other farmers?"

"As a seed distributor in the area. I think he did." There was silence for a while, and then Tongo said. "I will visit several farms this week and collect some more samples Dr Blake wanted."

Joseph clenched his fists and jammed them into the side of his khaki pants, "you said the farmers were happy with the abundance they received and applied fewer chemicals. I wonder what caused the issue.

We have all these conflicting views that don't make sense, and how can we explain?" Joseph paused.

"I don't know, and it's real," Tongo nodded. "I think there were two distinct seeds in the experimental plot."

Tongo realized the frustrations and tried to divert his attention. "You scientists are strange people, and I am sure you can solve the problems you created."

"You're right, Tongo. I was frustrated with how things were turning; the puzzle was one step ahead at each turn. "Wait." He held his breath. "Is there something we didn't know about this seed?" He continued before Tongo had time to respond.

"We need more information; I am sure Dr. Blake used different codes for all the seeds. Who planted them?"

"Other than the farm manager, Dr. Blake was the only one with access to the original seed stored in the cold room.

He does not allow anybody else to plant his experimental seeds." He then added. "Michael probably has access, too."

"By the way, I heard they have decided to discontinue the seed multiplication of the sweet corn variety. The instructions came from the big boss, William Stanley. Something terrible must have happened."

"Yeah, I heard it." Joseph glanced at his scribbled note. "They are tight-lipped, though. I heard that Dr. Blake made a blunder. They might fire him. If not, they might rethink his role in the Kenyan project they wanted him to lead."

"What?" Tongo choked on his words. "What did he do?"

"He disagreed with the company's plan for Africa. Please don't quote me, though. It's highly classified info."

"Can they fire him for that?"

"No, I think he's too valuable to let go. There was more than a simple disagreement. I suspect it has something to do with the gene. When you manipulate and edit the gene, anything is possible."

"I don't get it. Is that possible?"

"Sure, you can insert the gene you desire to have, turn it off, or delete the one you don't want. There is a possibility that he might have done some of those things. They believed that's what happened exactly, and those changes can alter the functions of a gene."

"I also heard that the company has a secretive plan for Africa?"

"They were some boot lickers promoting everything about the West and destroying the indigenous knowledge that we have, and they don't see anything good in Africa. The sad part is that some of our scientists and leaders were to blame. They can do anything to gain a material world and sell their own country."

"Dr. Blake has a good heart and cares about the people and their wellbeing."

"That's why he got into trouble with our company. I heard he was opposed to the idea of the African population project. They have all kinds of bizarre ideas for how to reduce the population.

"Our number is a great asset. We have a lot of young people, and they need jobs."

Joseph smiled," how many kids do you have?"

"Six. Four boys and two girls." Tongo proudly announced.

"The West is pouring money into the family planning campaign. They will tie any portion of aid or donation we receive from the West on condition that we implement a family planning program in Monge. You knew about the debacle of the program they introduced."

"I won't blame them. Our greedy politicians facilitated it. They didn't care about exploiting our natural resources as long as they benefited." He turned. "I am hopeful, though, the miracle seed might change the future outlook of our food system."

"Dr. Blake's miracle seed?"

Joseph wrinkled his face. "It's not like what you think, but they can always send experts to the field to assess it, and another team will work on the genetic lines of the variety." Eager to share more, Joseph continued. I wouldn't be surprised if they created one for use in Africa and other developing countries."

"What difference does it make anyway?"

Joseph hesitated. "Tongo, I think you're not so naive. We don't know the components of the gene yet, nor do we know what it does when consumed. As usual, the farmers get the short end of the stick."

Tongo's worrisome expression prompted Joseph to stop.

"Maybe we should switch the topic. Is there anything else?" He asked.

Tongo cleared his throat. "The other news in the village doesn't look good. The insurgents have intensified their efforts."

Joseph nodded. "The loathsome rebel leader." He mumbled under his breath.

Tongo kept quiet.

"It's getting late," Joseph put out the cigar. The evening had gathered a blanket of cloudy dust and covered the rays of the setting sun, spreading its feeble arm across the horizon. A few pigeons and some birds flew over to secure roosting spots among the dense thickets and tree canopies. The two parted. Joseph returned to the office, and Tongo followed the path leading to the village. He brooded over his discussions with Joseph and previous conversations with John over the phone.

The sticky issue with the farms beyond the valley dwelled in his mind. He tried to connect the information he gathered from his uncle and the farmers in the area. It appeared his uncle sold seeds for sure, and Tongo may have to track and trace the farmers who bought from him at the source. Why would his uncle become so much into this seed? He continued with this thought process. There was no negative issue with the same seed he planted at his uncle's farm. He applied the same chemical and had no reason to think it caused any problem. As he revisited the catastrophic news from the village, he could not think of any possible solution. Whatever the villagers believed about the chemicals Dare Seed Company used and the purported disaster it caused had remained a mystery. The village enjoyed the abundance for a long time until the news of miscarriages and stillbirth hit them and triggered panic. Not only did this shake the entire region, but the anxiety and worry it generated had reached an all-time high. Everyone was on the edge. In the midst of all this was the mystery gene. It's whereabout and the source.

***

It was more than 15 minutes since Samuel huddled on the toilet and listened. He stood on the toilet seat and peeped through the small opening between the roof and the wooden frame attached to the shelter. No one was visible around the area and on the path leading to the offices and village. He still had to recover from the shock and became more confused about the controversial seed and the secret activities of his colleagues he eavesdropped on. Field of ES seed? They were up to something big. He murmured and shrugged off the memory and wondered. What secrets of the gene did John hold in the lab?

On the way back to his office, he met field workers. Some returned the equipment from the experimental plots nearby and prepared to go home.

The shade of dawn had set in, and most of his colleagues had gone home for the day. Samuel joined the pedestrians along the way to the residential apartment where he lived. He had a small radio he always carried, listened to, turned on, and heard the news. Samuel hastened briskly, held the radio close to his ears, and cursed under his breath, dreading the momentum. The tumultuous uproar and unrest in the eastern part of Monge had plunged the country into civil wars for as long as he could remember. The rebellious activities did not bother him until recently when his colleague showed a leaflet distributed in the village. The predominant tribes in this region sympathized with the rebel leader Amos Jaja. Samuel hastened his walking steps.

Unease overtook his body. The pounding of his heart intensified and echoed with the rhythm of the evening news. He turned the volume down as he approached the apartment. A gripping shiver sipped through his nerves. He knew how tribal affiliations and sentiments could play out. The sad, dark taint of tribal killings and genocide was still fresh in the news in this part of Africa. He looked back and slowed down before he reached the gate. He showed his ID and entered through the entrance guarded by two guards armed with a knife, machete, and throwing clubs. Samuel stopped as he reached for the door to his three-bedroom apartment.

He felt it was time. He had to arrange with his wife to take his two daughters back to his hometown in the Western part of Monge, where he had a farm.

He shuddered as he recalled the insurgent incident in his mind in detail. He could handle the mystery behind the seed in the troubled village but not the pending civil unrest.

Chapter 6

ngrossed by a hunch, Dr. Blake pushed aside the worrisome thoughts. The fear of what would happen if they implemented the plan seized him. He sensed a sign of disappointment from William Stanley on the project's slow process. Still, John had made it clear and determined to promote the spread of miracle seeds and eliminate hunger in the developing world. However, conflicting thoughts occupied his mind as he stretched his curiosity further. A few additional troubling traits of the seed unsettled him. But it was too late to call off the project. William had used it as a decoy to lure multimillion-dollar donors into financing it

He understood the plan of initiating the variety that could serve multiple purposes. It required well-balanced nutrients and ingredients that enhanced virility. John had isolated some undesirable genes and aligned them with market demand for food production.

He took the utmost pride in his work and envisioned how the product would serve as a nutritious breakfast for the whole world in the form of cereal or pharmaceutical products. John stopped in his thoughts, contemplating the hidden meaning behind Tongo's messages, and nodded with satisfaction. He looked at his watch and realized the time was getting late. He had to check the rat experiment for disposal before he closed for the day. The lights in the main building were off, as most workers had gone home.

***

Tongo packed some items in the gunny bags and loaded them onto his Land Cruiser. He checked the car's readiness for a farm visit early in the morning. He then drove to the lab section of the science building and parked. The parking lot was empty, except for John's car. He strolled along the corridor and passed by John's office. He peeped through the opened door and knew John was probably in the greenhouse or recording data from the observations of the rats. As he was walking to the rat cage, his mind wondered about the mystery of the rat experiment. No matter how much John tried to disguise the activities of these experiments, as a curious observer, Tongo might have noticed how so many infant pups multiplied faster than the cage could hold. John sped up his strategy and disposed of the rats after he collected his data. He always did it when nobody was in the lab.

He had to terminate them after the study with less pain and suffering. John used the techniques of suffocation in cages with carbon dioxide when everyone was gone for the day. He dawdled and delayed his schedule that day until he was about to leave. He thought he had the lab to himself that evening and forgot to lock the door when he did the day's last part of the activity.

Tongo entered the lab when John was conducting the termination.

"What are you doing?" He stepped back and asked with a surprising gesture of excitement. This abrupt intrusion surprised John, who was not expecting Tongo.

"Oh. Disposing of the rats we no longer need; I could only do it this way."

"You don't release them to the wild?"

"No, Tongo, the idea would make sense, but the population would get out of control." John thought he had said more than he should and kept quiet, hoping Tongo would not get the message about the nature of the experiment.

"I have an idea," Tongo suggested.

John hesitated, not sure where that question would lead to.

"Have you ever eaten rodent's meat?" You know, some people would consider it a delicacy." John knew people eat all kinds of things in the village. "I would like to try it if it's safe to eat."

"It's safe to eat. We fed the rats the same corn seeds humans could eat and did not use any detrimental chemicals on the seeds, even if we gave the rats out to those who wanted to use the meat.

Are you serious?"

"Yes."

"The villagers would love the meat." Just imagine the nutritious value that people would get. If you don't have any use for them, let me take them?" I will leave for the village early tomorrow morning, and they will still be fresh to use."

John softened up and thought. If he can help improve the diet and nutrition of the villagers, he won't mind the ethical dilemma. As a scientist, John considered those rats subjects, and it would be unethical to do anything other than what the experiment intended.

"I will normally dispose of them after two-week intervals. You can come around and pick them up if you want." Tongo smiled and beamed with a joyful gait.

Hesitant to break his scientific, ethical rule, John became curious as his experimental mind leaped ahead. He could get unintended data and learn about its impact on humans. His face flashed with a glow and rippled into a soft half-smile. He instantly stretched and raised his hands.

"Tongo, the meat will not be enough for all the people in the village. By the way, which village do you have in mind."

"I have a rapport and strong connection with the village beyond the valley where we had the incident."

"Great! That was where you had your uncle's farm?"

"Yes, he owns ten acres of farm, and Monge Seed and Fertilizer Company used his farm for seed multiplications. They planted some different varieties there like the on-farm experimentation."

John stared at him, holding his breath.

"You didn't share this information with me before."

Tongo fidgeted." Monge Seed and fertilizer company people didn't allow a visit to their experimental sites." He paused. "I will figure something out when I go to the village tomorrow. I have somebody who can sneak me in." John kept quiet for a while, thinking about how much he didn't know about Tongo.

It never occurred to John that Tongo could keep a secret from him, although most native folks kept local issues from foreigners.

John understood how the mistrust and secrecy of the nature of this experiment clouded his decisions to focus and probably robbed him of his natural empathy. Instead, he sunk into apathy after failing to grasp the uncertainty of the situation he was dealing with.

"Tongo, let's talk after you return from the farm visit." He looked him in the eye. "Do you need anything?" With that, John wished him a safe trip.

After a fifty-minute drive from the Dare Seed Company's experimental site, Tongo asked his driver to take a small dusty gravel road towards the village beyond the valley. The dust poured in as the Landcruiser's shock absorber and suspension springs clunked, hitting the hard bumps, and the wheels pushed dirt forward, creating rays of dust. The vehicle held on, tilling through the rough edges, slowly dashing forward, forcing more dirt into the next bump. The motion threw Tongo up to the roof of the passenger seat and back.

The intense, blazing midday sun had moved from the center of the sky towards the west. When Tongo arrived at his uncle's farm, the sun had rested at a low angle in the sky.

No matter how much he distanced himself from the problem, Tongo found his name dragged into it through his uncle. Word had reached him that his uncle proudly claimed and traded seeds and agricultural materials with farmers beyond the valley and around the neighboring countries. Tongo kept this information to himself. As he traced his involvement in the on-farm trials and his little side venture, Tongo concluded that the seed his uncle traded had some unique potential that he could not explain. He won't know the good and the evil it harbored. He could only rely on what he observed and heard from the farmers who used them.

***

The Saturday market can get crowded. The farmers from all the areas and even those beyond the village of Tongo's uncle arrived early in the morning to capture the buyers' attention. They brought various agricultural products, including corn, manioc, tubers, sorghum, plantain, goats, and chickens, loaded on donkeys, donkey carts, and sometimes lorries. Tongo knew the best time to arrive. Just before lunchtime, the hassle of buying and selling and the commotion of bargaining for better deals slowed. He mingled with farmers and got more information about the ongoing issues.

Tongo passed by the regular vegetables and fruit vendors along the edge of the market. He decided to remain incognito and wore an overcoat and a wide- brimmed hat woven with straw. He stepped aside to let a woman carrying a potato sack on her head. The rows of people along the alley of the market stall slowed him. He stopped and bought a bottle of water. Everyone seemed to ply their transactions, hassling for a better deal. He stood and watched. From where he stood, a corn farmer tried to convince him to buy his sack of corn grains. Several people gathered around this seller, who appeared to entertain them with stories. Tongo edged closer and listened.

"Come and buy the latest miracle seed. Be the first to get it before it's gone."

"How come we didn't know about it?" A curious buyer interjected.

"They kept it a secret for three years. They won't release it yet, though." He looked around as if expecting a disagreement. I heard they might modify it."

"We heard about the village's problem beyond the valley, and no one could tell what happened. Why do we trust what you said." Another bystander chimed in with the discussions. It appeared the back-and-forth exchange of words had escalated into an argument. "There was always an aura of mystery and a grave gloomy situation surrounding this village." An older man said and moved on to the next row of fruit vendors. A mixed vibe about the statement emerged, and someone murmured a familiar sentiment. "The government orchestrated it to punish the village and supporters of the insurgents to discredit the rebel groups." The crowd dispersed, and no one said anything. The government's propaganda machine had painted a picture of a radical opponent of General Bukasa in villagers' minds and justified the military suppression.

Tongo observed at the corner of his eyes while looking over the sack of beans. The seller told him it was on sale for a day. Tongo shook his head and moved on to the next row. He made eye contact with the seller of corn seeds.

"Is it true?" Tongo whispered.

The corn seller ignored the crowd and continued arranging his products until the crowd at his stall thinned out. Tongo picked kernels of corn in the bins and examined them. He then turned his attention to a row of corn on the cob arranged by size. "You didn't answer my question," Tongo repeated.

"You know the answer," the corn seller replied sarcastically.

Tongo looked up. "I didn't know that you recognized me. It's from Monge Seed Company, right?" Tongo asked.

The corn seller remained silent.

"We need to talk." Tongo nodded and stepped aside when he noticed two women approaching. "I will be back before the end of the day."

"You know where to find me." The corn seller continued calling for customers to check out his products. "There is a high demand for the product from an unlikely source. A risky but lucrative business." He whispered. Tongo jerked his head. Two women stopped by and bought a handful of sweet corn. One of them was trying to tell what she had heard about the insurgent groups in the eastern part of the country.

***

Tongo returned to the corn seller later, before the market closed. The buying and selling activities had slowed. He then approached the seller and purchased a couple of ears of corn.

"I thought you didn't need to buy corn." The seller commented.

"I want to see your miracle seed," Tongo replied. "Why did you mislead farmers into believing you have a miracle seed? Where did you get them?"

The corn seller laughed. "I am surprised you didn't know that Monge Seed and Fertilizer Company has everything your company developed. I was not misleading."

"Are you sure?" Tongo pressed.

"I thought you're the same company."

"You know I work for Dare Seed Company. We are not the same. I need a sample package of their seed."

"We only have the sample for a pilot project that Monge Seed and Fertilizer Company gave some lead farmers to try. Here," he pulled out a few cobs of sweetcorn. "You can try this still fresh. He then added, "they will release the hybrid next year. They are testing the market at Kakai Farm Enterprise, their other branch. They would then have some more samples."

"Okay." With that, Tongo parted with the corn seller.

Chapter 7

The close collaborations between Dare Seed Company and General Bukasa had propelled the hatred the rebel groups had for him. Their strong aversion to foreign influence in the country ignited the rebel leader's desire to expel them. The most dominant and vocal group, "Monge Liberation Front led by Amos Jaja," had been in the news. The group staged a formidable resistance and inflicted severe casualties on government forces. Tongo sensed the anxiety everywhere, and people whispered about the impending civil war. The government considered the group as terrorists and has been suppressing the news about their activities in the forest. The government news rarely mentioned the name of the rebel leader, and everyone had their version of the stories about his activities and the terror he had leashed among the people. Some had mixed feelings and perpetuated various levels of understanding about the leader of the insurgent's activities. Tongo had observed the unspoken gestures and secret murmuring in a low tone.

***

Amos Jaja, a fearless and well-built man with broad square-shaped shoulders, stood above average in height and weighed 200 pounds. When you see him from far away, he appears heavy with lean, long, sinewy biceps, creating an impression of deadly stamina. A charismatic leader, Jaja seemed friendly to his loyal rebel groups but ruthless to his opponents. He looked older than his young age of forty, hardened by the rugged environment and the effect of many years of hardships and jail terms. He led the most militant group among the armed military insurgents. Jaja vowed to destroy and disrupt not only the ties between the Dare Seed Company and Monge but also General Bukasa and his family's greed and purported tyranny.

***

Amos Jaja concluded his brief midday meetings with his top counsels and reviewed updates from the small group of exceptional village cadres. His devoted team had exceptional skills for infiltrating the villages and recruiting new members for his fighting force of 5,000 members scattered in the eastern part of the country.

Jaja's obstacle had been other insurgent groups in the area, all fighting to gain control of the country. Each faction fought along tribal lines. He twitched his tensed facial muscles and clenched his fist. The mood around the people with him changed, and unsure of what next move he would make, they waited silently.

Jaja had just received a secret report about the other rebel factions with whom he broke the agreement. While their main goal was to fight General Bukasa's government, the rebel groups fought among each other and disseminated their energy and resources. It was no secret that the government of General Bukasa would like the group to finish each other off and play divisive roles along tribal lines.

Jaja stood up and paced the green camouflage tent, invisibly blending underneath the forest floor canopy. He used three tents, and even his close confidants sometimes did not know in which tent he resided. He concealed his whereabouts, taking all safety precautions. Some of his commanders were ambitious, and he needed to take care. The recent news about the fate of one of the rebel group's second-in-command leaders shook him. The second-in-command leader slaughtered his commander in broad daylight during one of the inner circle meetings.

The brutal reality of the inner power struggle he wanted to avoid became apparent.

Jaja walked back and forth within his tent, which stretched five meters long. His thoughts returned to the strategies he tried to incorporate. The terrain, jungle environment, and psychology of his men's readiness occupied his mind. He puffed on the Cuban cigar in the tradition of Fidel Castro style with an affinity for hand-rolled tobacco leaves.

The "Guerrilla warfare" doctrine by Che Guevara, a renowned Latin American revolutionary leader he admired, inspired him. Jaja underlined some passages in the chapter about the general principles of guerrilla warfare. He read, "It is not necessary to wait until all conditions for making revolution exist; the insurrection can create them." He contemplated how he could topple the government of Monge with all other factions fighting each other.

The conditions will never become conducive. Jaja had to force the situation to his liking. What bothered him most was the divisions and infighting between the rebel groups. Some of them got help and support from neighboring foreign countries. Even the CIA played a role by siding with one faction to cover and protect their interests. Jaja knew each section's tactics. Some had a vested interest and set their goals on securing the mineral-rich area for their benefit and greed.

The perpetual internal fighting that had caused havoc and a deplorable pile of destruction in the region had ruined the land's agricultural potential. Many lives were lost. Many fled, creating a mass exodus. The UN peacekeeping force had to step in, but the carnage of destruction continued to mount even with their presence. The vivid image and the picture of innocent children trapped on the backs of their mothers. People taking whatever they could carry on their backs and heads and fleeing their homes had become part of a daily routine. These innocent people got trapped and caught between the army forces and the rebels. When foreign governments stepped in to help individual factions, the matter got out of hand. Jaja's Monge Liberation Front group detested the alien factions' interference and often fought with them instead of the Monge government's soldiers. His group's goal kept shifting because of the insurgents mushrooming everywhere. Jaja's attempt to bring the groups together failed. Without unity, their effortless venture had diluted the cause of freedom and liberation of the country.

They all wanted to free Monge from the tyranny of a despotic dictator who clung to power for over thirty years. The casualties of the conflict in the area were unsurmountable. Jaja understood the situation; although he was sympathetic to his people's peril, he knew they had few choices. The civilian population had to languish in the overcrowded camps, escape into the jungle, or face the brutal acts of militias. Or, as often with the case of conflicts, the people fleeing their country-of-origin risk further persecution when they return. There was no better option available, and knowing this predicament, some of Jaja's captives surrendered and joined his force.

At his weekly meeting with his commanders, Jaja, who sometimes preferred to use the title of "Comrade," questioned the tactics his group and rebellious groups used and what they should adopt. He absorbed various guerrilla warfare tactics from different sources and wanted to try some of the tested principles.

He tapped the edge of the table with his middle finger. His commanders waited. Their attention on the edge, knowing the order would come soon. He turned to one of his lieutenants, whose assignment was to infiltrate the enemy using the elements of surprise and deception. He clenched his fist and puckered his lips. Sometimes more upset with the other rebel groups. Jaja deplored their relentless self-interest-driven strategy. His call for unity against the dictator evaded him. They focused more on the mineral-rich area of the country and didn't seem to care for the rest of the country. Most rebel groups fought to strengthen their negotiating positions. Jaja exuded confidence after getting a report that working secretly with the local community members had yielded positive outcomes. His small groups of ten to fifteen men with specific goals to achieve had delivered results. The group followed strict rules of engagement and never participated in direct battle with soldiers, and if they had to, only under favorable conditions. Their first goal was to avoid, retreat, and plan carefully, in line with a well-known guerrilla warfare tactic.

The meeting had extended beyond midday. Monge's tropical climate, characterized by high temperatures and humidity, did not deter Jaja from issuing directives and sending a scouting expedition to different parts of the forests. These tactics helped his group blend in and shift their camps. They utilized the elements of unpredictability, even within his group. Only a few people knew when the base could move and where they would go. Jaja used surprises to put off any speculations. The January short dry season had set in, and he had to shift his camp further into the forest. The diverse, dense vegetation, with multiple layers of forest structure, provided the protection the group needed. They camped under the forest canopy, with the tall Maobi trees hovering above with leaves drooping, showing a slight impact of impending drought. Jaja's constant shifting of locations had strained some of his loyal lieutenants who trusted the serenity of the forest. The large tropical trees with locked branches and thick canopies gave a sense of security. From above, they provided extra safety and protection from the prying eyes of the Monge's army helicopters. Their enemy, a low-flying harbinger of death, could not see the underground. The canopies even hindered the penetration of the sunlight from reaching the ground.

Above the canopy, he heard the sounds of the fabulous Great Blue Turacos. Not far in the distance, a massive Hornbill soared overhead with its heavy wings pounding from the high canopy. The calm, still air added an aura of confidence and security Jaja calculated. He always took one step ahead, never trusting even what he could not control. He had to devise a strategy by placing guards at fifty-square-meter intervals from the center of the camp. To overcome the dense forest's limited visibility.

Jaja checked the time. He expected the full report from all sectors during these briefings. He had been waiting for more information about the ongoing activities. He heard so much about the miracle seed. He needed to clarify the conflicting stories about the two villages. One village was blessed with a shower of bounties and prosperity, whereas the other one beyond the valley remained accursed and devastated. He heard life ceased to exist in that village. They blamed it all on the chemicals donated by the European government and sent there by the Monge Department of Agriculture. Jaja was convinced of the cover up propaganda, to divert attention. It was easy to remind the people of the faraway culprits. And yet the real danger was at arm's length.

Jaja had a trusted team of well-trained individuals working undercover to gather information about everything in the villages. The news had reached his ears about Dare Seed Company's future dominant role in food production in his country. There was a talk about the company taking over the country's food production. They had acquired farmland and monopolized seed production. He vowed to prevent this from happening.

Jaja lit his Cuban cigar and puffed to get his buzz. A habit he developed when he contemplated a severe issue. The council of advisers remained alert, waiting for instructions. "I want the miracle seed. Get it." With that, he dismissed the meeting.

Chapter 8

amuel Baraza tiptoed to the lab door and opened it. A question of trust had never crossed his mind as he reflected on his career with the government of Monge and Dare Seed Company.

A doubt of betrayal crept into his mind after the fateful eavesdropping encounter with Tongo and Joseph.

He stepped into his section of the lab and observed the plants closely. They appeared intact. The chemicals he applied did not affect them, and he noticed the absence of the peculiar phenomenon he identified in the field. He turned the plant sample around, looked at it, and wrinkled his forehead, wondering what kind of weedy plant they sent him.

As an expert specialized in plant science, he knew the weedy plant populations could change. Some weed species in the general plant population could survive because of their genetic makeup, which gives them the ability to withstand a chemical attack. He scrutinized the plants again and confirmed his fears as he expected them, unsure whether it was a corn plant or a weedy species.

It bothered him that the farm manager failed to follow his recommendations on the herbicide program. The weedy plant resistance issue was more of a management problem than anything else. He checked the next row of plants for diseases and insects. He then exited the section and headed towards John's part of the experiment. He called to find out whether anybody was there because the door connecting to his research was open. They were usually closed all the time. He entered the enclosure and stood at the edge. With hands akimbo, he surveyed many tiny, potted, robust young corn plants arranged in rows.

Samuel left the lab building and drove to the experimental corn field two miles away, towards the village. He rode a bike and followed the worn-out footpath used by laborers. The narrow path had the mark of exhaustion from continuous daily use by pedestrians. The markings of donkey cartwheels, bicycle wheels, and animal hooves were visible.

A dusty trail followed him. He stopped at the first field, walked across the rows of plants, and checked for any sign of abnormalities. Any symptoms of chemical or insect damage and took notes. He crossed to the field with scattered weedy plants and a clearing in the center. A patch of land was planted with sorghum and millet. The space serves as a buffer delineating the Dare Seed Company's area from the villagers' fields. He walked further into the field's length and took some time to examine weedy plants and insects. The field was spotless except for a few beetles and weedy species at the edge. He took more pictures and noticed the same deformity he analyzed in the farmers' samples. A few steps away, he could see where the farm laborers grew some vegetables. He ignored the small patches of the field and observed the plants in the center, where he noticed several pale-looking plants that looked exactly like the ones he saw at the greenhouse. He recognized it and knew it was a corn plant cross-bred with other cereals. He followed the rows to the end. All of them appeared the same and partially looked like sorghum. He pulled out the label. A letter code ES and a five-digit number that didn't tell him much. He moved to the next row, where the plants appeared different. He recognized it was a corn plant. Initially, but not anymore.

A series of questions raced through his mind, and he wondered what the new variety would look like. Samuel knew about the ongoing discussion within the regional team about the future use of sorghum for its higher protein and lower fat content. Sorghum is also grass known for its allergy. When he saw its bushy appearance and flowers, he didn't know what to call this plant. He scanned the field layout, took notes on the insects, and strolled along the edge of the field to scout for more insects. As he craned his head to get a clear view of the surroundings, he noticed two men waiting where he parked his bike. He approached them and recognized one of the men who worked with Tongo as a field laborer.

Mambo introduced the farmer. "Tell him what you told me earlier. Go ahead, you can tell him everything. His farm is near our experimental plots, and you can see it from here." Mambo pointed to a farm in the distance.

"It has been two years since we went through the deadly allergies." The farmer held two fingers up. "They did not report it in the papers and suppressed it." Samuel raised his eyebrows and knew people tended to exaggerate and flavor their stories.

"I also heard." He lowered his voice. "No babies were born in that village for the last two years." He held two fingers up again.

"Can you elaborate on what you mean?" Samuel looked on in a disbelief gesture.

"Life in that village was never the same after they planted the seed. In contrast, the village on the opposite side had a bountiful harvest. Everyone was happy and content." After a minute of silence, he continued. "What is happiness without crawling babies, a family with no offspring?"

Samuel jerked his head and frowned. His facial muscles bulged with lines of veins. Mambo looked at the farmer.

"I don't know how to explain." The farmer admitted. "In that village beyond the valley, people no longer produce children. The government has reported and blamed the chemicals from previous years.

Samuel remained in a reflective mood. The farmer looked at Samuel and his friend for an answer.

"Many people confirmed it." Mambo turned to the farmer. He hesitated and added.

"Did you say that there was more?"

"Yes. Everything that fed on the seed suffered a similar fate. Their chickens and goats did not produce young ones either. It was like a targeted plague on reproduction. You already know about weedy corn." He stopped. "People don't talk openly about these catastrophic occurrences. Blankets of doom had covered them and touched every living soul in the village. Some had abandoned their farms, and Monge Seed Company bought them."

Samuel acknowledged with a silent nod and promised to look into the matter but had no answer for him. When

Mambo and the farmer left; Samuel returned to the station with more questions on his mind to answer.

He transferred some of his notes and uploaded pictures of the plants he observed before he left his office. He walked down the building corridor towards the exit, where he packed his motorbike. Mambo saw him and waved. He waited until Samuel caught up with him. They walked with some of his colleagues out of the building. It was the end of the day, and everyone rushed to leave for home. Mambo turned and asked. "Did you know there was a problem in the village?"

"I heard those stories."

"I would like to visit those farmers if you could arrange a tour next week. I will have to talk with Dr. Blake as well. He knows more about the variety in question."

"No problem. Is our company involved?"

"I don't want to guess. We are not the only seed company in the market." Samuel preferred to keep his response vague. With unanswered questions, he took a silent approach following the internal memo from the headquarters. It reminded them of the company's policy regarding controversial matters. None of his colleagues wanted to talk about the events in the village. Like Joseph, Samuel came from Monge's western part of the country and spoke a different dialect. However, he made more friends with the local people in the area than with some of his colleagues at work. Only Michael, the regional director, had the authority to release information about the company. In his press release earlier, he denied Dare Seed Company had any role in the problems mentioned in the two villages.

***

On his way home, Samuel stopped by the local amusement center. This was where some of his colleagues and workers played while drenching themselves with all kinds of intoxicants and entertaining themselves. They gathered in groups, listened to the news, and watched soccer games. One group gathered around the TV stand at one corner, routing for their teams. Adjacent to the center were stores and shops with various items on display for sale, including paintings, sculptures, and some souvenirs. The closest town was 20 miles away, and most workers preferred to hang around this community center after work on the weekdays.

As an employee of an international company, Samuel automatically found himself in a unique category of an elite class of professionals. It was no secret that many equally educated people in the country coveted this job. Some were envious of this prestigious role he and his team at Dare Seed Company occupied. While Samuel was confident and qualified to get the job, he lacked the mantle of regional recognition. As he mingled with his friends, he understood his shortfalls regarding local situations. He knew the subtle, unspoken attitudes, and some strange whispers from his native colleagues in social gatherings. People usually talk in their dialects. He learned about the local habits over the years and enjoyed the social gatherings and funny stories. He ignored everything else and realized that people kept to themselves in an inebriated state. He learned to observe them and knew some colleagues who spread tribal sentiments and talked behind his back. Unlike what they believed, he got the job not because he and the president belonged to the same tribe. He did not blame them, though. Everyone knew the disease of nepotism that choked his country and the rest of Africa.

Samuel would never approve of or agree with what General Bukasa did, yet some of his coworkers felt uncomfortable around him. Still, he got used to the air of isolation and unspoken gestures. He noticed the look and the silence when he entered the room. A familiar, passive, fake smile and nods haunted him. Samuel worked with the Department of Agriculture before he got this job. As part of the agreement between the Monge and Dare Seed Company, he would work with the company for two years to gain research experience.

Samuel had a habit of going home on time to see his kids before they slept. He also promised his wife that he would be home after work. That evening, Samuel met many people at the amusement center. He would sometimes delay going home early when meeting his friends. He stood up to leave after thirty minutes and moved toward the exit door. Mambo appeared, panting out of breath. "Doctor!"

Samuel turned, rushed back to the building, and stopped when he recognized Mambo. Mambo motioned his hand to stop.

"The farmer's child." He gasped. "He needs help and can't breathe," Mambo said.

"I can't help, and I am not a medical doctor. You can send him to the clinic. What exactly happened?"

"He had swelling around the mouth, writhing with pain holding his abdomen, and vomited. He fainted several times."

"Did they call the ambulance? Did he swallow something?"

"I don't know. The store owner called the emergency services."

"Then, they have to wait. There is nothing I can do for the child."

Mambo went to the pharmacy store across the street.

Samuel stood and looked after him. The shops and stores were still busy with people hassling for the evening sale. The vegetable hawkers strolled along the street to make the final pitch for the last-minute deal before it got dark. He noticed Mambo hurried past him, jumped on his motorbike, and sped away. Samuel strode across the parking area and slowed down when he got closer to where he parked. And before he mounted his bike, he scanned the surroundings and waited. A billboard banner on the roof of the amusement center fluttered in the vibrating breeze. He pulled up his jacket collar, letting the gentle breeze dry his sweaty face. As he drove home, he switched his mind to a series of events he encountered and wondered what was happening to the plants.

Chapter 9

Back to his lab the next day, Samuel's suspicions escalated when another plant sample came to his attention. He paced between the rows of trays of plants. He picked one sample up and called out loud to the attention of the lab assistant.

"Who brought this sample with incomplete contact information? I won't look at it without a proper identification form." He repeated when he didn't get a response from the lab assistant working in the next stall.

"We cannot help farmers if we don't properly identify the samples. How do we know where it came from?" It was as if he was talking to a dead end. The assistant was out of hearing range and did not answer immediately but responded to him later when he returned.

"There are some samples worse than this. We have observed some strange-looking species that we have never seen before and didn't know where to place them. Even the weeds we struggled to eradicate with heavy chemicals remained strong and defiant. They survived and took a different form. Still worse." The assistant lowered his voice, "Some weird things are happening, and we have no answers. People are talking." Samuel locked glances and stared at him.

"People always talk." He brushed him off.

"There is some truth in it. What do you expect when we see all these deformities and obscure-looking features on the plant? We no longer recognize the corn plant anymore."

Samuel turned.

"Look." The assistant showed the article clippings about the high increase in allergy cases. "You knew what was happening. The sudden surge of allergies caused many people to worry; some ended up in the hospital. They said the emergency rooms were overwhelmed. The doctors have tried all known remedies to combat this deadly outbreak and failed."

He thrust the article towards him. "They blamed Dare Seed Company for the problem."

"Are you serious? How can you buy into this propaganda?" Samuel asked the lab assistant and tried to understand how everything he heard was connected. "By the way," he flipped the paper over. "Don't trust all that you read. The writer of this article inflated the story."

"I know you won't believe me. I am not talking about the old rumor of the donated obsolete pesticide that devastated the village beyond the valley. Something else is happening in that village, and we had to believe those people."

"We do; it's a hoax." Samuel gazed on. "Pass on the next sample," said Samuel. The lab assistant crossed over to the next row of the table, sifted through the piles of trays on the bench, and settled on one particular sample that caught his attention. He picked it up, turned the sample over, and looked at it. It was the same as the previous one he saw. Amazed by its fresh outlook, Samuel asked. "The new arrival?"

"No, an old sample that we missed to identify." The lab assistant worked silently for a while and then asked. "What do you think about the role of Monge Seed Company in all these issues that keep coming up?" Samuel harnessed a period of silence.

"I don't want to speculate, and I would reserve my comments. There are so many players in the system. Our company should have avoided doing certain things, like the on-farm trials. However, I don't think we caused all the problems and everything that went wrong in our country." Samuel appeared agitated, darting his eyes. Other workers were not close to hear what the lab assistant said. In Monge, people avoided issues associated with the president and his family, and mentioning his name could trigger a dreadful fear. The government had a secret network of spies who intermingled in all spheres and sectors of the workforce. People didn't trust each other and were fearful of anything connected to Monge's autocratic ruler. When the lab assistant mentioned Monge Seed Company, Samuel feigned ignorance. "You know there was an investigation pending, and the report was not yet out." He tried to downplay the incident.

"There were all kinds of speculations. They said Tongo planted some seeds and applied some chemicals that caused the problem, which could be true."

"It is still a guesswork, and Tongo himself denied it. Leave it at that. Is there anything else?" Samuel asked.

"About those plants." The assistant pointed to a tray in the corner. "They talk to each other."

Samuel stared at him once, then burst into a peal of laughter. "Wait a minute. Have we come to this level? Did I hear you correctly? I fear you will say they'll walk out of the door next time." He chuckled at his response with a frown.

"Anything is possible, and I know you won't believe it. At first, I didn't believe it until I witnessed it before my eyes."

Samuel stopped what he was doing and glared at him. "What did they say? What language did they speak? When do you people wake up and get real? Stop making things up and believing in this nonsense."

The lab assistant cowered, fearing further criticism, and lowered his voice. "You don't want to hear from my side of the story? I am sure this is not the first time it has come to your attention."

"Yes, many times and all of you pass on the same superstitious tales, and you want me to believe in them? No, I don't want to hear it and refuse to buy into this preposterous hearsay. Take the sample back and fill in the proper forms. Do that so that I can do the analysis." He pushed back the sample already withered to the assistant. "Bring me the next after you have identified all the sources. Also, identify the location and the distance from Dare Seed Company." He then pulled out another sample from the tray. He looked at it, and then his attention got distracted.

Samuel noticed the sample in the second tray appeared as if something was under it that made it move. He ignored it because some beetles and other insects came with the plant samples, and their movement under the leaves made it appear as if it was moving. Samuel scrutinized the specimen received earlier. On his left side was another sample; he could see a movement heaving as if breathing. When picked, the lifeless thing remained motionless. He smiled, thinking about the silly thoughts he had gathered about what he saw. Two plant samples close to each other had some movement, and he confirmed it. They appeared in motion, but nothing was going on when he looked at them. He brushed it off again, thinking that his mind was playing a trick on him. And of course, the silly stories he kept hearing about this ludicrous myth about talking plants had manifested in his mind. Samuel picked up the plant again and put it down. He moved to the next row behind him and looked toward his back.

Stacked in a corner were more trays with different kinds of plants. He sensed a strong feeling as if somebody was watching him. He heard whispers and turned around. A little distance away, a gardener was watering plants, and he could hear the hissing sound and thought it was what he heard as whispers. With his mind now diverted, he continued looking at the plants. Almost all of them looked different but drastically similar in appearance, lush and vibrant with leave firm and exuding freshness, yet the samples were two to three days old. What happened? He asked himself. The collected samples remained alive, still crisp, and supple, with all their features intact. They did not change. He turned around again to look at the plant on his left side. He thought he heard a whispering sound and saw some movement. When he picked up the sample and checked the label and the location from where it came, he stepped back. The sample originated from a small farmer far from the Dare Seed Company's experimental site. The corn he mistook for a sorghum sample appeared fresh and appealing. The leaves looked thick with various colors of the tropical soil. The underside was slightly rusty. He could see the stomata blinking.

The assistant who logged in with the information included a comment from the farmer.

"I know you won't believe this, and I am not insane. My plants whispered. They talked to each other. The head of the millet bent and looked at him." Samuel wrinkled his forehead and closely observed the handwriting, which was difficult to read. He hallowed across to the lab assistant to come. He scrolled through the comments before adding his own "Another bizarre incident." He shook his head and read further from the same farmer. "We fed the hens with the seeds from the same plant. They failed to lay eggs. It seemed as if they decided not to deliver eggs but kept their lives active and continued having fun, and worse of all, the cock still had an appetite and chased them around. It was as if the eggs refused to develop, or the hen did not want to produce."

Samuel placed the tray on the table and asked the lab assistant. "It seems this farmer clearly understood what he was talking about."

"Many farmers have expressed similar sentiments and were not from the village beyond the valley. The problem had spread all over the country. Otherwise, how can we explain this anomaly? Here, you can read what another farmer said and the comments by our lab assistant: "The farmer planted his corn to feed his chicken and goats, and the hens did not lay any eggs. They all failed to produce young ones yet were extremely healthy-looking with stamina and vigor." The note continued with an additional drawing of a skull symbolizing death. The comments indicated that the farmer was worried that he would soon starve if his chicken and goats did not produce young ones and needed meat. Finally, as one of his friends advised, he decided to burn the whole crop. Can you believe that?" The assistant ended his comments.

Samuel had enough and decided to leave the sample for another day. He then turned to face the assistant. "We must have a scientific explanation for all these happenings and investigate thoroughly." The assistant appeared not convinced. "Hey. The whisper you're talking about may be a hissing sound from all the beetles and insects that came with the sample, which is not a mystery."

"How could that happen?" The assistant asked.

Samuel looked up. "I said we will investigate."

"I know you wanted to justify the cause, but this phenomenon had never happened before until Tongo introduced some seeds to the farmers in those areas. There is no way that all the farmers from different locations decided to narrate a similar story."

"That's what we call rumor, and it spreads, gets planted in the mind, and people regurgitate," Samuel replied. "However, we can look into your point regarding some individuals who might have played some roles."

He picked the three-month-old sample again and looked at the data entered. There must be a mix-up of dates. We will never keep the plant that long without analyzing it. In any case, the plants would have dried up. He thought something was wrong, which he could not ignore, and it may no longer be a rumor. The material came from the village beyond the valley, and the problems emanated from two villages connected with John's experiments. Samuel knew coincidence could happen as a scientist, but he didn't have solid proof to back it up. With his mind still bogged down by all the recent activities encountered, he decided to do his investigation and not take things at face value. Samuel singled out the only incident that caused much friction and disagreement with him. He had always questioned the multiple roles Joseph, Tongo, and Fakir played. The mere mention of their names creates a look of pain on his face, and he decides to keep his plan of a farm visit away from them. Samuel knew Tongo's popularity and influence with farmers in the village. He twitched his facial muscles and twisted his lips. Samuel tried to push away the nagging thoughts of revenge and left the issue for another day.

Samuel strolled down the familiar path after work, his mind looping through the same thoughts as always. As an introvert, he cherished these moments of solitude, letting himself drift into deep reflection. He smiled to himself, recalling his discussions with the lab assistant. "The plants whispered," he repeated under his breath. The phrase stirred a distant memory—one of his father's old stories about a con man who tricked farmers when Coca-Cola first arrived in the village. The con man had convinced the villagers that when they burped after drinking Coca-Cola, the medicine hidden within the bubbles would purge disease from their stomachs and cure them. The first crack, fizz, gulp, and the frenzy that followed sent ripples through the village. By word of mouth, the news spread—distorted, embroidered with strange connotations—until it became legend. No one questioned its truth. The villagers rushed to the miracle drink, eager to get healed, unaware they were lining the con man's pockets with their belief.

Samuel thought the whispering plant phenomenon might succumb to the same fate. He knew better than that and wouldn't fall for similar trends of thought and slowly repeated the word until he reached his house. Samuel must find a better explanation for what happened.

Everything he heard was connected and Dare Seed Company or Monge Seed Company could be the source. He could not dismiss all the multiple events and stories he heard from farmers about their concerns. The issue of allergies and weedy maize plants kept coming to his mind, and even last night's incident with a child confirmed that the problem had spread beyond the village. And then there were the whispering plants to which he might have a possible answer. He then paused and smiled. When carbon dioxide escapes through the shrinking stomata of the leaves, it makes a similar sound. He struck his forehead, wondering why he didn't think of that, and almost bought into the crazy idea of superstitious beliefs. Before he turned the door handle to get into his apartment, he stopped and looked around, a habit he had acquired. He didn't want some people to know where he lived.

Samuel entered his house, closed the door, and put down his bag. One of his children ran up to him and held his hand. He looked up with a wide gaze.

"Did you hear the news? The allergy pandemic has hit the town."

"No need to panic. Everything will be fine." He consoled his wife. The news repeated the incidents of farmers beyond the valley and the recent cases of farmers around the vicinity of the Dare Seed Company's experimental fields. The broadcaster carefully calmed the situation by emphasizing that they would expect an allergy during this time of the season with all plants flowering. Samuel turned off the TV and focused on his kids. His mind was not at ease. Later, when the kids slept, he told his wife about his plans to tour the farms in the village beyond the valley. "I will be with a colleague who knows the area." He added when he noticed the worrisome look on her face. The kind of facial expressions and gaze he alone could understand.

"You must take our kids back to our village until things are settled." He concluded.

"Do you have to visit the farms? I don't think it's safe. You said your employer had instructed the employees to reduce farm visits." She lamented.

He nodded. "Some strange things are happening, and I wanted to see it firsthand. Mambo will take me to a farm. They reported that corn plants had become weeds, shrubs, and grasses. We won't take long. Everything will be fine. I have to get firsthand information." He winked and gave her a flirtatious smile with reassurance. In his mind, Samuel needed the information from the village for his other assignment.

Chapter 10

ongo knocked and waited. "Come in, have a seat." Dr. Blake turned around and faced him. "We are getting conflicting news from the two villages. Things don't look good. The headquarters wants answers." Tongo sensed the tension on Dr. Blake's face. "What's the latest news from the ground?"

"The village looks like a ghost. People are evacuating." Tongo then added. "Farmers are selling land at a throwaway price. You will be shocked by who the main buyer was. Our mutual friend and competitor, Monge Seed and Fertilizer Company." John rocked back and forth and raised his head to face him. Tongo sat with eyes raised and jaws dropping, wondering whether the words he used offended him. John's face twitched as he tried not to show concern.

"Interesting. Our mutual friend? Who?" Tongo kept quiet. Having been in Africa for a while, John knew Tongo's reaction could represent respect for a supervisor. Sometimes, people know about each other's habits but acknowledge them silently, using innuendos and nonverbal traits to convey the message. After eight years of working with Tongo, John became more conscious about what Tongo's nonverbal cues might imply. He could pick up what Tongo intended to express when he avoided mentioning the names he revered.

John understood the message behind the words the local people carefully selected. He can recall his personal experience of the hallway whispers and peeping eyes. He noticed numerous times how heads turned wherever he visited Lucy across the building. The talk about his relationship with Lucy reached his ears before he even proposed to marry her.

Fakir and the family of General Bukasa owned most of the shares in the seed and fertilizer company in Monge, and people grumbled about it. Still, everyone kept quiet and didn't question what happened in the area beyond the valley.

"Sorry, sir, I didn't mean to make you uncomfortable when I used the word our mutual friend. It's part of our culture that when a person marries from your tribe, we consider that person an in-law."

"Is Lucy related to Fakir?"

"I should say, a distant relative. Lucy's mom was one of the second cousins of Fakir's aunt. I don't know whether Fakir even knew it. They had a large family scattered all over East Africa, mainly in the coastal areas of Kenya. We are a small community, and most people didn't know Lucy was an orphan."

"I see. Do I need to know more?"

Tongo shook his head.

"Thanks for the heads up. We strayed from the issue. Let me take you back. Do you recall when we planted the first variety in the farmer's field? The variety you called cursed."

"Yes. I remember it very well. The neighbors on both sides of our farm planted beans, following your advice that they should not plant corn near our experiment. All the farmers planted different crops: sorghum, millet, beans, and cassava. There was a high price for millet and beans in the neighboring country, and many farmers rushed to plant those crops to capture the market." He hesitated.

John raised his head. "That would exclude our seed from the purported contamination and problems in faraway villages beyond the valley. Again, the pollen can't cover such a distance and pollinate those plants." John confirmed.

"I agree," Tongo nodded. He paused and added. "We discussed the possibility of Monge Seed and Fertilizer Company's experimental field.

"We need to get a sample of their seeds?" John instructed. "We must disprove the claim that the corn had turned into weeds or grass. We must identify what kind of corn and where the seed originated."

John noticed a doubtful look on Tongo's face.

"Is there a problem?"

"They said the variety is no longer in the market," Tongo confirmed and commented. "You can't find the seed in the store, either. They introduced a new variety during the last four seasons and sold the seeds at a lower price to encourage farmers to try them. They wanted to see how it does in the field." John did not speak for a while and remained in a state of bewilderment. "They are competing seriously with us and have gone a step further ahead." The trajectory trends of John's thought shifted, and he had to tackle two things simultaneously.

"Let's address the first issue regarding the concerns in the village. Is there a new problem other than the earlier one we knew?"

"The same issue. Allergies, congenital disabilities, weedy or grassy corn plants, and possibly chemical pollution."

"Tell me more about the village beyond the valley that we have been hearing about all the time?"

Tongo delayed his response. "They blamed us for the cause of the problems. Your name remained an enigma, but they were happy when you helped and funded a village water project." John glanced.

"If I understood you correctly. The problem persisted in two adjacent villages, and we never planted our seeds in those two areas. Why did they associate my name with the problem?" Tongo noticed the accumulation of anger on John's face and had to avert his gaze to a side peep. "I tried to direct the evil they associated with you to the chemical incident they already knew from the previous episode. The calamities they dreaded manifested within two months. It started after the first season when we planted the first ES variety, and they thought it was the chemical we recommended because of earlier perceptions." Tongo took a breath and continued. "It was easy for me to embrace and acknowledge the existence of the pesticide problem they knew."

"I think that was the problem. We had nothing to do with what happened in the past, and it was not our chemicals that caused the problem. Why do we accept this responsibility? I don't understand."

"I thought you did. Some things were beyond our control." He kept silent for a while and acknowledged. "You're right, and we didn't have any crops there. Someone did, and the government didn't want to hear our version of the truth."

John tightened his facial muscles and nodded. "There was only one truth, which was clear from the beginning. Our variety did not cause this problem. We need to know more about the component of this other variety that you said was pulled out and the composition of its genes. I need to have a sample for analysis. We cannot keep going around the circle. We caused the problem, or the Monge Seed and Fertilizer company did it. I want to prove it."

After a long thought, Tongo cleared his throat.

"As I told you, my uncle has a farm in that village, and I often visited him. He supplied seeds to the farmers in the area and those across the border. Some people thought I was the source, but he got his supplies directly from Monge Seed and Fertilizer Company."

"Your uncle's farm might be the source of the problem."

"I don't think my uncle even knew it. He's been a contract farmer for a long time with Monge Seed and Fertilizer Company."

"I wonder why people thought our seeds caused the problem?"

"The Monge Seed and Fertilizer Company representatives had created a flawed narrative about our involvement with the on-farm trials and implicated our company." He took a pause. "People remained skeptical because of the history of chemical pollution." He continued. "Before you came, the government poured a huge donation of pesticides from Europe into this village. There was a big scandal, and it involved a lot of money. Unfortunately, the thugs behind the event made it look like the government bought pesticides for the farmers. The money went into the wrong pocket." John looked on and allowed him to continue without interruption. "What do you think happened?" Tongo shrugged his shoulders.

"You tell me," John waited.

"The village got an expired pesticide intended for disposal. People have heard all kinds of stories about this episode. Some believed they rerouted it to the coast of Somalia in the Horn of Africa and finally made its way to Monge. You probably won't know the real story behind this pesticide fiasco and have heard various versions of this European pesticide donation.

"That was a terrible violation and inhuman act. You know our company did not use chemicals in the village, and I don't know why such horrendous things were allowed in the first place. What can I do to help them?"

"Maybe we could avoid adding more pain. People are afraid to discuss the pollution scandal because the government covered it up and silenced those who spoke about it." John watched with a melancholy glance.

"It is a crime, Tongo, and the sad reality is that your people are to blame. When I say this, it might seem like I am defending the Europeans who donated pesticides. There is no way of exonerating the heinous crimes the colonizers committed in this country. Still, your agriculture minister, and I assume an educated man, had a choice not to accept the expired pesticides if what I read was true. And no one was held accountable for this crime?"

"No, everything came from the top." Tongo looked around. John understood the local people didn't criticize their leaders and were afraid to express their feelings.

Having lived in Africa, John had learned how to cope with the prevailing vicissitudes and dealt with cultural necessities, as unexpected nuances often needed immediate action. One had to use connections and elders of clans or tribes, and it required small items of gifts to silence and diminish the intensity of the damage. Tongo played a major role in clarifying the issue. He had to do it fast before the whole country caught the fire of rumor.

John concluded that he had to play it low and pretend he didn't know what was happening. He thought over everything that was developing and didn't want to escalate this matter further. At the same time, he would investigate this variety and get to the bottom of it. He will do it in a way that would not draw attention.

Tongo turned and waited for instructions.

"Go back to the village. Here are some questionnaires to guide you. Bring as many samples as possible from the village beyond the valley. Confirm the sources of the seeds. I will arrange another follow-up visit with you." He paused. "First, could you get the seed your uncle sold? Does he still have them?"

Tongo nodded. "I could get that from his store easily."

"Good, let me have them this week." With that, he dismissed him.

Tongo hesitated. "I think some people have decided that your presence in the village will do no good. The irony is that you did more for the local people than anybody has ever done for them. Some people wanted to create trouble and connect it to our seed." John faced him again. Tongo continued. "Some people see our company as a threat. They are jealous and vile and hate anybody who brings even the slightest progress to the village. They wanted to keep people in the dark ages."

"I don't understand. Who are these people?"

"The people in the village beyond the valley. They had a strange analogy." John raised his head.

"I know you won't like this story, mixed with some beliefs in the Old Testament about the east wind that brought destruction."

"I don't get it." John waited.

"They believed that the wind from the valley carried death. Like the story of Moses in Exodus when he summoned the east wind to bring locusts that plagued the Pharaoh of Egypt and helped Moses and his followers to escape the tyranny of Pharaoh's army?" They believed that God brought the east wind to destroy the wicked."

"It's another diversion to distract from the real truth. What else?"

"Last season, they experienced an outbreak of allergies when we planted the crop. Many people had chest tightness, shortness of breath, and cough, with swollen lips, tongue, eyes, faces, tummy pain, and vomiting.

Twenty-six people died due to some complications, and fifty-five ended up in the hospital. It was the worst pandemic outbreak in the country. They strongly believed the wind blew the chemical vapors to their area and caused all those problems."

"I have no doubt it is that kind of season when the wind blows, but that does not make the story true about the wind blowing chemicals 20 kilometers away. It seems far-fetched. John twisted his lips. "What's the real story behind this?" He shook his head.

Many unanswered questions settled in his mind, and he didn't know how to address the new emerging threat. The range of events that happened had distorted his reality of scientific thinking. He downplayed and dismissed what Tongo had said earlier. The latest development made him reassess the whole project. John doubted whether Tongo had told him everything and whether he could trust him entirely in this incident. Some things did not add up.

"We need to collect more information from those villages. First, I would like you to reassure the people in the village beyond the valley that we will help with the investigation. We would look at the issue of chemical pollution and find out what the problem was from their records on public health."

"I am confident the farmers will receive us with an open hand. The elders will treat your case lightly, and the in-laws are honored in this community." Tongo said. John looked up with a doubtful facial expression. Tongo's ways of seeping unrelated bits and pieces of information into the picture did not go well with John's level of patience. "You're now tied to the village by marriage. Lucy's relatives lived in this village."

"One thing at a time, Tongo. I was not at fault, and I didn't expect any favors. We can investigate and correct the errors if there are any." He ignored the ringing phone. "Here is the least we can do. Go ahead and plant our seed."

Tongo acknowledged with a nod. "When people try to find mistakes, they will find them. Monge seed and fertilizer company people are digging dirt on you. This company is our only competitor. They don't want anybody from our company to get involved with the villagers." Tongo paused. " Samuel also visited the village, and his tour didn't go well."

John raised his eyebrows and stood up. He moved the chair back and pressed it down with both hands. The look on his face and the changes in his demeanor signified a stormy response. He ushered Tongo to wait. "Do you have anything else to tell me?"

"I don't know whether I have to bring this up. It's something that happened in the past. It may not mean anything to you now."

"What is it?"

John waited.

"Someone looked into your past and connected you to an incident during your Peace Corps years in Kenya."

John's calm manner and desolate composure prompted Tongo to add. "We can fix the record. I have connections." He studied his facial reactions for a clue that never showed up. He then looked up.

"What incident?"

"They said that you facilitated an abortion."

"No need for that." John raised his arm with an open palm. "You can go."

It took a while for John to normalize these attitudes of diversions and avoidance of confrontations—the habit of going around the points. The act looked awkward to him, but John found it worked. He had compromised his principles in the name of diversity, immersed himself in cultural norms, and toned to political correctness. Now, he had to question what impact he had during the last eight years of his life in Africa. The Monge farmers remained the same, with no improvements in their lives. They live from hand to mouth, and his involvement might even take away whatever little they had over all these years. Their offspring and future generations had yet to mourn the loss of their exotic genes to the wild. They had also not yet reckoned with the continuous exploitation of their natural resources. This exploitation was worsened by the degradation caused by the greedy foreign companies he represented.

John knew the forces beyond his control. He also knew the secret danger of his innovations, and the power that if used with good intentions, can make the world a better place to live. In the wrong hands, a destructive silent force of weapon of mass extermination. He had a tool in his hand if he wanted fame, prestige, and world recognition. He tried to push away the gloomy thoughts creeping into his mind. The built-in guilt he had suppressed and kept dormant was now itching to erupt. John no longer needed to slow his gut-retching feelings.

He sat down with heavy thoughts, clasping his hands behind his head as he reflected on the events.

Tongo's words reverberated: someone was trying to dig into his past and unearth secrets from his Peace Corps years. The times that he hoped would stay buried.

Who would like to know what happened during the Peace Corps years, he fumed with irritation and brushed it off. Tongo's words echoed in his mind again. "Can he fix the record with connections?" He stretched his hand to pick up a phone and then had second thoughts about it.

They won't keep a record of 25 years ago in that small town anyway. He thought the people who knew him were probably dead or retired by now.

Chapter 11

⟨ongo felt proud of his roots in the village beyond the valley, where his grandma lived. The village's history etched a fresh memory in his mind—a picturesque contradiction of the bygone days. His last visit was a year ago when Grandma was still alive. Tongo mainly kept close contact with his uncle, a retired army major, the only older surviving relative. His uncle often refreshed his mind with events in the village and stories during colonial times and vividly portrayed them. He would retell his nostalgic reminiscence from the events he wanted to forget during the Civil War.

The village beyond the valley consists of a small farmers' settlement named after, its geographical location. *The Village Beyond the Valley.* History did not favor this village of 900 people. The government of Monge may consider them an outcast, stubborn-headed, and rebellious group. Other people may also admire them for their courage and determination to fight oppression. They are independent-thinking people who fearlessly fought the colonial regime and now resent the mighty rule of General Bukasa. The inhabitants of this village sympathized with the current rebellious activities against the government of Monge. One might raise eyebrows as to why the problems persisted in this village. Some outspokenly accused the government of creating the issues. They believed that General Bukasa had a hand in everything that happened to them because the rebel leader had a connection to the village.

Tongo spent two days in the village visiting elders. He collected some samples of the seeds, sent them to John with his driver, and remained behind in the area. Most people he talked with had no clue about what caused the problem, and few dismissed it as a propaganda plan to confuse them. Some took advantage of the situation and wanted compensation when they heard rumors that the foreign company would solve the problem. A local insurance agency tried to convince them to purchase farm disaster insurance so that they could sue Dare Seed Company.

The people in the village had mixed feelings about their contradictory views. Some believed that the earlier pesticide pollution caused all their problems. Tongo acknowledged their grievances and played along until the grumbling subsided.

***

In the meantime, John worked late into the night in his lab and ran the genetic analysis of the seed for the third time, getting the same results.

He paced the office corridor back and forth. There must be a mix-up; one thought led to another. It was identical genetic makeup to the seed he created. He was the only one who knew the component of the gene that went into his experiment. He pulled out the results of his earlier analysis from Tongo's sample. The outcome was the same. He had confronted William and Michael about the role of Monge Seed and Fertilizer Company and the secret association with Dare Seed Company.

Where did Monge Seed Company get its seed?

John pondered and then checked his to-do list on his schedule. He planned to visit Kenya for three days, and by the time he returned, Tongo would have all the samples from his uncle that he wanted to run for the comparison.

***

Tongo spent one week cajoling and pampering the villagers with gifts until they settled—the trap of soft bribery that John wanted to avoid.

He then gathered some elders, talked with them separately, and addressed them together in a gathering. He had prepared and rehearsed his speech in the best traditional eloquence of the local community dialect.

"My esteemed elders," Tongo began. "The rainy season is around the corner. It will soon be that time of the year when we all get busy putting back seeds into the ground to generate a new life. I know there was some misunderstanding about the last couple of seasons. Dr. Blake generously sponsored many students in our schools and donated to this village. We know the people who wanted to tarnish his name. They spread rumors and said that the seed that devastated the village came from him. That was false. There were already some problems with the soil due to chemical pollution before he came. I have the report here as a source of evidence. You all recalled the contamination fiasco, probably nine years ago."

A retired military general who served during the colonial era raised his hand. "Those who have lived long knew the affliction and multiple problems since the colonial era. The civil wars still raged unabated, not to mention the strange diseases and a calamity that visited us

99

in recent years." He expressed his utter helplessness with a wave of his hands. "We don't even have a name for this thing. You can see we are all healthy, but the horrors of the unknown have sunk into our hearts. Is it true that the chemical you used in the soil, or the seed destroyed life?" He adjusted his sitting position. The crowd surged in anticipation. The uncertainty intensified with murmurs spreading like a cloud of jitters within the group, creating more unease and anxiety. No one spoke. They looked at each other. The elder who raised his hand continued. "Let me tell you the truth. We feared the loss of the future. Our offspring." The grumbling shifted to one corner in the back row. "We heard this thing could dry up the seeds in the loins." Another elder picked up from where he had left.

"How can we survive as a community if there are no children after us?" He held his hands up in supplication posture and showed a dejected expression. "I have had a long life, but I want my line to continue." Several people nodded. Tongo held up his hand in silence.

"I do understand your concerns. We took the soil samples and waited for the results of the analysis. Dr. Blake had promised to find out what caused the problem. We believe it was not associated with the seed we introduced in a few areas. We did not plant our seeds in this area last season or apply any chemical linked to the problem. Every year, I plant seeds on my uncle's farm and use it as a demonstration for farmers to learn farming techniques. We will invite all of you after the harvest to see for yourselves." Tongo handed an envelope to an elder of the village. "Here, a small gift from Dr. Blake is enclosed in this envelope." He ended the meeting and, before he left, turned around and faced a village elder who pulled him aside and whispered.

"Are you sure about this? Tongo asked in a low tone of voice.

The elder furtively darted his eyes at the departing crowd and edged closer to Tongo. "Yes," he mumbled, and another two elders interrupted before he said anything else. They wanted a private conversation with Tongo.

Tongo stopped and apologized that he had to leave and reassured them that he would be back after two weeks. He then faced the elder who whispered to him. "I need proof, and I will still be around this evening. Meet me at my uncle's farmhouse before sunset."

***

On the way to his uncle's farm, Tongo detoured and surveyed the farms. He noticed a familiar terrain of land plowing in preparation for the rainy season. The topography of vast rolling plains extended as far as eyes could see. Some farmers used oxen plows, and very few used small tractors rented from the large farms in the area. Most farmers lived on a few hectares of land and used hand hoes. The only implement they could afford. He lifted his gaze, rolled the window down, and asked the driver to stop. A speck of weary dust poured in. Tongo came out of the Range Rover. With his hands akimbo, he stared at the pillar of dust that rose and stretched above. It lingered in the atmosphere and created a thin blanket of rays of hues against the faded blue background color of the clear sky. He muffled his face with a handkerchief as the wind blew a trail of dust in his direction.

Several farmers were waiting for him when he arrived at his uncle's farm. He addressed some of their concerns, mostly the same thing they discussed at the meeting. Some had personal and financial issues and needed school fees and financial help. He learned not to promise anything he could not deliver. They didn't know he had little authority to change significant policy-related matters.

A lone figure rose last and approached him but hesitated. He wore an oversized military coat with a hood, dark sunglasses, and a partially covered face. "You got my message," Tongo recognized the voice.

"We want hard evidence. You know, people say all kinds of things." He waited.

"Why can't we sit?" Tongo pointed to a chair.

Tongo cleared his throat. "I didn't even know your name."

"You can call me Farmer Charles. Let's keep it simple that way."

"Do you have anything for me?"

"I will, before planting season."

"You want something in return, I guess."

It took a while for him to respond. "Yes, the seeds of your new variety. The other one."

"Which one?"

"The one you don't want to talk about. The miracle seeds. I have an offer that you won't refuse." He stood up. "I will be back," he said, leaving before Tongo asked a further question. Tongo rushed after him.

He pumped into the watchman. "Which way did he go?"

"Towards the store." His uncle had farm equipment supplies in the store, and a small kiosk was adjacent to the store selling household goods and materials the farmers needed. The crowded store was a center of meetings for farmers to exchange goods and socialize. Tongo held back. The man kept going and disappeared into the milling crowd.

***

The watchman looked down when he saw Tongo.

"Sir, a note for you."

With everything that happened this week, Tongo's mood mellowed as he tried rearranging the various events and unanswered questions that kept propping up in his head. He wondered how the man knew about the variety. What did he know about it? "Let me know if the man returns."

The guard replied with a startled voice. "He said he will return soon."

Tongo spent the night at his uncle's farmhouse, which sat on a sprawling fifty-acre farm. He used the guest room wherever he visited the family-owned farm. The farmhouse included a complex of a family residential house of six self-contained rooms, a guest room, a farm laborers' quarter, rental rooms, and stores. The building towered above the dwarf dwellings of the small-scale subsistence farmers. The residential house looked impressive, with a formidable structure enclosed with barbed wire intertwined with thick bamboo hedges. Tongo surveyed the erected fenced wooden poles at the corner, with one of the poles connected to overhead power lines dotting the neighborhood. Like a sentry on duty, a Red-

Winged blackbird patched on the pole post and looked down.

The setting rays of the fading sun percolated through the fence and created an image of bouncing spotlights. Tongo's mind remained unsettled, with the dry season dwindling and overtaking July. He paced the compound, trying to recall what he knew and what else he didn't know about the variety. A question of a variety mix-up never crossed his mind, and John would not allow it. A watchman approached him.

"Sir. The man is asking for you."

"I am back," the man announced. "I need the seed, and I can pay you well."

"We don't have the seeds for sale. You hinted that you knew how the problem in the village started, and can we address that first?"

The man smiled. "First thing first. At the meeting, everyone believed Dare Seed Company had something to do with what happened." He took a deep breath and asked, "Who planted your seeds?

"Why? I did," Tongo said. Wait a minute. We didn't plant any seed in this village."

"It doesn't matter. You probably had some laborers who planted your seeds elsewhere.

"Yes, but I supervised them. What are you up to?" Tongo wrinkled his face and waited. He hired laborers to plant the seeds and left them unsupervised only during lunchtime when he went out for lunch at his favorite restaurant in the village.

"Okay, get to the point. There are no seeds for sale. What else can I do for you?

The man looked him in the eyes and replied. "Are you sure they planted the right seeds?"

"Get lost, man. Are you out of your mind? We had everything labeled."

The man smiled and quoted an African proverb. Judge not your beauty by the number of people who look at you but rather by the number of people who smile at you. He then added. "Let's wait until harvest time."

He stood up, prepared to leave, and turned. "By the way, " he winked. Someone you know will contact you soon." Tongo looked on. "You'll play it safe," he squinted his eyes and whispered. Watch Monge Seed Company." With that, he left.

Tongo considered what the man said about the seeds during planting. He heard the rumor about seed pirating, but he trusted his workers.

Over the months, Tongo cleverly used his uncle's reputation to weave compelling stories about the seed, ensuring it gained traction. He put all the harvested cobs in a bag, labeled, and guarded. Tongo then bought egg-laying chickens and reared them on the grain. After two weeks of feeding, the miracles blossomed before their eyes. The hens produced healthy, giant eggs, not only one per day but sometimes two. It was not normal, and it never happened. At most, a hen lays one egg, but not every day. They could only attribute this result to the ES corn's miracle seeds.

The news spread beyond the villages and even extended to neighboring countries. The bounty seed appeared unstoppable and destined to eliminate hunger from the region. A sign of relief appeared. The rumor also twisted and stretched the truth, confirming that the miracle seed contained a secret potency of aphrodisiac quality.

While the villagers did not forget the severe, lethal allergies that caused havoc and demise, the news revived the excellent reputation. It left a mystical aura around everything that John was associated with.

The big day came, and Tongo sent a team of his loyal employees and friends to visit each household in the village and invited them to a big feast. He arranged for cooks to prepare fufu, ugali, cornmeal, matoke, cassava, rice pilau, chapati, and all the main East and Central Africa dishes, with chicken and goat meat stew.

The villagers came and enjoyed the feast. Tongo took the opportunity to strengthen the relationship. He proved to them and emphasized that what happened during the previous seasons was not the problem of their seed. He asked the person who took care of the farm to explain what he did in the field, and the villagers were satisfied with his explanations. They concluded and agreed that what happened in the previous seasons and the two villages beyond the valley was the fate of unexplained phenomena and had nothing to do with John or the Dare Seed Company.

John did not attend that gathering. He wanted to give Tongo to own this event and convince his people. Tongo did the assignment excitedly, understood public relations, and encouraged his team to intermingle and gather information. Many came from different villages, and

Tongo later learned that some were from Fakir's Monge Seed and Fertilizer Company team. They were the same people who spread the rumors about John's experiment. Tongo kept a close association with them, a position that had worked to his advantage as he played the middle ground. He felt the meeting went as planned.

Tongo had long expected that something in the gene might have caused the problem in the two villages, but there was no way he could prove it. As he eagerly waited for John's analysis, Monge Seed and Fertilizer Company released similar seeds into the market. He confirmed with the farmers and recorded their concerns. He proved that the number of allergic incidents increased in the areas where the farmers planted the seeds from Monge Seed Company. This knowledge came to him earlier during one of his visits, and Tongo waited until he heard from the farmers themselves.

In the meantime, the news of all these happenings had reached headquarters in the USA. The second wave of news that William and Michael at the regional office did not anticipate.

***

John summoned Tongo to his office once again. "Have a seat, and I have the genetic analysis of the seeds you gave me."

"Dr. Blake, the secretary interrupted. There is an urgent call waiting for you from the headquarters. I will transfer it." She hurried back to her seat. Tongo stepped out to allow him privacy.

"Okay, "John said as he picked up the phone. After a lengthy discussion with William Stanley, he sat silently and thought.

Tongo noticed the change in John's demeanor and hesitated. It appeared to him as if something heavy weighed on him. "I can come back another time. There is something I want to tell you, "He said.

John looked up and ushered him in with his hand. "It's alright. There may be a drastic shift in our program. Our jubilant mood may be short-lived. The people at headquarters are not rejoicing. We confirmed the existence of the miracle seed and put a smile on the faces of the village, and now everything has turned upside down." Tongo stared in disbelief. "Something happened?"

"The headquarters wants me to stop everything and discontinue the program, threatening to cut all the funding," John murmured.

Tongo had never seen John in this mood. His face turned reddish, and his facial veins bulged. He thought it was not the right time. "I can come another time," Tongo said.

"It's okay. What is it that you wanted to tell?"

"It's about the rebel leader."

"I am afraid the maniac will take over the country."

Tongo paused. "He wants to get the miracle seed, too, no matter what."

"What?" John wrinkled his nose and did not respond immediately. In normal circumstances, he would have crawled with a belly laugh. Right then, he could only stare.

After Tongo left, John remained preoccupied with his thoughts, considering the next steps.

Chapter 12

ongo groped around in the darkness for a flashlight and waited. The tap on the window grew louder, and he lifted the window curtain and looked through the glass. On the other side of the window, a dark figure tapped the window three times and showed him a number. Tongo opened the window halfway and lowered a burlap sack. The dark figure grabbed the package, draped it over his shoulder, and slithered into the morning jungle. Tongo looked on without uttering any word until the faint image disappeared and merged into the dark shade of the distant trees.

A dog barked in the next house, separated by a high protected fence. Still sleepy from the exhaustive day, John raised his head. He rolled out of his bedclothes, dropped his feet to the ground, and shoved them into his accommodating sandals. He walked to the restroom with his eyes partially closed. The recent remodeling and interior design of his house, akin to the American style, disoriented his views. It magnified the outlook of his curtain, which changed the look of his entire room.

The long, draping curtains glide effortlessly open or closed, featuring a grommet top and broad, elegant folds that exude a dreamy charm. He pushed it to his left to get an outside view of the African living quarters where some local company employees lived. He craned his neck when he noticed a movement along the edge of the fence and followed with his eyes. The thing disappeared. He thought it was a deer or a wild animal. John looked at his watch and noticed that similar things had happened several times in the early morning at four o'clock.

The dog's barking woke him up twice in the past, and John saw a figure like a person walking across. Tongo brushed him off when he told him what he saw. John then ignored the incident but shared with Joseph and his colleagues the moving figure he saw early in the morning hours of the night. They floated the idea of ghosts and other forest things that had haunted the local people. John remained skeptical. He suspected the rebellious groups had some sympathizers in the village who might sneak in and out under the cover of the night and play multiple roles.

In recent years, the anti-government guerrilla groups opposed to General Bukasa had intensified their forest activities.

They engaged with government soldiers for control of the area, although they remained friendly to the community around the region. Monge suffered the ravages caused by insurgents that included foreign and homegrown rebellions. The North and Eastern parts of the country had experienced continuous invasions since General Bukasa took over the country thirty years ago.

The country's vast natural resources and minerals have been the center of unrest. Each group claimed a portion of the country and turned the territory into a battlefield of brutal war. The war had escalated and intensified the tribal tensions that led to what some called acts of genocide—one group against another. With a level of inhuman atrocities unparalleled in the history of that part of the world. Zombie-like child soldiers roamed the forest with their killing machines. And the rest of the world, while appalled by this senseless carnage, only condemned the act but kept watching the brutal massacres, rape, and daily atrocities that had spread across the region.

Many foreign-owned companies, including Dare Seed Company, had laid their strategies to tap into the vast resources. They scooped the lion's share of the lucrative mineral business. They grabbed and influenced every sector of the economy of Monge. With one bloody hand dipping deeper into the dirty politics of tribal conflicts. And with the other, sharpening the killing tools of destruction by facilitating secret arm deals through third- party vendors based in the neighboring country. The company had carved a role and relied heavily on the government's support. They had General Bukasa's army for protection. Dare Seed Company took this opportunity to broaden its sphere of influence beyond agriculture. The company had acquired a monopoly to access vast resources.

Dare Seed Company had even secretly ventured into unchartered territory. They dealt with all kinds of shoddy underground activities in the region. They even plotted an exit strategy under the pretext of peace initiatives and contacted the rebel group leaders. In this uncertainty, they had to look beyond General Bukasa and align with the emerging leader. However, their ambitious plans did not succeed due to the grave danger looming in the atmosphere, lack of overall stability, and lawlessness. It then became apparent that the company had to heed the warning signs and focus on agriculture for the next five years.

***

The rays of morning sunlight seeped through the window and lit up the corner of the room, casting a rosy hue across the wall. John raised his head, rubbed his eyes, and stretched to reach for his watch. Cooing doves and humming from behind the house caught his attention. Lucy was up earlier than he did. His servant, Mafuta, clipped plants in the garden and rearranged them. He stopped when John peeped through the window.

"Good morning, sir?"

He did not hear any response from John and continued with his work. Some Europeans he worked for earlier did not want to be bothered. Mafuta had no complaints. At least John would confide in him and reward him with bonuses.

He clipped the last plant for the day and switched his task. He changed into clean clothes. Mafuta then prepared a breakfast menu list. He gave the note to John to select what he wanted for breakfast. The lists included: a bowl of sweetcorn mixed with fresh-cut vegetables, a glass of milk, a fried egg with turkey bacon, a slice of bread, porridge, and a glass of juice.

"A slice of bread with honey and a boiled egg." He turned to Lucy, and she ordered the crumbled egg and toast.

John browsed through the one-week-old papers. He read the section that condemned genetically modified crops. It highlighted some demonstrations around Europe and the United States of America. He turned to the next page and found another article from a religious leader who denounced genetically engineered products.

"A bunch of fools running around claiming that the scientists have distorted the work of creation. Nonsense. What use does a plant or animal have if not for the exclusive use of human beings? What is wrong with putting a gene from human beings into a plant and transferring genes between plants to improve our lives? God had granted humans the full capacity to develop and master the universe." After each paragraph, John paused and made some remarks.

"There is nothing wrong with transferring and rearranging genes. That happens in the natural environment. What do you think?" John read further when he did not get a response from Lucy or his servant, who was busy washing in the kitchen. The evidence indicates that most transgenic crops are environmentally harmless, as opponents made us believe. Most of them are beneficial. "Yes, I agree with that," he continued.

Some sections of the article reported the great success of some of the genetically modified crops. The article's writer recounted an event during the early research when the news media reported about genetically modified potatoes spliced with DNA. The detailed information about this old report confirmed that the rats fed on the products had their vital organs and immune systems damaged. John kept reading. In cooperation with big corporate sponsors, the scientists worked in total secrecy and would never reveal the true nature of their experiments to the public. They would stop at nothing. Companies compete and would like to be the first and be at the head of the curve in a world where business, technology, and DNA drive future progress. The article concluded. He tossed the paper and turned to his servant.

"Mafuta, have you ever heard about cows that can produce the milk of human proteins?"

Mafuta jerked his head. "Eei."

"I mean, we can make cows' milk to secrete human protein for the use of pharmaceuticals. This can provide a continuous reservoir of drug factories right here in Monge. We don't need to look far away. We have a conducive environment for this work here." John lifted his head, ate a little, picked up a Time Magazine, and browsed through.

"As you said, sir, anything is possible."

John looked up when Mafuta placed the juice on the table and fixed his eyes on the sweetcorn breakfast.

"Tongo gave this to you?" He stretched his hand to pick it up.

"Let me see the label. No-tag!"

Mafuta pulled a brown bag from the waste bin, "it says, E.S. field F. I placed them in separate bags, as Tongo instructed, and the label was on when he brought them, and probably it fell off when I transferred the bags."

"Did you put back the right label? It's critical." Mafuta

lowered his head, "Yes, Sir, I did. I am sorry."
He rearranged the tablecloth and passed a glass of water, just in case.

"Is everything okay?" Lucy asked.

Mafuta cast brooding glances in his corner as he wiped the kitchen sink.

"It was the labels, Madam."

Lucy glanced at John, " Let me try it."

"Not now, honey, until I confirm it." He said with a sly smile.

Her eyes twitched as she noticed the worried expression on his face. It was sweetcorn, after all, and it looked yummy!

"Sure, these are the sweetcorn varieties we planted in our experimental and farmers' fields. There were two types, and I would like to confirm again."

"Are you not satisfied? Oh, what about the other seed the villagers called cursed seeds? Do you plan to experiment with that seed as well?"

John laughed. "Yes and No, and we discontinued that particular one from the on-farm trials." He noticed the expression on her face changed with raised eyebrows.

"I heard people are still talking about that season, and they said life continuity ceased to exist and blamed Dare Seed Company. The wound from the deep resentment due to the past activities of the Ministry of Agriculture regarding chemical pollution did not heal," She shot him with a pleading gaze. "I am glad you didn't open the wound."

"Things have gone beyond what I expected. It isn't easy to sift truth from false. All that we heard was hearsay mixed with truths and falsehood. Unfortunately, people continued to believe."

Lucy hesitated to ask the question that bothered her and what people talked about. "I heard with my ears how a man narrated the story from the village and uttered exactly the following words," Everyone wants to leave their seed behind for posterity and family line. A doomsday awaits us without future generations.

"I saw the fear in his weary eyes filled with dejection and hopelessness." He then added. "Not only men, women too." With the same pleading glance, she said. "What exactly did you create?"

John raised his eyebrows. "Common, honey. Did you believe that? She looked at and sat in sullen silence. "Are you serious? Okay, I get it." He tried to cheer her up.

"You didn't believe it when Tongo told you the same story?"

"No, honey. Not that I didn't believe. I needed more evidence to prove those people wrong. In less than a month, I took it upon myself to provide the miracle seed for a demonstration. Tongo planted it on his uncle's farm and got the results we expected, and the villagers were happy." She turned abruptly. "Wait a minute, hold on until I finish." He calmed her down. "And then the little success we had tumbled. There will be no miracle seeds. The program will end. I don't want to go into the details, right now."

"I guess that's the same with egg-laying chickens.?"

John nodded. He sighed and twitched his eyebrows when Lucy showed a surprise gesture.

"Are you trying to say something, honey? "Different versions of the same story are circulating"

"A farmer fed his chicken on the grains and got no egg after two weeks of continuous feeding on the seed? What do you have to say about this?" He ignored the direct response and thought it through for a moment. "We don't sell seeds to the farmers, but some were supplied by Monge Seed and Fertilizer Company. I am not pushing the problems away. The whole country needs to assess this issue. We may have a bigger problem than we think. It's about the gene factor in the environment. You can call it cursed or blessed; both exist."

Mafuta went outside the house while John and Lucy remained at the table. He watered the flowers at the edges of the compound. John stood up and entered the bedroom to get ready for work. He took some samples from the two bags of grains from the recently harvested field in the village sent by Tongo. The kernels looked fresh, and they were from the variety John coded green. He took five ears of corn from each sample, put them in separate small plastic gunny bags, put the bags in another container, and took them to the office.

Chapter 13

When John arrived at the office, he checked the data Tongo had entered on his computer and the messages. He walked to the greenhouse section of his potted plants and peeped through the small window hole to glimpse rats in the cage without disturbing them. Conspicuous differences stood out in the behavior of the rats fed on seeds coded green and red. The rats fed on the seed-coded green had developed aggressive, irritable behavior with an intense concentration of high fecundity. They were extraordinarily prolific and produced twins or triplets. The aggressive behavior of these rats had already led to infanticide. A strange reaction that he had never anticipated.

He looked closely at the previous notes Tongo took when he was on vacation. It took a while to discern the meaning behind the detailed note because Tongo had a creative way of describing what he observed. He singled out each rat and recognized how each of them behaved. He reasoned that the lot on the seed-coded green was aggressive, prolific, and exhibited strong dominance. Their aggressiveness led to killings, and that shocked him. His note on the other group on seed-coded red was as follows.

"These rats were different. They were docile and kept to themselves, cuddling and accepting your presence and friendship. They seemed excited, as if they would miss seeing you. They would make great pets. The strange thing about them was their lack of interest in mating. They no longer produce any young ones. Whatever was in seed-coded red will eventually make them extinct. I am sorry for my strong aversion to their behavior. Regardless, these rats remained miserable and lonely and had no offspring. John looked at the detailed notes with admiration. Tongo's descriptions of the behavior impressed him. His suggestion about them being less interested in mating surprised him more, not because it was the wrong observation, but because of how he assessed and concluded. He reread the last sentence and raised his eyebrows. Tongo wrote. "What if we allowed the two groups to mix and pair them up? It was as if Tongo had read his mind.

***

John stepped out of his office and into the corridor and noticed Tongo reading the display on the bulletin board near the front office. He beckoned him over to join him.

"Thanks for your detailed notes on the report." He scanned his notes and pointed at the line that read, "We planted the crop in the year of beans." He then read further. "The first complaint we received came from a farmer with six sons, who lost all his investments and remained bitter. He got his seeds from the Monge Seed & Fertilizer Company."

John opened a file in his computer folder and browsed through the screen, reviewing the DNA analysis results. "Bingo!" he exclaimed. The same anomaly in the sex chromosomes caused the problems and contaminated the gene pool.

"Tongo sighed. "I told you; it was not our seed?"

"We now know the source." Tongo leaned over, eager to hear what he would say next. John held his hands over his head and leaned back on his chair. He remained in this position for a while. "We have a problem. We don't know what's already up there in the field."

Tongo jerks forward. "Maybe the free seed sample they gave the farmers caused damage. Some farmers also saved their seeds from the previous seasons." Tongo added.

John held his chin in a reflective mood. He took a pencil and circled one area of the village map. The village beyond the valley was where the high concentration of problems appeared. He drew another line in the area where he had the on-farm trials and the farms of Tongo's uncle.

"There is only one way to stabilize the situation. We have to survey the whole area. It's time-consuming and requires a lot of resources.

John raised his hand. "I will need to schedule a time with you to visit this village," he said, drawing a line through the village beyond the valley.

"It's the work of Monge Seed and Fertilizer Company, right?" Tongo asked

John smiled a dry smile that showed contempt. "Do you know the African proverb?" *Do not look where you fell, but where you slipped.* Tongo felt ashamed that an American man knew an African proverb that he didn't know. He gave him a blank stare. "I knew they were working on something." He rocked his head. "I do not doubt their abilities. Not this first, though. He shook his head. "They couldn't produce a seed with the same genetic makeup as mine." John puckered his lips. "I don't have any malice against anybody. We all steal from each other." And then he stopped. "I have to trace back where I slipped. Anything is possible. A common error, data breach, and all sorts of things might have given them an edge that contributed to this outcome."

Tongo blinked through the corner of his eyes. A futile attempt to say something failed. The correct word evaded him, and he mumbled, his mouth dropping open. "Is something wrong!"

John lifted his head. The color of his face turned pale. He looked Tongo in the eyes.

"I want to hear the whole truth. Don't flavor it or justify anything. Spill it out. That would make me happy." He propped his chin with his left hand and waited.

Tongo shifted his seating position and looked past John. He removed a handkerchief from his hip pocket and wiped his entire face. John looked up at the buzzing ceiling fan.

"Tongo cleared his throat. "I should have told you earlier." He hesitated as if trying to look for a better word. "My uncle had a miracle seed and might have another seed with opposite traits." He grabbed a bottle of water and emptied it without a break. "Monge seed and fertilizer company is using my uncle's farm as a demonstration site for their on-farm trial." He stopped and then continued. "As you know, our sweet corn seed multiplication experiment was also nearby."

John sat up abruptly. "No wonder the gene mix-up disaster right under our nose. What's your share in this business?"

Unexpected questions jolted him to leap forward, and he knocked the table. The empty water bottle tipped over.

Tongo let out a long sigh of uncertainty. "It's through my brother-in-law. Alfred and my wife co-own some shares." He wiped streams of sweat.

John kept silent.

"We harvested the corn three weeks ago, and the sign of prosperity is already on the horizon. The miracle seed is back." He adjusted and recovered his tone of voice. "The word had gone out, and you heard about the news. The demand for seeds escalated. The sale of the grains from the corn variety as chicken feed had gone through the roof. We couldn't cope with the demand."

"Really?" John stared.

"At the same time, we are hearing the surge of the story of the cursed seed on the rise." He shook his head. "You know the results." With his face down, he rumbled. "A tragedy. I know some farmers and friends of mine who used these seeds. Their chickens, fed on these seeds, did not lay eggs until now."

Tongo remained quiet for a while and looked up. The only sound he could hear came from his breathing and the buzzing sound of the fan.

"How widely spread are the distributions of the seed with undesirable traits?" John asked.

"The farmers in the village beyond the valley received this seed." Tongo rubbed his forehead as if trying to squeeze the answer. "There was some inconsistency in the behavior of chickens. Some have developed aggressive behavior, like rats. My uncle noticed this first, and some ate their eggs. Some roosters don't show interest."

John rolled his eyes with a resigned air of Deja Vu. "Not this again. We have gone through that with those rats," He paused. "I am not a poultry expert, but a lack of calcium can create this appetite for eggshells. I appreciate your detailed, constructive observations." Tongo smiled with satisfaction.

"Can you identify the rooster and chicken you suspected of being different?"

"We labeled them with a permanent marker and will monitor them."

"Tell me the truth about the pesticide. Did you believe it?"

Tongo kept silent for a long time and finally faced him. "No, it was the seed and something in it."

John exhaled a long sigh. "Why did you tell them it was the pesticides?"

"People already knew the pesticide problem, and I didn't want them to go after us." After another pause, he continued. "There is something else," John raised his head attentively. "The variety releases a toxin, which may be the source of whatever happened to the village beyond the valley."

"Are all these seeds from Monge Seed and Fertilizer company?"

Tongo wrapped his neck and, with a barely audible voice, confessed. I don't know whether something I did might have played a role."

John stopped in his tracks with a gaping mouth. What did you do?"

"I planted from the seeds you told me to dispose of. They remained viable and sprouted."

"Do you believe the pollen from this plant caused the problem in the village beyond the valley? Unbelievable." He shook his head in disbelief.

Tongo scratched his chin and held on to it, his habitual tactics of deflecting attention. John knew the trick and waited. "I think the pollen has polluted and changed the seed. I don't know the genetic identity of the seed they planted in the village beyond the valley and the one I planted." John sucked in his breath and let it out steadily.

"Why didn't you tell me immediately?" John continued with his series of questions. "Did you give me the sample of the seeds you harvested from the varieties that you planted?"

"No."

"I need the sample, and I need to know everything. Did you plant all the seeds you are supposed to dispose of?"

"Yes, I saved them for next year and shared them with some farmers, too."

"You can't save these hybrid seeds; you know the losses of vigor and various benefits if you do."

"At my uncle's farm storage. The farmers told me they also saved and replanted the seeds the following year."

John took a deep breath and continued. "Is this also the variety you dubbed cursed?" Tongo looked down.

"Yes. The same quality, and it's widely spread." He mumbled.

"You know Intellectual property laws will protect our seeds." He held his face with an air of confidence.

"These are no ordinary seeds, and they have something in them that we don't understand. It caused damage and will wipe out the whole population. The seed had transgressed all the rules of biology. The deadly allergy combined with this life-sucking trait worries me. We need to take urgent action to stop further destruction."

"I don't get it." John gave a snorting grunt. He bit his lips. "Tell me. Did you plant the seed in the village beyond the valley?"

After a long silence, Tongo replied. "I don't know. I mean, I didn't do it physically with my hands."

"What? You don't know? How can this be possible?"

"Farmers might have planted the grains that I provided." Tongo sighed. "I don't know if the farmers I shared the seeds with have planted the seeds in the village. In any case, that's a minimal number of seeds." John shot him a glance. "Where did the widely spread distribution of seed that you're talking about come from?" John shook his head.

Tongo pulled on his beard with a fake smile, but his attempt only showed a stale grimace. He could see the anger on John's face mounting. "Farmers were worried about how the government pushed the hybrid through. They complained that they can't afford to buy it yearly because it's expensive and not feasible for small farmers." He stopped to take a breath and proceeded. "You heard the news?" He glowed with excitement. "Monge seed and Fertilizer Company have provided free seed supplies this year. They announced it over the radio and TV news."

"Yeah, you're right. Farmers have had enough of this facade of government support." John didn't show any excitement. "They put conditions in place that farmers should not grow local maize." John was not surprised. The plan was already in place, and he was waiting to find out how they would implement it.

"The loss of identity and ownership of Monge farmers had become evident. The Indigenous bits of knowledge handed from generation to generation are disappearing rapidly, leading to extinction." John lamented and then added. "I believe the exotic maize varieties that survived and remained with farmers can still exhibit superior quality. Didn't you tell me that a farmer who mixed it with the hybrid variety improved the vigor and quality?" Tongo gave him a nod.

"We no longer have the exotic maize seeds left. All gone. We noticed that they have turned into weedy plants. Something had entered the genes and changed them. I saw strange things with my eyes and didn't know where they originated." He took a deep breath. "All these changes came after we introduced our seeds to the farmers."

"Okay, I understand these are some serious issues we must address. We will revisit this topic later. In the meantime, did you send me samples of those seeds?"

"Yes, all of them, including the recent free sample from Monge Seed and Fertilizer Company and the ones I saved in my uncle's barn, which I shared with some farmers. All are labeled and ready.

"Don't do anything with those seeds." John's face flushed a reddish shade, and he squeezed his lips tight as he stared down at him. "I don't know why you didn't get it!" He raised his voice, clenching his fists tightly. My reputation is on the line." John stood up from his chair and looked one more time at Tongo. "I don't know how I could face Dare Seed Company with this information if our seeds caused all these problems. I can only ask you one favor for now. Until I figure things out, this information should remain with you. Can you promise me that?"

Tongo nodded with a weary look.

"Thanks, you're dismissed, and you will wait to hear from me regarding the farm visit."

Tongo mumbled something and abruptly turned.

"There is commotion in the forest. Do you want to wait until things settle? The government soldiers are losing control."

John understood how the local people reacted to the conflict. They avoided discussing it. General Bukasa's divisive tactics planted in their minds over the years had psyched out the population and created a deep-rooted mistrust and fear among them.

"Anything else?" John asked.

Before Tongo responded, John received a long-distance call. He blocked the microphone on the telephone receiver with one hand and dismissed him with a wave.

***

Later, John went through all the data analysis and the information he had about the analysis of the gene, including some anecdote notes. He sat for a long time and pondered. Beads of sweat trickled along the veins of his forehead. His face flushed as if an invisible hand tightened his throat. His whole body remained tense and stiffened, almost trembling. He stared into the distance vacantly, for what appeared to be a frozen time. He tried to hold his fury and slammed his fist into the cushion of his bulletin board. He barely realized the impact until a sudden pain hit him, and blood oozed from his knuckle.

Chapter 14

The next day, John's meeting with Tongo took longer. The series of events in the area had left many questions unanswered. Tongo entered the office and stood in the doorway. John pointed to the chair and remained composed and thoughtful.

John began by apologizing for his actions the previous day. He thanked Tongo for the detailed information he had provided and asked him to feel free to tell him everything he knew about the problems in the village.

"Tell me anything that you can remember."

Tongo appeared confused and perspired. "I don't know where to start. The recent news was overwhelming, and I told you everything already." With his head tilting down, he held his chin and paused.

"The panic in the village had intensified. It is now fully confirmed." The look on his face appeared hopeless. "We are seeing the long-term impact of seed consumption. Child mortality is high, and the report suggested that women in that village do not get pregnant." He stopped. "Monge Seed and Fertilizer Company have been experimenting in this village for three years. One of the samples I slipped through was from the Kakai farm enterprise. I labeled it."

John screwed up his eyes, trying to peer through for better understanding, and nodded. He began to titter. "Wait, this is not the same old story, right? We have to move past these unsubstantiated myths."

Tongo stepped back. "The complaint came from women."

John wrinkled up. "Interesting. What was it about?"

"Consumptions of grains."

John looked up with a penetrating gaze. The results of his analysis confirmed what Tongo had been saying all along, and it will also exonerate Dare Seed Company's role in the spread of the problem in the village. The question that bothered John was the level of advance that Monge Seed and Fertilizer Company had shown. He wondered who helped them reach this level.

Tongo glanced at John, eager to cover up his mistakes, and added. "As I always thought, there was something in the seed." Tongo stopped and then continued. "The village elders blamed our company. They considered it a trap." John raised his eyebrows and waited. "They believed it was the chemicals. However, as I said, the root cause of destruction was the thing in the seed. Take the case with my uncle's chickens I told you about." John remained silent, trying to process the piecemeal information. The African ways of communicating important information sometimes irritated him. Tongo diffuses the complicated tension by going around the issue. John considered this approach a waste of time and attempted to say something but paused until he finished. Tongo wiped streams of sweat from his forehead, stood up, sat down, and stood up again as if his legs could not hold him.

"Can you sit down?" Tongo looked on and mumbled inaudible words in his mother tongue mixed with an expression of Swahili. *Naomba msamaha*. I will ask for forgiveness." A chilling atmosphere hit the room. A deadly silence came over the tiny space. No one spoke. Tongo kept darting his eyes back and forth. Their eyes met in search of answers, and they remained in a state of limbo. The long silence did not clear up the mystery behind the village debacle. Tongo dreaded the outcome but wanted this off his chest.

"I gave out a few red coded packages of seeds to my uncle."

"Tongo. You're not allowed to give out experimental materials. Never." The forceful words vibrated in his head.

"I apologize for the mistake."

"Did you consume the grain products from the experimental site?"

Tongo shook his head and looked up and then down. "No."

"Why not?"

"I figured it out."

With intense wrinkled facial expressions and anticipating the worst, John asked. "What else do you know?"

"What happened with chickens scared me." Another moment of silence and guilt filled the room. Their eyes met again, and both understood what the other one was thinking. John bit his lower lips and stared at the space in the room. There was only one question on his mind. "Who else knows about this quality of the seed for real?"

"Everyone affected believed something linked to the seed or the chemicals used caused the problem. They seemed to accept the narrative that the previous chemicals used in the soil caused the issue." He darted his eyes and knew that John was not convinced. "My lips are sealed as far as the components of the genes are concerned. Nothing will come out of me." He looked at John in the eyes and looked down, and John lifted his head, thinking how he could believe him.

"Monge Seed and Fertilizer Company people knew the properties of the seeds. The analysis of their seed proved it."

"What about your uncle?"

Tongo kept quiet.

"I see, so we are not alone. Your uncle is my biggest concern for wider publicity, which we don't need." John looked him in the eyes." I still need to know how my seeds ended with Monge Seed and Fertilizer Company. Did you share the information with them? Or any of their acquaintances."

"No, some people think they worked with our company."

Tongo hesitated and continued, "If we have a pure line of the fertility gene, can we introduce it in the same village and see what results we can get?".

John sighed and rolled his eyes. "I thought we sorted out the issue, planted the miracle seed fertility booster, and made them happy last season."

Tongo took his time and slowly responded. "Yes, the problem is in the other village beyond the valley."

"That's too big of a mess for us to get involved."

Tongo kept silent for a long time. John knew Tongo had not shared everything he knew and decided not to pressure him. He then asked.

"What else do you have in mind?" In the manner of his usual reaction, Tongo fidgeted.

"Do you remember the farmer who burnt his crop? The one who believed that the corn seeds he planted had produced a crop of weeds?"

"John acknowledged with a nod of the head and asked. "Where did he get the seeds?"

"Monge Seed and Fertilizer Company. The case is under investigation. The government was involved."

"Did you know how many farmers had a similar issue?"

Tongo shook his head. "The news mentioned several farmers. Again, I don't want to speculate. So many things have happened in that village. I attribute all these to Monge Seed and Fertilizer Company."

"No doubt we all now know and wonder who provided the information."

Tongo's whole body swept, his hands closed, drained with sweat, and his heart palpated. His body remained hunched.

"I have moved on. No need to worry. Anything else?"

"I wanted to ask why we must withdraw the miracle seed. And Monge Seed and the Fertilizer Company also have the miracle seed, right?" He glanced at John and asked.

"Are we replacing the miracle seed with the cursed one? He paused and added. I mean the red coded one." John hesitated to answer right away. As a scientist, he should have relied on facts, not intuition, to make decisions.

"Sure, based on the results of the analysis, we have both the miracle seed and the one you called cursed."

He stood up and walked to the window, his mind drifting. How had he missed the signs?

John stiffened as memories surged back. It was the strange thoughts that had nagged him for weeks. The telephone conversation with William about the sweetcorn for breakfast. His confrontation over the role of Monge Seed and Fertilizer Company. And then, something in him snapped.

How did Monge Seed & Fertilizer Company get a replica of his work? He tried to retrace his steps, searching for any overlooked clues. He couldn't recall anything and did not suspect anyone at this point.

But one thing was clear, he needed to eliminate the field factor first.

Someone must have hacked into his computer and retrieved the data code. He sank back into his chair, gripping his chin as he stared into the empty space before him. Then, another chilling possibility crept into his mind. The original sample was in cold storage. Access was restricted. Only two people could reach it, him and Michael

Tongo broke the silence. "What do you want us to do then?" he asked.

"Right now, the attention is on what your government would do. We don't want to create bad publicity." With a solemn expression on his face, he added. "We better not get involved, as you hinted."

John thought over what Tongo had said and realized the political implications of the current situation in this village. Michael, the regional manager, warned him about the activities in the area. And with the government's involvement, there is little he could do. John had to agree with Tongo and protect his company's reputation. He turned to Tongo. "I would like to visit this village if you could arrange it." He paused, "What do you know about the guerrilla fighters in the forests? I heard they get support from the local people in this village?" There was a moment of silence. John could sense the uneasiness, a subject that many people like to avoid.

Tongo quickly looked around. "God forbid." He crossed himself by putting his thumb, index, and middle finger together and then touched his forehead, the center of his chest, left shoulder, and right shoulder in the manner of Western Christian practice. "He mumbled. Why do you even think of something like this." He murmured. "No," he nodded.

John stood and watched how Tongo's demeanor changed.

"I had to go." He tried to downplay the scene and released him.

Chapter 15

John picked up the buzzing phone in his office and paced the room, grinding his teeth. He had to swallow the unpalatable, sensational stories about this seed with many unanswered questions. In a place where truth and falsehood are equally embraced and accepted, he had to sift through and can't take things at face value anymore. John could think of probable causes for the numerous problems cited and would never dismiss any of the allegations. He could cite the report of the evidence of chemical exposure in the area. John stood up and walked to the bulletin board word wall lists he created (fertility, allergy, weedy corn, miracle seed, local exotic maize, pesticides, herbicides & GMO). He twitched his muscles around the mouth, and a moment of truth hit him. It is a known scientific fact that the chlorinated pesticides they used, and herbicides could damage and disrupt fertility. He shook his head, amazed that chemical use had even increased in Monge.

Some chemicals banned in developed countries found their way to Africa. He was shocked to learn what they used for malaria spray. A chemical that was forbidden because it tends to remain in the body. He went through Tongo's notes again and underlined the statement, "Women don't get pregnant." Such a vague statement didn't make sense. However, on a broader scale, John did not overrule the gene factor in his calculations. He circled allergies and weedy corn. His first task was to isolate the gene that caused allergies and weedy plants—a tall order in the list of haphazard activities that had occupied his mind. The numerous reports of untreated allergies continue to ignite the rumor that points fingers at the GMO presence in the area. The fear that prolonged allergic reactions could weaken the immune system. This would lead to further complications for dangerous bacterial or fungal infections in lungs, ears, or skin. The least Dare Seed Company needed at this time was negative publicity associated with their products. John stretched his hand to pick up the buzzing phone.

"Can you come to the lab? I want you to see this." Samuel insisted when John told him he would be late for his staff meeting.

John picked a sample of a stunted plant from him and examined it.

"I have been bombarded with calls and overwhelmed with samples similar to what you see here. What do you think?"

"Did you identify what this was about?" John turned to him.

"It's obvious this is a form of a distorted corn plant, partially turned weedy and presented as a weed. You know this is a corn plant, although we avoided calling it so, and I will not call it corn anymore."

"Where did this one come from?"

"The same area. From the village beyond the valley. The corn seeds the farmers planted sprouted this weedy plant.

John nodded. "Tongo told me about this a couple of times, but it's hard for me to believe the extent of the damage." He placed the sample on the table.

"This has nothing to do with our experimental seeds, right?" Samuel asked.

John hitched his right shoulder in a shrug and did not like the look on Samuel's face. He then commented.

"You know the history of this area and all the controversy surrounding the expired pesticides and Monge Seed and Fertilizer company's involvement. We better keep out of this dilemma. Let them handle it."

Samuel shook his head in disbelief and wrinkled his brow. "We cannot pretend to look the other way. There is a strong indication that your involvement with the on-farm experiments might have played a significant role. The seeds Tongo distributed might have caused the problem." After what looked like a long recollection, John kept silent and shrugged as if to say there was nothing he could do. He responded as an afterthought.

"I did not have any experiments in that village. Tongo is a farmer like most of you, and whatever he did with his village life was none of my business. For your information, his uncle distributed the seeds supplied by the Monge Seed and Fertilizer Company. You seemed to get that wrong."

"Regardless, we have problems, and people are looking up to us for solutions. There is a perception that the seeds we introduced have destroyed the local seeds and changed the plant's ecosystem, and they blamed us for it. I have to be frank with you, John: avoiding this problem won't solve it. You have to come clean."

"What!" John swung his hands up. "Do you believe that I had anything to do with it?"

"I don't know. You did your things with farmers. Maybe whatever you did with on-farm trials." John started to move to the door before Samuel finished his words.
"I had to go." John turned. "If you want to know the truth, check with Monge Seed and Fertilizer Company."

***

John briefly met with his staff and administrative office personnel. He checked about the upcoming dinner at a local hotel to celebrate the annual agricultural show. He agreed to give brief updates and represent Dare Seed Company. He was even ready to address the controversy surrounding the misunderstood term of genetically modified crops. The company's internal policy discouraged staff from talking about GMO crops. A newspaper title caught his attention. He picked up a daily paper and browsed through it.

Contrary to his expectations, the world was no longer inaccessible, even to a small village in the African jungle. Negative news about GMOs has penetrated the wilderness. He flipped through the papers and read about the ongoing highlight of the agricultural fair.

He stopped when he came across a statement about the miracle seed, extolling the benefits and the unforeseen danger it could cause. He scowled at the topic, expressing his displeasure through a scornful grimace.

John tossed the paper across the table and opened the window. His mind was not at ease, entangled in the maze of gene discord. The encounter with Samuel about the weedy corn added another layer of surmounting problems. He pieced together the mystery, from gossip to reality he can no longer ignore. He thought the incomplete, innuendo, false, and misleading information about the village tales would disappear rather than turning into a roadblock. John referred to Tongo's field note for further clues. Tongo is stressed. "Farmer's chickens had failed to produce eggs, and there was no record of childbirth in the village for the last two years. Something terrible had happened in this village. We need immediate solutions.".

***

John sat and mused over everything he had encountered that week. He then swung around to see who had knocked at his door.

"You came at the right time, Tongo; I was thinking about the farmers' episode regarding your observations. You didn't mention the weedy corn plants in detail. What's this issue about? Did you know anything about this latest upsurge?"

"Yes, I wanted to find out before I could give you any information. The farmers who planted seeds saved from the previous crop got the crops of weedy plants. The village had great commotions, and the loss of their local seeds became imminent." He noticed John was not satisfied and then added. "They planted the seeds supplied by the Monge Seed and Fertilizer company."

"I see. Monge Seed and Fertilizer company will have a representative at the meeting this evening?"

"Yes. The company will dominate the agriculture exhibit display with a greater representation. They have advertised their seeds in the news media. It is the only seed company the government has promoted. You will most likely meet Fakir, one of the owners of the Monge seed and fertilizer company."

"I would love to see what they offer."

"Fakir has the government behind him, a well-known family with broad business interests in various enterprises. The giant of the farming industry in Monge, with extensive interests. I was surprised that you didn't meet with him."

"He was in the papers, and I read and heard about his business expansions and influences in the neighboring countries. Some people accused him of illegal activities like human trafficking. He regularly visits Michael, but we were never officially introduced."

"His company had got involved in some controversial issues in the past. Do you remember the famous story of the pesticide pollution scandal?"

John wrinkled up. "Sure?"

"The government contracted him to distribute the pesticides." Tongo lowered his voice. He's also one of the owners of the Monge Seed and Fertilizer Company.

After years in Africa, John had picked some strategies and learned ways of getting the information needed. He didn't need to ask direct questions; sometimes, an indirect hint or question can lead to the desired outcome. "What else do you know about Fakir and his company?"

Tongo began to chuckle and cackle with glee.

"The relationship with our company is complex."

"What do you know?"

"They knew everything we did. I wondered how they knew."

Tongo's eyes darted around the room. "There are all kinds of stories circulating about this close relationship." He gave a little chuckle while throwing his arms up in exasperation. "I took notes on what I observed. I don't know what to tell you. Some things were exaggerated." With a pensive facial expression, he added. "The report came from the farmers who used local variety."

John tilted his head, leaned in, and asked. "Did you see the weedy corn plant in the farmers' field?"

"We are noticing more and more farmers reporting it now than any other time."

"Did your uncle notice this phenomenon on his farm?"

"Yes." he nodded.

John noticed a familiar pattern of behavior and kept quiet for a while, staring at him, his narrow eyes widening. Wherever he had something to keep to himself, Tongo would change his voice and look down, avoiding eye contact, blinking too much, and looking sideways. When this happens, John usually waits and pretends not to catch him in this mood, but he sympathizes with his demeanor.

"Tongo, let me ask you one more question. "Is it fair to say that Monge Seed and Fertilizer Company supplied farmers with the seeds that caused problems and tried to blame it on the Dare Seed Company?" He threw up his arms in disbelief. "This doesn't make any sense if we are collaborating as you seemed to suggest. Who exactly are they collaborating with?"

Tongo weighed his response before he spoke. "The most likely candidate is Samuel. I caught him stalking our experiments in the greenhouse like a peeping Tom. Uuf." He twisted his mouth.

With a jolt of surprise, John straightened his back. "I was suspecting Joseph. Did he ever come closer to our computer?" he then interjected. "He's knowledgeable about computer science; he has a diploma."

"No, I never suspected him. I noticed Samuel snooping around the cage."

Tongo got the opportunity to unleash all his grievances against Samuel. John shifted the topic to the upcoming agriculture fair and assigned Tongo to gather more information about farmers who reported weedy crops.

Chapter 16

ohn had no time for preliminaries and long, endless speeches. He plunged right into a brief introduction about how scientists produced genetically modified crops and inserted genes. He answered the general questions and attempted to say a few words in the Kiswahili language, and his wrong choice of words generated a burst of laughter. The applause gave him enough courage to continue.

"Let me take you through the scientific jargon about insect-resistant crops." He continued.

"The scientists first isolated a gene called Bt from bacteria in the soil. The Bt gene will then cause the plant to produce a toxic protein that can kill some insects. At the same time, the scientist would insert another gene called "marker" into the plant to identify the cells that had taken the Bt gene and provide protection for the plants. The genetically altered cells would grow normally." John paused, thinking that he had lost the attention of the crowd. "The seeds from these plants will, therefore, produce cells containing Bt toxin, and when insects feed on these plants, they will die." John sipped a glass of water and beamed with satisfaction that the audience was with him.

He often used scientific jargon but tried simplifying his statements: "The transfer of species happens all the time in nature. Winds or insects can carry pollen to different plants and fertilize them if they are close relatives, regardless of whether they are weeds or crops."

Someone in the crowd spoke, and people tried to murmur. The people who sat close to the speaker encouraged him to speak up. "No wonder that's why we have all these deadly allergies. We are encountering strange diseases, and the hospitals are overwhelmed and need help. We heard that the local farmers' maize had become a weed." What's going on? We need some answers." The speaker shouted.

A participant followed up with a question about pollen from genetically modified maize. "Will this pollute our exotic local maize species?" John assured the audience that it would not happen. The participant shot his hand up again. "Are you saying there is no gene mix-up and pollution risk?"

John wanted to avoid discussing this question in detail and using highly technical terms and jargon. "Let me say this," he began.

"Crossing over genes between plants is possible if the species have the same number of chromosomes, similar life cycles, or ecological habitats. However, we do everything possible to minimize this activity and surround our GMO crops with rows of non-GMO crops as a barrier to trap the transfer of pollen and balance the resistant trait." He avoided other questions about GMO conspiracy theories. After his session ended, John mingled with the crowd.

The people moved around in the big hall, checking posters and exhibits from local chemical and seed companies. Several stopped to ask him questions, and John walked with them in the hallways. A small snack cafe was in the corner where some of his colleagues gathered. Joseph and some of his friends sat in a corner and appeared agitated in a heated debate. John walked to the booths, where international companies displayed all their products. He strolled to the Dare Seed Company's pharmaceutical section site.

"Hei," Joseph caught up with him.

"Let me introduce you to my friend." Mr. Fakir." Joseph announced.

John turned around rather unexpectedly. He looked at Joseph's friend for a second. An instant recognition from the papers struck him. He stretched his hands to greet him. "Nice to meet you. I have heard a lot about you." The hand grip was rough, and a scar on the side and the missing little finger caught his attention. For a second, John had a flash of recognition. He couldn't be sure where he had seen this hand before, but somehow, he recalled having seen this hand with a missing little finger somewhere. John waited, hoping that Fakir would remind him where they met.

"Ah, everybody looked at this hand and wondered what happened." He held his right hand up, showing the missing little finger. "I got this unexpected gift for the rest of my life. The result of an unforgettable event from a crocodile hunting expedition in the Tana River-Kenya." He smiled and continued. "Don't ever play with a live crocodile." Joseph looked sideways as his eyes met with John's. Fakir introduced himself to the other two people in the group and moved closer to participate in their discussions on genetic engineering. In the corner, towards the end of the row of the exhibit posters, a lone figure held a placard, "Stop GMO!"

"We don't need to listen to the community's few misguided, lonely voices. They were up against an impossible feat." Fakir pointed to the lonely demonstrator. Someone jeered in support of the statement and added. The gigantic muscle of the corporate world, in cohort with the government, will crush any voice that dares to oppose these greedy parasites.

"What can you say about the opposition, Doc!" Fakir interjected.

"I guess it would be fine if scientists used bacteria to help cure cancer. Right? Do you know we have used bacteria to obtain human insulin for diabetics? Sure, no one seemed to complain about that, but when the same scientists worked hard to make vaccines that increased milk production in dairy cows, it became a big issue. Why.?" John paused in his steps and turned as he spoke. "You must have read numerous reports about how we put technology to good use, from curing human diseases to cleaning up oil spills and recycling waste." He glanced at the missing little finger again. Fakir nodded.

"Unfortunately, people are always pessimistic about everything. It's not a question of whether they are with or against you, Doc. I read that we already have the ingredients of these genes in our blood. We are all living proof of free specimens for experiments that we can succumb to because we had little choice." He turned to John. "There is one thing, though," Fakir emphasized. "The juggling of these genes, some with possible toxins with potential for allergies, may be the scariest thing scientists have yet to deal with."

Joseph sipped Mango juice in a plastic cup and looked on. He did not participate in the discussions until then and only nodded when he agreed with either of them or kept to himself throughout the talk. He checked his time as if he was expecting someone else. "Fakir, with time, this fear will be over. It is impossible to prove the experiments while the media and some fanatics worldwide kept bombarding scientists with questions about the possible problems of genetically engineered crops before the problems appeared." John nodded and agreed with what Joseph said. "There is nothing new, and everything was in place already. The scientists modified and improved what humans had done over the generations." The group moved to the dinner table together and continued with their discussions. Only Fakir seemed interested in the debate on genetically engineered crops. "Doc!" he called out to John for another attention. "We hear strange stories. The farmers in one region are losing crops. Their local maize plants are disappearing. What do you think about that?"

John faced him. "The preliminary results confirmed that Dare Seed Company was not the source, and we did not supply the farmers." Their eyes locked, and the rest of the people waited.

"That leaves only one company then." Joseph hinted.

"Your company distributed seeds in this area. Perhaps you could share what you know," John suggested.

Fakir, trying to deflect, ignored the question. "I'm hungry," he muttered. A tense silence followed. After a moment, Fakir glanced up and added, "We're the only two seed companies in the country. Our success depends on working together. That should be our focus."

He brightened and exclaimed, "What are we waiting for?" With that, he headed toward the food stall. The array of cultural dishes was clearly labeled, and cooks worked behind the counter, serving up the various selections. John chose a plate of barbecued goat ribs.

*****

As he prepared to sleep that night, John revisited the events of the evening in his mind. He picked up a notebook and jotted down the plans of action that came into his mind. A newspaper sub-headline caught his attention. It was about the drought and hunger that persisted in the northern part of the country, and they predicted the regional impact on the whole of East African countries. He scribbled some words in the notebook and listed what he needed. The same question that popped up in his mind earlier came back. Can the traits of the seed be reversed?

While that would have been the right approach, John feared the unpredictability and uncertainty of the variables he could not control. He did not want to fall into the trap of an internal political game and become a pawn in international bickering tactics.

As John mulled over his options, his mind raced through every possible scenario. His best chance was to stay hidden, execute his plans covertly, and keep his movements under wraps. But to pull it off, he needed volunteers from the village—reliable people he could trust. He flipped the thoughts in his mind thinking how to collect data on the individuals who consumed the grains of the experimental seeds.

His focus drifted to the events of the day again, replaying each interaction over and over in his mind. Yet, despite the apparent calm, a nagging feeling gnawed at him.

Something about Fakir triggered a deep unease, an

151

instinct he couldn't ignore. Fakir, the wealthy businessman, seemed to know too much. He's a dealer in seeds, fertilizers, and international trade, with a keen interest in GMO technology. He carried an air of expertise that made John uneasy. But it wasn't just Fakir's knowledge that unsettled him, it was the eerie
sense that he'd seen this man before. Somewhere in his past.

The memory flickered, but it was elusive, like a shadow slipping just out of reach. Then it hit him: the missing finger. His pulse quickened as he recalled one of his students in Kenya. He tried to remember the name of a student with a brother who had a missing finger. The memory was faint, buried beneath years of dust. John tried to place it. The name wouldn't come, and after 25 years, people, faces, names, and even memory can fade away. Yet, something about Fakir's presence, the way his hand moved when he gestured, kept drawing John back to that missing finger. The pieces weren't fitting, but the tension in his gut told him they would soon. He had to figure it out before it was too late.

The final week of his Peace Corps service left him with a haunting memory. The young man with missing finger frequently came to school. John vividly recalled one particular incident when the young man had asked for his address in the U.S., explaining that he dreamed of studying at a U.S. college. It seemed innocent at the time, just another hopeful student, but now, looking at Fakir, the memory felt like an eerie premonition. Was it possible this was the brother of his student? John tried to push the thought aside, but it lingered, growing more unsettling with each passing moment.

At the agriculture fair meeting, Fakir vehemently denied having a brother at Milima School in Athi River, Kenya, 25 years ago. He claimed he had never been there. John, however, wasn't convinced. He knew how complicated African familial relationships could be. Cousins often called each other brothers, uncles were referred to as fathers, and aunts as mothers. Fakir's response felt too quick, and dismissive. Then, in a subtle shift, Fakir admitted that one of his uncles lived in Malindi, a coastal town in Kenya. The abrupt change in subject was enough to make John pause. Something didn't add up. The way Fakir dropped the topic made John suspect that he might be hiding something or perhaps avoiding it.

As John considered this, another incident from his departure in Kenya flashed through his mind for the second time, sending a ripple of doubt through his thoughts.

The week John finished his Peace Corps service, a major scandal erupted at the school where he had taught. Three of his students were accused and charged with serious criminal acts. He first learned about it while reading the newspaper at the airport on the day he flew back to the U.S. The news hit him like a punch, and he kept the clipping for the first year after returning. But eventually, his notebook containing the contact information and that crucial article was lost. The memory disappeared, buried in time. The haunting recollection of the incident, which led to the tragic events, lingered in his mind. At the time, John had felt utterly powerless, consumed by doubt. He had no idea who the father of the aborted child was. The guilt of indirectly facilitating the abortion weighed heavily on him. He had been too frightened to confront the situation in a foreign country, surrounded by an unfamiliar culture.

For twenty-five years, John managed to forget most of the details of his experience, until recent news about a rebel leader's early life rekindled the memories. Speculation grew that Jaja, a notorious figure, might have been a student at the school where John taught biology during his Peace Corps service. John was certain he never had a student named Jaja, but the thought gnawed at him, what if Jaja had been one of his students?

The possibility unsettled him, plunging his mind into a tempest of confusion. The pieces didn't fit, but the nagging feeling that something was wrong refused to go away. Could the past he had tried to forget be catching up with him?

***

John glanced at his calendar and saw an upcoming meeting with youth programs. He turned off the light and settled into bed, his mind still racing. He hoped to learn more about Fakir from Tongo. There was something about Fakir that didn't sit right with him. He couldn't shake the feeling that Fakir was hiding more than he let on.

As he drifted off, John's thoughts wandered once again. Who was the insider working with Monge Seed and Fertilizer Company?

Chapter 17

John habitually interacted with local community organizations and occasionally talked with youth groups. Even as a researcher, he demonstrated his leading role as an educator. The youth who met him wanted to know more about future farming prospects in the age of genetically modified crops. As he intermingled with them, some shared with him the local problems and concerns people had about the country's current situation.

Unlike the older generation, the youth were bold and forward-looking. They were unafraid to point out the government's mistakes and condemned Dare. Seed Company for exploitation. They blamed their government for allowing Dare Seed Company to control part of the forests.

The youth were skeptical and detested the aggressive and exploitative attitude of the company. John knew of this resentment and the severe battle with the shrinking forest that caught the local newspaper headline. This was the subject of the youth's discussions. "Did you know what happened to the journalist who covered the disappearing forest?" Everyone turned and looked toward the voice. The animated youth enjoyed these unfiltered discussions with John, who was a representative of the foreign company. Dare Seed Company discouraged its employees from participating in local politics and community issues. Regardless, John believed that people had the right to know and considered youth education as part of his educational outreach program.

The rest of the youth members waited to hear what John would say. The silence in the room prompted him to react.

"I think we all agreed to stop further devastation of the forests. I acknowledge that you lacked the resources and courage to reinforce the rules." A lone voice interjected. This was a vocal youth who frequently interrupted the discussions. John tolerated and enjoyed his presence, although the rest of the youth members considered him a nuisance.

"Why do we always blame the outsiders? We invited them and allowed them to do whatever they wanted in our country." Some youths grumbled and didn't like what he said. Some were delighted to hear his point of view and encouraged him to continue. "Look at our pathetic population. We don't know how to manage it. The farmers had encroached on the forest in search of new lands, and the tropical forests of Monge would soon disappear. Can you believe that?" He stretched his arm, projecting it like a beggar's posture. The mimicking gesture caused a burst of laughter. The resounding voice of the energized, restless youth echoed through the chamber. Like the cackling laughter of a hyena in the wilderness, it might seem blissful, but it is, in fact, a distress call of frustration.

The village dwellers regarded the forest resources as a natural gift accessible to their needs. They looked at it from the survival point of view. They depended on it. They cut wood for fuel, sold charcoal in the town, and made their living. They opposed the ownership of land by foreign companies. The government foresters protected the forests and discouraged people from what they called poaching. With their meager salaries, the officers often looked the other way when offered extra money. While Dare Seed

Company volunteered to help, their approach looked suspicious, and the locals did not trust them.

Everyone knew the government's goal was to fight rebels in the forests, and clearing part of the forest would help their cause, although they would not admit it openly.

***

The next day, John decided to stop at his manager's office. Michael had recently returned from his vacation in the USA, "Come in, John," Michael stood and offered a handshake. The incidental contact should have brought a cheerful mood, but it ushered in a dark feeling, reviving the old lousy disagreement relationship between them. "Do you have a minute?"

"Sure."

"I heard you met with the youth group."

"Yes, this was a routine educational program I arranged. The people were curious about GMO crops and the disappearance of the forests. "He waited to see what Michael would say and continued.

"There is a lot of resentment out there. The local people blamed us for destroying the forest and Monge's natural resources. I think we have to own our share of the blame. Don't you think so?"

Michael was not ready for this today. He had previously given his peace of mind about what he considered interference with local issues and knew John's stubborn stand. "We talked about this in detail, and you know our company policy and the role we play."

"Yeah, the policy is one thing, and we do something different. What's the point if we don't enforce it? We allowed the destruction of the forest and enabled the dictator and facilitated the oppression of his opponents."

"Hei, chill out. We don't want to interfere with local politics. We are in Africa?"

"You're right. Only when it serves our interest."

He saw the look on John's face and wished he could retrieve his words. "We are revising the clauses in our policy in the light of the recent upheavals. Your concerns are real. The forest trees are disappearing. Our new policy guarantees and mandates that we plant another tree for each tree they cut and introduce some buffer zones to protect the primary forests." John's posture remained tense as Michael continued. "We will not support all the requests the government made and will not recommend using chemicals on the trees. You must understand that we are not naive in our game and relationship with the host country. We should avoid and not interfere with local politics and ever-present conflicts. Our goal in this part of the world is clear."

"That is the problem, Mike."

Michael waited until he got full attention.

"You know as well as I do that Dare Seed Company has helped Monge with the balance of payments and hard cash inflow. We helped Monge grow its industrial sector. The country desperately needed capital, technology, management expertise, and access to Western markets. We have successfully negotiated all that and facilitated it. One of our branches of Dare Seed Company has already taken care of car manufacturing, tires, chemicals, and fertilizer. And this will boost Monge's economy and put the country on the right track."

"Yeah," John shook his head. "The foreign companies will kill all local companies, replace them with mega conglomerates, and take over everything: storage, shipment, packaging, transportation, and marketing. You know, that's where they made the bulk of the money. And we leave them dry and make them dependent?"

"Let me finish. Michael raised his hand. "You have strayed. Let's stay on the topic. Our company would not do the Monge government's dirty job of eradicating the rebel hideouts. We are on the same page here, John." With a sneering tone, he stared.

John was not ready to back down. "The tropical forests of Monge are nature's gift to humanity. Many people depend on them for their livelihood" He shook his head. "Unfortunately, desertification had encroached and choked the earth under their feet. Nothing was left on the soil surface to bind the soil together. It's sad that the once fertile lands had become barren due to soil erosion."

"We are doing the best we can to help them." Michael interjected.

"Not enough. We had the leverage to influence the government to introduce alternative income-generating ventures for local people."

Michael cut in. "We are already putting a lot of money into the development of Monge as stipulated in our policy."

"Mike. Don't even go there. We thwarted their efforts and intensified the appetite for more vicious greed." He paused. "Who do you think benefited from the aid for the community projects? We knew it and yet dispatched all the funds through the government officials. They diverted the funds to the areas of their interest or shifted the focus to some dubious projects that the government considered a priority. With no accountability and no proper follow-up."

"We followed the protocol."

"This reminds me of a South African proverb. When you bite indiscriminately, you'll eat your tail," John said.

"I understand that we cannot do much as a private company. You have made up your mind on this anyway. If there is nothing else, I have other things waiting." Michael prepared to leave.

John pulled out the report Michael referred to earlier and was glad that the company paid attention to how the government of Monge used the money the company gave for projects. Their favorite cash cow was various road projects and dams in the president's hometown. The government officials responsible for the project were eager to show pictures of the dams, road construction, and low- income housing projects. In contrast, the local town remained impoverished and alienated. A week later, after John wrote and sent the report, he received a memo from the company headquarters telling him not to get involved in local politics and to focus on his job. He wondered why his company pretended to look the other way while the solutions to pesky problems and injustice remained unhinged. The causes were obvious to notice everywhere in the area—the scene of small plots of land dotting the flat topography of the farming landscape. The highly weathered soil, typical of humid tropics, remained neglected and exhausted from frequent cultivation without fertilization. As such, there was not enough income from the land. He wondered what happened to the initial promise of bounty and miracle seeds from Dare Seed Company that many had hoped to receive. The first few farmers who tried it on their farms got mixed reactions and put their plans on hold. They realized that the company targeted only the large-scale farmers and never intended to benefit the small farmers. John understood all these concerns, but unfortunately, nobody else from the company supported his idea and grasped the way he reasoned.

The peasant farmers in the area with five to nine hectares of land had toiled for ages. They grew all sorts of crops and tried different varieties. When his company settled in the area, the farmers felt pressured to conform to new compliances and were no longer free to choose as they used to. John's earlier memo to the company about empowering and investing in the local farmers got shelved. The company saw the activities of the local farmers as a danger and pollutant. They considered it undesirable that it had to be restricted. Mike and William were the architects behind the aggressive plan that decided the fate of the farmers. As he sifted through the old company memo, John came across the statement, "Dare Seed Company would buy off all the lands in the vicinity." He remembered his opposition to the idea and how they ignored his advice and isolated him.

In the meantime, John kept wondering what William would do in the coming week when he arrived in Monge. He checked his monthly calendar and noticed that the planned district tour with the regional agriculture officer would happen in two days. His colleagues at work joked and accused him of not knowing anything beyond the gate of the Dare Seed Company farms. They didn't know that he learned many things from Tongo, who played the vital role of farmer, and arranged for John to use one of his on- farm experiments in the village.

As he pondered over the whole episode of the farm visit, chilling thoughts about the rebellious activities in the forest crossed his mind. At one point, he thought the conflict had nothing to do with Dare Seed Company. Contrary to the notion held by Dare Seed Company employees, most people in the opposition group came from around this region. The area, with a population of about 10,000, comprises a vibrant, growing community. Dare Seed Company was a significant source of income for them. However, the local people had their share of resentment because of the favor the company had granted. Many local employees of the company came from the General's home area. It would be a matter of time before the situation could erupt into an ugly scene. Tribal conflicts, repressive government, unemployment, and corruption have become part of daily life for people in this country. General Bukasa had tightened his iron grip on the local people. The international community knew but looked the other way, even when he exterminated his opponents. The Western world and Dare Seed Company want to keep the status quo. They wanted the old General to die peacefully in his old age. However, in this part of the world, anything can happen.

You might wake up in the morning to find a new government. Insurgent and violent confrontations could occur unexpectedly. The government of General Bukasa had made deals with many local and foreign companies, enticing them with unlimited opportunities. Some stayed behind and exploited this country's untapped natural resources, and as time passed, they continued exploring and venturing further into the dense forest. They worked closely with government officials and made deals only known to the close circles of the General. Things happened behind the scenes, and vocal leaders who complained and raised the issues vanished.

The general population, kept in perpetual darkness, naively accepted the only government version of the news as truth. The government-controlled media kept praising the General and his policies. General Bukasa had loyal government employees from his tribe who swiftly executed his orders. There were rumors about prominent opposition leaders who disappeared or ended up in jail without trial. People would only read the brief news about their disappearances later.

As John reflected on all the past events, the urge to venture more into the farming life of the local people propelled him. In the back of his mind, he still wrestled with the puzzle of the wandering gene and how far it spread.

Chapter 18

The tour team left the station in John's Toyota Land-Cruiser. The agriculture officer took them to prearranged farms, where they usually held bi- weekly educational meetings with progressive farmers who adopted newly introduced agricultural programs.

They also stopped at farms along the road. John had visited one of those farms and learned how the agriculture officers prepared farmers close to the main road for publicity.

"The farm where we are going is on the right. You won't miss it. Pass the first two farms and then take a left at the road's junction." The agriculture officer instructed and turned to talk with Samuel. John slowed down and turned when he saw a woman working on the farm on the right side. He thought visiting farms scattered in rural areas would be a good idea.

"Not this one, and it's the next on the left," said the agriculture officer.

"We are already here. Let's see what's on this farm."

Not expecting any intruders that day, the farmer stopped pulling weeds and raised her head. She held her hand over her forehead, shielding the rays of the morning sun for a clear view. She waited until they approached her and came closer to the edge of the farm. She thought they got lost and needed directions.

The woman observed to ensure she did not miss anybody she might have known. The faces looked strange, and even the agriculture officer, who had never been to her farm, had a peculiar look and was ready with questions on his mind. The woman, with a puzzled gesture, stood still. The visitors trudged slowly and stopped at the edge of the unbeaten path. They crossed the ruined fences with overgrown invasive weeds. John pulled out the weed burs that clung to his khaki pants. He scrutinized closely and noticed a weedy plant alien to this region of the world. He wondered where it came from. John turned to the agriculture officer and asked. "Do you have this type of weed species? A native to northern Europe? Common Burdock?"

The agriculture officer laughed and commented. "I hope you don't feel offended. This particular species did not exist before you came." The team erupted with laughter.

"I see. I do have the honor now."

"I meant Dare Seed Company. We have witnessed strange happenings and worse."

The unfamiliarity of the surrounding area stood out. The farm was about seven acres, with all portions planted with maize, beans, bananas, mango trees, and some vegetables. Two cows were grazing in one corner of the farm, and close by stood an old barn with the roof curving in. A goat, tethered by a long rope beneath the shade of a tree, bleated. One could see some chickens foraging and chasing each other near the water tank. A typical picture of the farm that John wanted to see. As they came closer to the maize field, the tour team stopped. Samuel and John exchanged glances. A familiar site they noticed in the lab emerged.

"What's this?" Samuel scanned the vegetation. "The exact replica of what we saw in the lab-weedy corn plant. Here, let's see what the farmer had to say." Samuel pointed to a woman.

The woman called herself Mary. She was small, perhaps above average height in her youth, but the burden of rural life and years of physical hardship had taken a terrible toil on her posture. Her bow-shaped shoulders stooped forward, her chest caved inward, and she sagged under the weight of time. With a baby strapped on her back, she hesitated and stretched her crooked hand when the agriculture officer offered to shake her hand. She grabbed part of the cloth, holding the baby with one hand. The entourage took turns. Samuel took her hands, detached himself quickly, and stepped aside. John stretched his hand to greet her. She looked so fragile, but her handshake's strength surprised him. She withdrew her grubby hand, hardened with permanent calluses. Mary waited, her presence whispering both sorrow and innocence, and yet a blissful expression lingered on her face. A small boy and a girl joined her. They tugged at her tattered dress. The children looked pale and unkempt. Flies swarmed around their eyes and noses, fighting over what looked like dried yellowish mucus. A man came out of the circular mud hut and joined them. Francis, the agriculture officer, told him that the team was on a tour of the farms in the area and stopped by the farms along the way. Shortly after, Mary withdrew and took shelter under the shade of a mango tree.

After a few questions about his farming activities, it was apparent that he had no clue about what was happening on the farm. The farmer admitted that his wife took care of the farm. He was mainly in the town looking for jobs. A hired laborer with a low and erratic income, barely getting enough to feed and clothe the family of seven. He worked hourly for a construction company. Every morning, he left at four O'clock to take up a queue at the company. Some days, he got turned down and did not work because there was no work, but he kept hope and went to the town daily. The big farms occasionally hired his family members. His older children, aged ten to fourteen and a young adult, had already joined their father in bringing whatever little they could scrub from anywhere.

"I will have Mary tell you more," the man yielded.

Mary sighed. "They gave us seeds to plant and this was what we got. We expected maize but we got grass instead. They said the government will introduce a new crop and asked us to sign a paper for a free food."

The agriculture officer looked the other way, when John shot him a glance. The rest of the team members kept quiet.

"Ask her who gave her the seeds, or whether she still has some seeds?"

She looked at her husband. He said something in their tribal language. She stopped. The husband then told the agriculture officer that his wife did not remember."

John cast a skeptical glance at the agriculture officer. Samuel smirked, letting out a chuckle, and said, "Do you believe that?"

John looked around the exhausted farm and wondered how they could survive. At one point, his question aroused laughter. He turned to the agriculture officer.

"Ask her whether she heard or is interested in growing genetically engineered crops."

The agriculture officer put him off, telling him that it was evident that this farmer had never heard of genetically engineered crops. Surprisingly, the woman confidently answered the question and shook her head vigorously. "We heard of strange crops and could not afford them because of their requirements. They said that it needed chemicals and fertilizers to feed. We also heard strange things brought to the farmers beyond the hills in the valley. They said the pollen consumed their crops and turned them into weeds." She paused and added. "We are seeing the same thing here, as you saw it." The agriculture officer laughed aloud as the woman waited without emotions. She then continued. "Why don't you produce crops that should sustain themselves without help from everything you tell us to buy?"

"What was the cause of the laughter," John asked.

"It was the way she expressed herself. The crops can't eat each other, but the message is clear. Words spread quickly, the incident in the village beyond the valley spread to all corners, and some people twisted the message."

John may not have fully grasped the underlying tone in her words and innuendo. The agriculture officer had deliberately withheld the true meaning of what she said. Was he protecting John? Or hiding something? Either John played dumb, or he truly had no idea about the history of these farms.

As far as he knew, and from the company records, the Monge government set aside a chunk of land for research and turned over to Monge Seed and Fertilizer Company. The documents indicated that the company purchased the land from the government, and the truth was that the government confiscated the land from the local people around the area without compensation. The farmers still clung to one or two acres of land around the land now owned by Monge Seed and Fertilizer Company.

The woman swung her hands over her farm. She pointed to the neighboring farms and gazed towards the direction in the far yonder and beyond. "Everybody knows the history of this land and how they stole from the rightful owners. We still weep, our tears fresh and wet, hoping that we will return to our land one day. At least to our children or our grandchildren." She passed her hands over the little boy's entangled hair gridlock. Two other children were pounding maize or cassava into flour near the kitchen. Nearby, some chickens fought over the pieces of a spill-over pounded chef of maize dropped on the ground.

"You are also aware of the strange diseases that afflicted the village after the company arrived at the scene." The agriculture officer and Samuel looked at each other.

"People were lamenting the loss of their lands everywhere around the village." Agriculture officer said, to what amounted to his translation of what the woman said. "The village beyond the valley had experienced a unique tragedy of its kind, and stories kept changing, and they don't have any explanations." He added.

John walked through the farm, and the woman explained what crops she had grown last season and what she had used. In her farming practices, John noticed that she maintained the farm well, using crop rotations every season and applying manure from cows' and goats' droppings. She also planted some of her crops together in a mixed stand. He saw these techniques in Kenya with small-scale farmers, and the practice helped her reduce pests and get enough yields to sustain her family. However, there was little left to take care of her other needs. Still, the rural farm situation illustrated the tragic poverty that had befallen the majority in Monge. As they left the farm, John turned to the agriculture officer and asked whether they had a school in the village.

The only school in the village was located near the road and in the small trading center. John wondered what terrible curse had visited the area. He looked at some children loitering around. They, too, would join the cycle; they inherited. The sins of their fathers, their poverty, and their daily toil.

"John," Samuel interrupted before John was about to ask again. "Are you aware that all the land occupied by Monge Seed and Fertilizer Company used to belong to the farmer we have just seen and those other farmers in this village?"

John turned abruptly, unsure how to respond to that statement other than shaking his head. "No," he said.

They drove between the farms slowly along the dusty road. They stopped by over 20 farms. All of them had similar experience with their field crops turning into weedy plants.

Occasionally, they had to stop to avoid people going about their daily lives. At one point, they almost crashed into a woman. She was bent over, and her head was covered and loaded. She put a heavy load of firewood on her head and a Jerrican of water on her back. She staggered forward, unaware of her surroundings. Had the car not stopped as they came closer, John might have mistaken her for a tree swaying in slow motion. Her back was burdened and stubbornly unyielding, as if resisting gravity itself. She moved beneath what looked like a low-hanging tree branch, her frail form fading into the shadows.

John asked no one in particular. "I see only women working on the farms and everywhere all the time. Where are men?"

"Men are in towns either looking for jobs or some of them working in timber and mineral industries. These women do all the work, and they work close to 16 hours a day." Samuel answered.

"No wonder that's why these rural women have many children to help on the farm," John hinted.

"I'm sorry. I did not mean this negatively." He apologized after Samuel gave him a mean look.

After a short pause, John wanted to ask but decided against it. He reflected on what he had seen, heard, and now fully confirmed what he feared all along.

The danger of relying on a single source of food controlled by foreign seed companies is becoming alarmingly clear. The era of farmers freely choosing what crops to grow is over. Monge Seed and Fertilizer Company, in collaboration with Dare Seed Company, will now dictate what farmers plant for food, ultimately controlling what the population eats. These destructive shifts were deliberately orchestrated, paving the way for a swift takeover. By creating a dire need and a vacuum, the companies positioned themselves as saviors poised to rescue the nation.

In John's view, even nature seemed to share the anger of a doomed world burdened by oppression. The evidence of natural calamities was unmistakable as his eyes swept across the barren terrain. The topsoil, stripped of its inherent nutrients, lay exposed. Torrential tropical rains poured relentlessly, soaking the earth and washing away what little remained of the fertile soil. Valuable minerals had long since leached away, leaving the land stained with the rusty red hue that marked the tropics. Fallen leaves, once a source of renewal, decomposed too quickly, their nutrients disappearing as fast as they arrived.

Working in such an environment was a daunting challenge. The air buzzed with an incessant, irritating reminder of the region's pestilent inhabitants including mosquitoes, blackflies, tsetse flies, and sandflies. This land seemed cursed, a place destined to suffer under the weight of its natural and human-inflicted tragedies.

John kept silent for a while and considered his company's policy. He concluded that the company should prioritize women, give back to the local community, and uplift women's living standards.

During the last part of their tour, the group's discussion turned to developing countries.

"What do you think so far?" Samuel asked John.

"It's a tough life. I wonder what the farmers would gain by producing the same commodities while the yearly prices keep decreasing?"

"The sad part is that we import all the materials needed to produce agricultural products from Western countries." Samuel commented.

"I sometimes wonder what the purpose of the developing world's economy is when they produce products merely to serve Western countries," John grumbled.

"Yep, to earn foreign exchange, and this was not even enough to repay the loan we took. There is an ongoing debate about whether anyone would loan us anymore." Samuel lamented.

"I think they would loan you and choke you in debt. The only reason they kept offering Monge at least something little was the fear of drastic chaos that could engulf the whole country in flames." John sipped a drink of water and continued. "And to avoid any new government taking over. They don't want to deal with a new government that may not honor the debt or even refuse to pay. In reality, that won't happen because of an international law on trade." John corrected himself.

"I think they should forgive the loan," Samuel interjected.

"Oh, no, that's a bad habit that will take them back to debt again. The solution they have is to bring the big lender to pay the debts and come to the rescue."

"No, no country will survive after the big lender stepped in." Samuel winked. "Africa had its share of this with the devaluation of the currency, which led to expensive imports, high food prices, and inflation. Everything will go through the roof, with dreadful consequences. A recipe for a disaster."

"You have already gone through that; what is there to lose?"

There was a long silence when the topic about General Bukasa was brought up. Samuel sometimes resented how he led the nation. At one time during the discussion, John mentioned how the developing countries did not follow any rule of law. And military soldiers seized power at their whims. Samuel waited and when the agriculture officer kept silent, he changed the topic.

It was a heavy-handed rule of the General that prompted the question. With the recent upheavals in the forest the General had tightened his grip and increased surveillance. He had silenced some rebellious young military officers. Several attempts in his life failed. The Tuba tribes in the eastern part of Monge, with their rich agricultural lands, were dissatisfied with the rule of General Bukasa and staged numerous uprisings. They wanted to carve a separate state of their own.

The rest of the people in Monge were indifferent. The lack of job opportunities, landownership crisis, and overall poverty had created a group of societies that had nothing to lose. They had no interest in defending the country and the General. Their frustration had reached a level where some groups took matters into their own hands. The people who were promised many things throughout the years remained deprived.

The General divided people into groups and changed their mentality. He made one group fight against the other, favored one side and exploited the other side. People under such conditions resorted to individual solutions. Some leaned against one or two influential individuals from their tribal members in cohort with the General. It was a well-known fact that the General doled out some tokens to coerce the whole group. He used proxies and gave orders in small increments, keeping them in suspense. Others blamed scapegoats for their multiple troubles, including the foreign investors, and considered them enemies of the people. At times, John felt the anger directed at him as if he was the cause of their miserable life. In a way, John had come to accept that he represented the economic power of the Western world.

After a brief lunch stopover at a farmer's field, the tour team headed back through the windy road. They followed a different route through the diverse landscape, dotting lush valleys. John focused on the road and carefully navigated the rough, winding terrain. Everyone appeared tired and silent as John encountered a sharp curve at close quarters and slowed down. The roadside shimmered with the sparkling gleam of orchids and various lilies in full bloom. A light breeze swept through their yellow petals, setting them into a gentle dance and infusing the air with a kaleidoscope of bouncing colors. Despite their exhaustion, the team members could barely contain their excitement about the farm experience.

John learned certain things about Africa that he didn't know before. For obvious reasons, he had relied on his employer for information about the area rather than the local people and natives of the land. The briefing from the CIA and the Western news showed him a despotic world that could go on flame if left unchecked. Nevertheless, his approach to the solutions differed from what his employer envisioned. John had created an alliance, a trusted group of locals, and he was not afraid to learn the indigenous knowledge from them. As a result, he gained the trust and loyalty of the local farmers and Tongo.

The recent news and activities of rebel groups and the brutal incidents attributed to them sometimes bothered him. John knew what those rebels could do. He saw what they did to each other, an act of savagery and loathsomeness beyond any human imagination.

Chapter 19

J ohn took time to mull over a week-long activity. As he lay down devoid of energy from the exhaustion, his body floated in a surreal sensory experience bordering between sleep and awake. One tiny proposal by Fakir, the statement he hinted at during the agricultural fair event, crossed his mind. John turned down the idea of partnering with Fakir to own a lab. He never thought of this venture and was unsure if it was even legal for a foreigner to operate a business. Fakir believes in the American business model and wants skills and investments in American business. He had much to say about everything, including the future of farming in Africa, and argued about modern technology.

"You wanted to keep our people in subhuman status and primitive ways of life and exploit them, eh." John recalled the statement how a simple argument could spark a racial sentiment when he tried to encourage the traditional and indigenous ways of doing things. He had seen how people belittle their cultural values and compete to acquire Western values regardless. Even if those values are destructive to their ways of life.

In looking at the whole picture and the historical context of the regions of the colonized world, John was not surprised. Fakir's rejection of his own local peoples' ways as primitive was not probably a rejection of his cultural values. It may be a defense mechanism professed by those who had tasted power and gathered influence. They used this strategy to deflect attention from the real problem they caused their people. The problem that they created with the help of the Western powers. People like Fakir and many others in Monge kept one foot in their traditional ways of life and enjoyed all the pride of their tribal ways wherever they could when it suited them. At the same time, they stepped into the world of modern amenities, where they developed a taste for a different kind of lifestyle. They have developed a ferocious appetite for amassing wealth and indomitable pleasures the Western world provides. The paradox of life here seemed apparent.

The history of colonization and missionary indoctrination in education had left an indelible mark on the people's way of life in this part of the world. John had seen how deeply people believed in and clung to Western values. The colonists instilled a sense of inferiority, making people view their own traditions as of lesser value. Over time, this influence led many to abandon their traditional ways, accelerating the erosion of their cultural identity and the decline of their nations.

He interrupted his thought process with a pause. Fakir was right about one thing. Dare Seed Company and the world of the West want to enrich themselves and exploit the developing world's natural resources for their greed and unsatisfiable whims.

He walked to the staff launch to get a cup of tea. Samuel, Joseph, and other staff members chatted and discussed heated topics about African politics and social issues. "Let's hear what John says," Joseph waved to John to join them.

"Not in the mood today; just needed a cup of tea to wake up."

"Common, John, you're more of an African than a native African; join our discussions about African politics." John looked at him with a dismissive gesture and ignored the comment. The others tried to encourage him. "A question came up about your youth outreach program. They said you have energized them, and some think you're giving them revolutionary ideas, a dangerous territory to tread on." Joseph warned.

John knew local discussions sometimes sparked nationalist sentiments and didn't want to dwell on such a topic. However, exchanging words with Samuel brought up the implicit biases people harbor. "Why do you care so much about Africa? You will never understand our situation," Samuel retorted during the discussion.

John's emphatic response raised eyebrows, "I never claimed to save the people of your world from the misery they were born into. They don't deserve to suffer on this earth while they have everything to make their lives comfortable. Your country is rich in mineral resources, natural resources, and possibly crude oil. Yes, you're right. Why should I care? Do you care?" John asked. A hush fell over the room as heads turned into eerie silence. Joseph raised his hand to stop Samuel from responding. "I think we all need a break," Joseph filled his cup. John did the same, and the rest of them started to disperse.

With a steaming cup of hot tea, John returned to his office. It never occurred to him that he could feel guilty about what he did or his work. Deep down, John had a long yearning to help humanity. That was why he went to volunteer for the Peace Corps some years back. Times have changed, and the desire to uplift downtrodden societies disappeared from his heart after completing his terms with the Peace Corps. The urge to help those in need is now resurfacing.

He shuddered at the thoughts. What would he tell William? He shifted his thoughts and looked forward to seeing him.

***

In the meantime, John closely reviewed the summary of the data he had received from Tongo. He concluded the analysis and prepared a brief report for the meeting with William. While John trusted his data, the dark, negative news from the field observations or reports circulating about the seed contradicted the positive achievement he wanted to portray. Still, something about these genes bothered him. At this time, John was tight-lipped about the nature of the gene in seed-coded red. The gene can affect multiple traits. He studied it thoroughly, knew the component of the gene, and kept the data close to his chest, although he lacked the confidence to report it. Tongo, who helped him with all his experiments, had no idea what the details of these genes were, but one would never underestimate Tongo. No matter how much John tried to disguise the activities of these experiments, as a curious observer, Tongo knew what those seeds were capable of. He observed the experiment with rats and how many infant pups multiplied faster than the cage could hold.

John hastened up his strategy of disposing of the rats after collecting his data, but he always did it when nobody was in the lab. He had to terminate them after the study with less pain and suffering, using the techniques of suffocation in cages with carbon dioxide. John carried out this task when everyone was gone for the day. He remembered that day when he dawdled and delayed his disposal schedule.

Out of nowhere, Tongo stepped into the laboratory when John was conducting the termination. "What are you doing?" he asked with a surprising gesture of excitement. This abrupt intrusion surprised John. He thought he had the lab to himself and did not expect Tongo. He thought he had locked the door.

"Oh. Disposing of the rats, we no longer needed them, and I could only do it this way."

"You don't release them to the wild?"

"No, Tongo, the idea would make sense, but the population would get out of control." John thought he had said more than he should and kept quiet, hoping Tongo would not get the message about the nature of the experiment.

"I have an idea." John hesitated, not sure where that question would lead to.

"Have you ever eaten rodent's meat? You know, some people would consider it a delicacy." John knew people eat all kinds of things in the village. "I would like to try it if it's safe to eat."

"It's safe to eat Tongo. Are you serious?"

"Yes. The villagers would love the meat." Just imagine the nutritious value that people would get. If you don't have any use for them, let me take them?"

John softened up and thought. If he can help improve the diet and nutrition of the villagers, he won't mind the ethical dilemma. As a scientist, John considered those rats subjects, and it would be unethical to do anything other than what the experiment intended. He fed the rats corn seeds that human beings could feed on. The experiment did not use any detrimental chemicals on the seeds, which could not harm the rats or humans, even if he gave the rats out to those who wanted to use the meat.

"I will normally dispose of them after two-week intervals. You can come around if you want, and I will leave them in the gunny bag near the storage cabin." Tongo smiled and admitted that he ate rat meat in the village and enjoyed it. John initially hesitated to break his ethical rules but became curious when his experimental mind leaped ahead. He could get unintended data and learn its impact on humans. His face flushed with a glow and rippled into a soft half-smile. He instantly stretched and raised his hands.

"Tongo, the meat will not be enough for all the people in the village. By the way, which village do you have in mind?"

"I have a strong connection with the village past the valley, where the incident occurred."

"Great! That was where you had your uncle's farm?"

"Yes, he bought ten acres of farm in that village last year. Monge Seed and Fertilizer Company used his farm for seed multiplication, basically like on-farm experimentation."

John stared at him, breathing, "You didn't share this with me?"

Tongo fidgeted." They restricted visits to their experiments, and they didn't allow me." He paused. "I will figure something out when I go to the village tomorrow. I have somebody who can sneak me in." John kept quiet for a while, thinking how much he didn't know about Tongo. It never occurred to John that Tongo could keep a secret from him, although most native folks kept local issues from foreigners.

John felt the weight of mistrust and secrecy clouding his judgment. The ambiguous nature of the experiment had stripped him of his natural empathy, leaving him adrift in a sea of apathy. The uncertainty bogged him down, making it hard to focus, and the more he tried to grasp the situation, the more it eluded him.

"Tongo, let's talk after your farm visit," John said, fixing his gaze firmly on him. "Let me know if you need anything."

He turned to leave but stopped abruptly, as if struck by an idea. Turning back, he locked eyes with Tongo. "I need one favor from you."

"What is it? Sure, no problem," Tongo replied, his tone light but curious.

"Can you document the names of the individuals you give the meat from the rat? Keep track of them and let me know."

There was a brief pause. Tongo nodded, though his expression hinted at unease.

John's lips pressed into a tight line. "Thank you. Have a safe visit."

As Tongo walked away, John remained still, the request lingering in the air like an unspoken warning.

Chapter 20

ongo stood in the doorway. He waited a little and slowly closed the door. He tried to assess the vibes in the room. John turned and ushered him to the conference table. Tongo expected to hear some unpleasant news, but John did not show it.

Their recent meetings had become a series of speculative interrogations, each one more probing than the last. Tongo couldn't ignore the shift in mood. He picked up on the unspoken gestures, stiff, calculated, and devoid of the camaraderie they once shared. What used to feel like friendly collaboration had dissolved into something colder, more detached and distant.

Tongo had accepted the new dynamic as part of his routine. But he couldn't shake the sense that something deeper was unraveling. The luster of their friendship had faded, replaced by a quiet, unspoken tension.

Unlike other foreign employees, John had always stood apart. He'd built genuine relationships with the locals, particularly the rural farmers. His support carried weight, and enough to sway decisions with a word, if he chose to. That influence, once a strength, now felt like a looming shadow over their conversations. An eerie silence stretched between them, heavy with unspoken meaning. Tongo could read it clearly. He had learned to decipher John's subtle cues, the weight behind his words or lack thereof.

He understood that the experiment was consuming John, heightening his obsession with the seed. Tongo could sense it wasn't just curiosity anymore, it was something more urgent, almost desperate.

Tongo opened his field notebook and flipped through the pages, pausing briefly before lifting his head. John nodded, signaling him to begin.

"I had a productive visit," Tongo started, his voice steady but with an undercurrent of tension. "I discovered that Monge Seed and Fertilizer Company is distributing a seed variety with traits identical to what we've observed. Whether it's the same as yours or not, only your analysis can confirm." He took a deep breath, his expression darkening.

"The elephant in the room is Monge Seed and Fertilizer Company. Their seed is at the center of the problems we're hearing about, including those allergies."

Tongo hesitated, glancing at John for reassurance before continuing. "There's a plan to halt its release until next year, but the reason isn't clear. The government is involved, but they're secretive, and the details are sketchy." He fixed his gaze at John, the question in his eyes sharp. "What's the deal between Monge Seed and Fertilizer Company and Dare Seed Company?"

John leaned back slightly, his tone dry. "We're competitors. There's little I can share about the complexities of the collaboration. However, we do have a bilateral agreement with Monge's government, and we've provided support in the agricultural sector."

Tongo's brows furrowed. Something wasn't right. "The DNA analysis you conducted confirmed that the samples I sent from the farmers' fields contained the same gene components as your seeds. I've also confirmed with farmers that Monge Seed and Fertilizer Company supplied those seeds. And those seeds caused the problems we discussed."

For a moment, neither of them spoke. The weight of the implications hung in the air, unspoken but undeniable. Tongo finally fell silent, his face a mixture of thoughtfulness and unease.

John cleared his throat, breaking the silence. "Tongo, you're aware that developing a seed variety takes at least ten years, right? Our seeds were produced through genetic engineering, and the foundational work started long before I arrived here." He paused; his voice steady but tinged with a hint of defensiveness. "When the scientist who held my position left, I inherited the project and continued the work he began."

Tongo leaned back slightly, his expression shifting. The revelation lingered in the air, and for a moment, it felt as though an invisible line had been drawn between them.

"There were a lot of rumors about what that scientist worked on," John admitted, his tone cautious. "Mostly about biochemical engineering and genetics, even whispers of bioterrorism. But that's all hearsay. I don't know the full story." He stopped, as if weighing how much more to say.

"Are you working on the same thing he did?" Tongo asked, his voice laced with suspicion.

John shook his head. "It's not what you think. The scientists followed standard practices for plant breeders—working with genetic engineering and genomes to produce new plant varieties. By the time I arrived, the project was already five years in."

Tongo's eyes narrowed. "What did you do differently?"

"I refined the work," John replied. "Tweaked and edited some genes to develop what we now call the miracle seed. Our research team has also invested heavily in the other seed, the one you're calling cursed. That project received funding from a philanthropist who wanted to help reduce the global population."

Tongo leaned forward, his expression shifting from disbelief to something bordering on anger. "Help reduced population?" he echoed, his voice rising. "That seed isn't a miracle. It's the ultimate destruction of humanity. How can you allow that to happen?"

John held Tongo's gaze. The weight of the accusation, hanging heavy in the air. For a moment, neither of them spoke, the room filled with unspoken tension. John remained silent for a long moment; his gaze fixed on the floor. Finally, he spoke, his voice reassuring. "As the lead investigator, my plan was never to release this gene until we could fully reverse it. I needed to understand how it interacts with the environment." He clenched his jaw and added, "But now, the matter is between your government and Dare Seed Company."

Tongo leaned forward, his fingers resting on his chin as he tilted his head. "Is the gene in the cursed seed the same one that made those rats docile and unproductive?"

John's expression tightened. "Tongo, I can't discuss that. This program is still confidential," he said with a shrug. "Maybe in the future."

For a moment, the silence between them grew heavier. Then John stretched and leaned forward, locking eyes with Tongo.

"You've been in the lab, and on the field. You know the type of experiments we've conducted," John said, his voice low but firm. "The analysis of the seeds you collected confirmed it."

The air between them crackled with unspoken truths, leaving Tongo visibly unsettled

Tongo appeared composed and at ease. "Yeah. The unknown elements still linger with Fakir of Monge Seed and Fertilizer Company.

John wrinkled his face and nodded in agreement. "Monge Seed and Fertilizer Company will soon be the sole seed supplier for the whole country, and sadly, our company will provide all resources."

Tongo squeezed his eyes shut and hesitated. "What about the miracle seed?" He asked again.

"The miracle seed is still under scrutiny and will not be released. Not many people even knew the component of its gene."

Tongo remained silent with an apparent sad gesture on his face and then asked.

"What exactly is the gene about?"

"Right now, our investigation has to take a multifaceted approach. The allergy issue, the weedy corn, and an elusive gene that we could not bring back. These are the unresolved pending issues we must deal with first."

John watched Tongo's slouch posture.

"I am still confused. Are you abandoning the miracle seed?"

"Yes, the government is behind it. There is very little I can do." John held a little back. He knew his company's plans had a hidden agenda. They will replace the miracle seed. He didn't want to disclose what they would replace with.

Not sure what to expect, Tongo remained silent.

They both understood the gravity of the situation.

"I think it was a done deal, and it could even happen this year." Tongo tilted his head and poured out every little piece of information he held. "You know our farmers still hold on to their old tradition of saving their seeds to plant the following year." And it did very well. They were delighted with the results. The farmers will always do that, and it's no big deal."

Tongo these are the second generation of hybrid seeds. You expect different vigor and high yields. Remember, the variety is patented, and the genes belong to our company."

Tongo brushed it off with a side glance, and John understood and felt a sense of betrayal.

"I have to know if they used the seeds from our experimental variety seed to replant again. I need to know everything." John's facial expressions changed. "You should have consulted with me from the beginning."

"Sorry, I thought you wanted to know more about how the seed behaved in the field. I wanted to witness the success and joy of seeing the miracle and prosperity under my watch. Not in the lab but in the open farmer's field."

"Yes, that's why I am conducting this experiment. However, there are specific scientific steps that I need to follow." His face turned reddish.

"Is there something you know that I don't know about this seed?"

"Joy and misery. Similar things we observed in the rats." Tongo said with a subdued undertone of uncertainty.

John understood his vague attempt and did not press for further clarification. "Bring me the samples planted from the hybrid seeds. Collect some kernels after the harvest. I want to see them. Label the sample and provide detailed information." He checked his calendar of events for a farm visit and declared his intention. "Do you have something else to add.?"

"Fakir and his teams are aggressively promoting their seeds in the village as a local variety that farmers can rely on. They have extended their free offering."

"Wait a minute. What kind?" John asked abruptly.

"I am not sure."

John remembered that Michael had mentioned the Monge Seed and Fertilizer Company developing a stable variety to launch in the coming year, and the country would only be ready to sustain itself for a short time.

"Tongo, I stopped paying attention to hearsay, but I heard Samuel lamenting that the Fakir company knew everything about our company, but we knew very little about what they were doing in the field." He twitched his facial muscles and asked. "Do you know how long ago they were planting?"

"Probably about two seasons," Tongo replied.

"Find out how you can get access to their seed. I need a sample of it as well."

"My uncle had planted these seeds and used them on three acres. He's a progressive farmer and wants to try new things."

"Is there anything else that I need to know?" John asked again, suspecting that Tongo had something to say.

"The problem in the village we discussed earlier is getting out of hand. Spreading to other areas and it's getting worse. The fatality has increased." He paused. John looked up as if he knew what to expect. "A university student was conducting research and reported no birth records in the hospital for the last two years. The area had more allergies linked to this seed than any other time in the village's history." He took a deep breath and noted. "The researcher strongly recommended that the variety be discontinued and banned in the region and considered it a pandemic health hazard."

"Tongo, people here all have bizarre notions. They don't even go to the clinics for delivery and keep recycling one little piece of information that happened in the past. I wanted us to be on the same page. We stopped planting our seed immediately after the first season, yet we kept hearing these stories. Remember, we controlled everything, and there was no way our seeds could cause problems related to allergies or infertility. We have the culprit, as you alluded to. The Monge Seed and Fertilizer Company."

Tongo shook his head. "They don't want negative publicity. The word is out. Dare Seed Company produced the variety. This was a fact. Who owns it is irrelevant at this point."

John grinned, his face twisting in distortion as the undeniable truth of Tongo's statement jolted him.

"They can get away with this. They are protected, and nobody can touch them." Tongo added.

John knew the politics of the area and understood what Tongo feared. Like most countries on the continent, Monge faced persistent intra-state conflicts and unconstitutional changes that no one could predict. He had a hunch about Monge Seed and Fertilizer Company's mischievous plans but underestimated how far they had progressed. They must have had a helping hand from inside, and he wondered who their source was.

"I am curious, Tongo. You knew these activities all along?"

Tongo appeared caught off guard. "No," he looked up, dazed as a deer about to leap out of the lion's chase. John let the initial reaction slide by. "I heard people discussing it and the government's collaborations with our company," Tongo added. He glanced at John and felt an awkward silence and the need to explain.

"I don't know whether the seeds farmers saved and planted had defects or genes that caused the anomaly. The viable seeds could have spread the deadly pollen."

"That won't happen." John interjected.

"Strange things have happened through the air." Tongo tried to change the topic again.

"There is no reason for alarm." John reassured him. "After the last season, as we agreed, there was no trace of our seed in the farmer's field. Whatever caused the problems had nothing to do with us." He needed to see the progress report from the village where Tongo had compiled the information. After a long silence, Tongo commented.

"We must admit that Monge Seed and Fertilizer Company produced seeds similar to the one we have, and they have distributed them. You already figured it out. How did they get them remained a mystery?" He shrugged. Tongo sensed how his statement weighed on John.

John lifted his head. "It's my responsibility to clear up this issue. As I mentioned, the analysis of the results confirmed that the seeds were the same. However, I was unsure what role your seeds played." While he had appreciated Tongo's knowledge and how much he knew about what was happening in the area, John suspected a bit of reluctance and how Tongo was not forthcoming with clear answers. Tongo had probably tried experimental seeds without John's knowledge and knew the real problem. And yet he tried to deflect the narratives and diffuse the situation.

Chapter 21

That same week, John embarked on an ambitious plan to implement his plan. He had gathered enough information but could not affirm the extent of the gene's spread in the area.

He strode into the main office past the secretary and stormed into Michael's office. He closed the door behind him and held on to the doorknob. In a split second, he halted and appeared to pause. "Is it true that we are working with Monge Seed Company to promote the new variety we haven't released yet? And you don't even have a bit of courtesy in letting me know about this decision? I developed this variety!"

Michael was temporarily set off and astounded by what he considered an uncouth sudden intrusion. "This is Dare Seed Company's product, and it is a matter of policy decision."

"You know what it does, don't you?" He pursed his lips.

"Sure, we know everything about it. We have partnered with Monge Seed Company and the Monge government to facilitate the distribution of seed and marketing to the rest of the world in the future. A great population control plan."

"I don't know what kind of government could accept this offer. How can we make the life of humanity so cheap?

It would be a genocide if we allowed this to continue and affect the unsuspected innocent people in the name of government policy on population control."

"You still don't want to sit?" Michael pointed to a chair. He sat up straight, with his hands on his red oak desk in the opulent surroundings of his spacious office, adorned with artwork from different African countries displayed on the wall. A carved cylindrical shaped stool engraved with a lion's head stood on his right on a mat. Nearby was an African drum, Masai shield, African tribal Akan mask, African sunset wall art canvas, and many other collections. "You know as well as I do that agriculture is Africa's most important economic activity. It contributes over sixty percent of the country's gross domestic product. We have to tap into these resources. With Monge's partnership, we can expand further to the whole continent and beyond."

"How can you achieve that if your goal is to reduce the population? Didn't you quote in your report that Africa will have the world's largest working-age population, less than 15 years from now? What a contradiction! A facade of lies. Don't we learn from history?" John sat down and continued. "We have done this in North America, China, and India did it. A familiar scenario of marginalizing people from having children. A deliberate coercive population control." Michael raised his head. "Common, John, you're taking things to an extreme level."

John appeared not finished with his trends of thought. "We have started abusing technology. Now, we can achieve all this fantasy with a simple manipulation of genes."

"Stop this nonsense. The world would not sustain the rate at which we add the number of people, which would create havoc and increase poverty. Imagine the impact on the environment and access to food and water. We are already in a crisis with climate change."

"No. There is an aging crisis and declining fertility rates in North America and Europe. Why don't we address that first? We don't need to control Africa's population. We can create abundance and have the means to do so with the fertility gene. It's sad that you still subscribe to this fallacy of pseudoscience of eugenics?" John didn't like the look on Michael's face about what he said. He sat still and waited.

After the furious exchange of words with Michael, John felt good about his stand; something had to come off his chest, and his attitude towards the whole program changed. He stood up to leave.

Michael watched and, before he left, added. "I hope you don't make stupid mistakes. Stick to your role and keep away from policy issues. Let me handle and deal with those; that's why I am here. If you need any help, let me know."

"I don't need your help," John shouted with a dismissive hand wave and left.

***

Tongo arrived at the village before the market closed. He knew what he was looking for and, with specific instruction from John, approached the chicken owner and purchased two hens. The seller tied the hens' legs and asked whether he needed a frame cage to keep the hens in for easy transportation. He knew Tongo from a previous encounter on the farm and initiated a conversation. "They have started giving out seeds for the upcoming season."

"What seed?" Tongo pretended as if he didn't know the news.

"You didn't know? Everyone was talking about it, and even the farmers from the neighboring countries wanted to participate. The government is behind it."

He got closer and whispered. "If the government is involved, it must be bad, right?"

"Why do you think so?" Tongo asked.

Another customer interrupted their conversation. He wanted to know where the distribution center of the free seeds would be. Tongo and the chicken seller looked at each other. They had no idea where and when this event would take place. Tongo volunteered and predicted that it would be before the rainy season.

"I heard they are going around the farms to take records, and some papers to sign. I will be away and don't want to miss it." The man confirmed.

"Oh, you knew better than we do," the chicken seller said through laughter. After he left, the chicken seller caught up with Tongo and asked for a ride to Kakai farms and the estate in the next village.

"Okay, I am heading in that direction." Tongo had passed through this village many times before but had never been to Kakai farms and estate's office, located about 20 miles from the trading center of the small settlement of shops and a market. He heard Monge Seed Company had its principal office and research center at this location. He spent a couple of hours in the market and trading center.

The man appeared excited, as if he had never been in the front passenger seat. He looked around in the car and admired the interior features of the Land Cruiser. Tongo offered him biscuits and a bottle of water. After they drove for a while, the man asked Tongo to drop him at the market. He had few chickens to sell. "What's happening at Kakai farms? Do you know?" Tongo asked. The man jolted out of his seat and leaned forward with a dreadful expression; his face bathed with perspirations.

"I don't know." He shook his head. Surprised by his emphatic short answer, Tongo asked.

"Is there anything wrong?" The man shook his head, and when Tongo kept waiting, he started to talk.

"I heard the government and foreign companies had secret activities at these farms," he said in a low tone. Tongo wondered why he murmured in a soft voice. He could barely hear him, yet they were the only two in the car. A few minutes of silence passed, and Tongo focused on the road as he approached the next trading center. He slowed down, and ahead of him, he could see people crossing the street with donkey carts loaded with gunny bags of maize cobs, probably returning from the market.

"What do you think they do at these farms?" Tongo asked.

"Some kind of miracle seed, people thought it was an experiment to change people."

"Have you been there?"

"Oh, no. You can't get near those farms. Imported ferocious dogs from Europe guard them, and they would release them to devour the intruders. There was a whisper in the village that they genetically bred those dogs, and they didn't look normal. Many burglars had lost their lives. Some believed they kept a vault of hidden treasure-gold, diamond, copper, and cobalt underground in the bunker.

***

For the next few days, John stayed late at the lab. He got the same results as the one with the rats. The hen fed on the seed with the miracle gene produced more than one egg per day and multiplied. He reviewed all the previous data and tweaked the narrative to eliminate the emotional component. He left the report on the rat feeding experiment without any change, except for the part where he had discussions with Tongo about possibly using it as meat for villagers. He checked his earlier results from the on-farm trial and added anecdotes from the farmers' success with the variety. He pulled out the sample Tongo brought recently from the village. He counted twenty cobs divided into five small bags containing four cobs each. The label indicated samples from different farmers.

The final part of his report included DNA testing that proved the results of Fakir's seed lot, which Tongo presented for analysis. John then browsed through the handwritten notes from Tongo's observation log and added the statement he had underlined. Some hens did not lay eggs, while others did.

He reread the report and made corrections to reflect on the latest update. It irked him to redo and fill the gaps. His cheeks turned reddish, and his eyebrows narrowed. The irritation had reached a boiling temperature. He acknowledged the destructive trait everyone talked about. He paced the length of his office space, stood before the window, and opened it. A stream of warm October air engulfed him.

John speculated that there might have been a mix-up in the color-coding of the seed varieties and suspected Tongo had mistakenly swapped them during planting. However, Tongo was certain about the color codes of the seeds he had planted. To verify, John reviewed the instructions he had given, checked the rat-feeding experiments, and confirmed that Tongo had followed the color-coded packaging of red, green, and orange correctly in all assignments.

Tongo's observation notes revealed an intriguing pattern: rats fed with seeds from the green packet multiplied the most, those from the red packet did not multiply at all, and the results from the orange packet were mixed, some multiplied, while others did not. What did this mean?
Tongo underlined the statement and placed a question mark beside it.

John called another meeting with Tongo to discuss the results. His main worry was about Fakir's seed lot, which he suspected might have caused all those problems in the village. He closely scrutinized the results and concluded that the mystery of the destructive gene originated from Fakir's farm. John turned to Tongo.

"We have enough evidence to conclude that Fakir's seed company engineered all these problems." He sat back with his hands behind his head and cast him a triumphant grin.

Tongo watched silently. He didn't have anything to add. John glanced and noticed Tongo's appearance shrunk with his eyes darting back and forth. John turned around.

"Tongo, I am not here to blame you or anyone. If the blame has to go around, I will be the first one to take it. I developed these varieties simultaneously. Our initial goal was to develop the miracle gene. The seed in the green color-coded lot and eliminate hunger, where farmers harvest bountiful crops enriched with well-balanced nutrients. The red color-coded seed lot was already in progress before I joined the Monge team, and we perfected it. The third variety in the orange color-coded seed lot was a mixture of the other two in equal proportion. We confined the red and orange color-coded seeds at the lab and only a few plots at the station."

He looked at Tongo and noticed his surprised facial expressions. Tongo knew all along that there were some secrets about these seeds. He followed instructions while planting those seeds at the company's experimental sites and the on-farm trials John conducted. He distinctly remembered three color-coded seeds— Green, Red, and Orange, which he identified as miracle seeds, cursed, and balanced seeds.

After a quiet moment with his hands folding across his chest, John straightened his back against the backrest, stood up, and stepped aside from the chair. He held his hands behind his back and wrinkled his face.

"I made the most significant error of my career when I allowed you to dispose of the variety, and you used it for your gain. It was a blunder of the highest magnitude." While listening, Tongo realized and understood why John gave out the seed to dispose of. It was not because of his humanitarian sympathetic feelings for the hungry, dying people who needed food. He wanted a human Guinea pig for his experiment and selfish, maniac fame-seeking goal. And, Tongo became handy and fulfilled his desires.

Tongo looked up, and their eyes locked. "You thought I used them?" Tongo asked.

John leaned forward. "What did you do with them?"

"I sold them to a trader across the border. Some farmers who bought the seeds have saved them for the following year."

John shook his head. "These were the seed lot from the red color-coded." He shook his head repeatedly with folded lips. "Those were not to leave the lab. Not at all."

Tongo remembered all the events and activities and how John got excited when Tongo offered to use the seed.

Tongo tried to break the silence. "You didn't believe me when I told you everything was fine."

"No, I am sorry. I didn't believe it. I suspected you were hiding something. On my part, I had to swallow my pride. The problems became bigger than we expected. The rat experiments, the chicken feed, and you told me about the women not getting pregnant. I had no clue what caused all these issues if our seeds were confined only to the lab. Where was the source? How did it happen?" Tongo kept listening. "When the issue with Fakir's seed came up, I confronted Michael. It became clear that Monge seed company was behind all these problems.

"Are you sure they had the red color-coded seed in the market?" Tongo asked.

"I don't know, Tongo. They seemed to know what I was doing. I discontinued the red color-coded seed lot. The problem, as you can see, did not come from me. It must be from somewhere, and the fingers point at Monge Seed and Fertilizer Company."

He stopped and then continued. "The outcome confirms our suspicion. "We don't know how many seeds you sold had survived and transmitted the genes to the wild." He paused and took a deep breath. "Further testing won't help. God knows the extent the gene had traveled." John stood up. "We are back to square one." He shrugged.

"What do you suggest we do?" Tongo asked.
John took a while before he responded.

"Tongo, my biggest worry is about the red color-coded seed. Once the genes are released, that would be the end of maize in Monge." John stressed

"What do you mean the end.? It will disappear for good?"

Tongo appeared shocked that his favorite crop with such a long history will disappear. He knew farmers have always conserved seeds and passed on from generation to generation. His forefathers before even colonists set foot on their land had grown maize in this part of the world. He heard that the crop was introduced to Africa by Portuguese in the 16th century.

"At this point, we understand what this gene can do to reproductive cells. I fear that manipulating it could accelerate the end of the human race as we know it, and I don't want to be on the wrong side of history."

He hesitated and then added. "It maybe too late. In the meantime, keep monitoring and documenting all the information you receive. I need it for my report." He turned, "You know we will have an important visitor next week. The General Manager- William Stanley."

When John left, Tongo sat down and thought for a long time about what to do. He held his hand under his chin in a reflective mood. His intuition had always guided him, and he knew from the beginning that there was a sinister plan with those experiments. John never disclosed the gene behind those colors. Tongo coined the terms miracle seed and cursed seed after he saw what happened. He now understood why John was so protective about the red and orange color-coded seeds and the genes they contained.

Tongo stared at the vacant ceiling, unmoved and unblinking. He breathed, contemplating the tragedy that could have happened if he consumed the seed. He still had to recover and couldn't help to hold the shock. His scary thoughts turned to anger.

With his heart pounding, Tongo struggled to determine if he could restore his trust.

Chapter 22

William Stanley landed in Africa, hoping to have the most secretive venture. He did not expect any negative news about genetically modified crops. As soon as he arrived, news coverage hit the media airwaves with a group called Save Our Crop, inflaming the information with negative publicity.

William attended a European meeting earlier and flew from London via Paris to Nairobi, where he would meet with Kenya government representatives and the Dare Seed Company management team. He would then fly to Monge.

The trip to Africa was his fifth and second time to Monge; visiting Africa was not his first choice. It became clear to him only when the European market and groups opposed to the genetic modification garnered support for a universal ban on some gene products. He then decided to attend the European meeting and use the time to explore African markets further and investigate the mysterious anomalies that John reported about the gene and its impacts. As the brain behind the Dare Seed Company, William believed that the company should not tolerate misguided groups who disrupt their accomplishment of noble activities. However, he weighed the sensitivity of the current situation and requested not to have any publicity during this trip, especially on his way to Africa. He planned to meet with the business industry group to discuss business deals and extend the long-term contract with the Government of Monge. He would also negotiate an agreement with the

Government of Kenya on behalf of his company.

William Stanley arrived at Nairobi Airport on a KLM flight. He met Michael Smith, his company's human resources director, and Dr. John Blake.

"Do you have any baggage to claim?" Mike asked after the initial preliminaries.

"Oh, no, this carry-on luggage and the briefcase. That's all."

"This way," Mike ushered him towards the airport exit, where a Mercedes Benz 600S awaited. A well-dressed chauffeur stood at the door, ready to welcome him in.

"John, you look different. I wouldn't have recognized you. Working hard?" John looked over his hairy hands, now with bulging veins that crisscrossed the knuckles of his fingers. His skin had turned a little darker.

"Getting old," John remarked.

"I am glad you settled. William felt awkward commenting, but John responded quickly with a smile to diffuse the uneasiness in his mind.

"Sure, I did. This time for real."

They walked to the waiting car in silence for the next few minutes.

"Mr. Stanley, Sir, do you have any comments regarding the escape of the pollen gene from the GMO crops to the wild as reported in some press? What can you say about the pandemic in the village? The deadly allergies from your seed in the village?" Another person shouted. "What brings you here to Africa?" A reporter from Reuters shoved a microphone into his face.

William dodged the unwanted intruder. The unexpected commotion put him off balance. He jerked his head away from a lone figure stretching to reach him. A dazzling flashlight blinded his eyes.

"What? Stop that," he yelled. Before he realized it, a heavy hand moved him away and shoved the reporter aside vehemently, but it was too late. The photographer got away. The two muscular-built bodyguards stood aside, somewhat embarrassed. They were supposed to keep away anybody who seemed to bother the VIP visitor. They will not exercise their heavy-handed job fully because of the police presence at the airport, but from their appearance, one would not doubt what they could do. William looked in their direction and felt a little shiver down his back. He thought he would be incognito, but the arrangement gave him some thought.

"I did not expect Paparazzi here in Nairobi, and I instructed that there should be no reporting on my trip to Africa. At least not this trip." He fumed.

"We will execute the order. Your pictures won't appear in the Daily papers here. We have our people inside to keep out any publicity we don't want. I am concerned about the foreign reporters eager to report anything out of the ordinary to their home country." Mike said with a tone of apology.

"How are the situations here?" William asked.

Mike paused and continued walking. "Well, if you know the right people to deal with, you will get anything you want." With amusement in his eyes, John looked at him, wondering whether that was any different from the

USA. "What I meant was," Mike somewhat hesitated again as if he would not like to say it.

"They don't mind as long as we provide the right conditions."

The statement was ambiguous. William waited. He understood that the company policy on paper differed from the company's actual policy in developing countries. In Monge and Kenya, the company wanted land and an uninterrupted duty-free transaction with no government interference or restrictions on how they should manage the land they acquired. They wanted a long-term project. In return, the country would get some loans for development and trade relations with the nations of the West.

William had been in Kenya and read about the country. When asked, he would say, "I won't call democracy, but that seems to be our only choice in this part of the world. They will never adhere to democratic values. We have to deal with what we got." Unlike Monge, Kenya appears relatively stable. The company needed stability to function. In the past, it had operated under shoddy deals drowned with secrecy. The company turned its back on internal problems even when it had leverage against repressive governments. They held to the colonial policy of not interfering with local government and worked with despotic leaders of the developing world. Their activities, including the recent unexpected events and criticisms, shook the company. Dare Seed Company would never remain mute on what was happening around the area. It no longer pretends to exist in a vacuum. The world is changing quickly, and even in Monge, supporters demanded a democratic process, a free-market economy, transparency, and accountability.

William had witnessed rapid changes occurring in developing countries. The competitive partners had taken advantage and ventured into all areas of genetic engineering. The need for food production to meet the demand of enormous growing populations has taken center stage in the company's planning process. Dare Seed Company had placed itself at the forefront with advanced biotechnology to meet those needs.

***

Michael checked his time. He had two more hours before the dinner with William and Dr. John Blake. Michael reviewed the lists of items to discuss and omitted some that only William could see. He put those under miscellaneous lists and circled the amount of petty cash kept in different denominations. Michael tapped the top of the desk with his middle finger. He re-read the statement about the spending justification he applied for and nodded. The local non-profit organization under the government's jurisdiction remained the beneficiary. He glanced again at the cash flow statements. The miscellaneous spending items listed was aligned with the expenses between Kenya and Monge. Michael had lived in Africa for over 15 years. He acquired deals, and got things done to benefit the company. Nobody asked him how he spent, nor did he volunteer to tell what he did with $250 million allocated for projects in Africa. However, the last-minute deals he made and the swiftness with which he closed the deals raised eyebrows.

Michael did not expect William to question or bring up the financial issue in Kenya. He briefed him about the overall situation and highlighted the projects' activities. Dare Seed Company supported many local agricultural projects in the country. William read the Kenyan report and familiarized himself with the country situation. Michael Smith had met with a representative from the president's hometown. He had earlier met with the powerful minister of internal affairs to discuss land issues for the company and secretly negotiated the deal. The minister insisted on a fixed amount of cash he would deposit in a Swiss bank account in hard currency. Michael used the discretionary funds to finalize the deal.

"I have arranged a private dinner with the minister without the presence of the press. It would be in a private hotel room. The minister will present our deals to the president. Frankly, the minister runs the government. Bimo can do anything and get away with it." Michael said. "Here," he handed him a newspaper headline where Bimo, the internal minister, was given full coverage. "The paper highlighted his background and his long relationship with the president. His picture was in color, and there was a tendency for the media to use his earlier ten years younger-looking photos. His enlarged and professionally done photo took half of the page in the Nation paper.

"This is another profile of the minister. You can get acquainted with his work and business interests before we meet with him tomorrow morning." Michael handed him a magazine.

Chapter 23

The next day, as they were waiting in the hotel lobby to meet with the minister, William glanced at the minister's photo on the cover page. He had studied his profile and was ready to meet with him. Michael shared the minister's mysterious habits, equivalent to paranoia, and William didn't know what to expect from his unpredictable behavior.

Michael introduced the minister briefly to his team, and they walked to the conference room. William tried to strike up a conversation with the minister. He noticed the minister's wit, sense of humor, and likability.

The minister craned his neck as they spoke to look up at William. No matter how much he tried to prop his height with high-heeled shoes, William's six-foot towering height put the minister in an awkward and uncomfortable position.

***

John arrived just in time for the meeting ten minutes earlier. After the preliminary introductions, which included the general overview, William told the minister, Mr. Bimo, what the company could do for the country. He emphasized the clause in the bilateral agreement that stipulated the mutual benefits and the economic advantage for the farmers. He looked at the points he underlined.

"Dare Seed Company will support the local area projects, collaborate with researchers, and provide professional development training for agriculture professionals. I am sure this was what Your Excellency the president wanted." Having been trained in the manner of speech accustomed to the country's norms, William attempted to make his point. He looked at John and continued.

"Dr. Blake, our senior regional scientist-in-charge of the plant breeding and genetic department and a project coordinator in East Africa, will attest to this." John acknowledged with a nod.

The minister started his remarks by extolling the government's role in establishing good relationships with the Western countries during the Cold War and the stability it enjoyed since independence. He cleared his throat. "We encourage foreign investments, and many companies worldwide have their headquarters in Nairobi. I am proud to announce that our economy is one of the fastest growing in Africa." William gave him a smile of approval. He read a lot about the country and acknowledged their positive actions.

"We applaud your government's support for our small businesses, energy, and agriculture sectors. As a result, our economic growth and trade are robust." The minister sipped a glass of water.

John could not wait any longer. He tried to jump in.

"What kind of partnership do you have in mind?"

"I am glad you asked, " the minister said. As you know, we are open to diversifying our economic sectors. Since your expertise is in genetics, any project that will advance our economy and give us an advantage is welcome."

"Do you have specific project ideas in mind?"

Michael and Stanley raised their eyebrows when John pressed the minister for specifics.

"Sure, we can work things out." The minister nodded.

"We support all the local projects decided by the people who live in that area," John concluded, looking directly at the minister.

" Dr. Blake, we are making every effort to unite our people. As you know, our small country is home to over 40 tribes living together, and each day, the pressure on land, the economy, and basic human needs is growing. We are doing the best we can, and believe me, when I suggested a project, the project would go to the area of your choice, but as government representatives, we can only advise on priorities." He glanced towards William. "Please rest assured that our close association will remain intact and grow as we expand our mutual interest. On behalf of the government and His Excellency the President of the Republic of Kenya, I thank you and welcome Dare Seed Company to this great collaborative effort."

William and Michael looked at each other. "Minister, Bimo, we know you have been in touch with our competitor and know what they offered. Our final offer is on the table, and we can make a good business partner. Let your Excellency, the President, know we still have more business interests in the country. We have expanded our interest into many areas beneficial to our countries," William paused and assessed the reaction from the minister, who stood still without emotion. William had training in behavior psychology to look for body clues, but the African leader sat rigidly, stone-faced, numbed, and without any reaction. The decades of life of lies, dishonesty, and corruption had become part of his life and hardened his heart and drained off all emotions. William got a briefing about the minister's tactics and his intimidating, piercing, blood-stained eyes. The minister's eyes remained flickered, darting from one to another. They said the minister used his eyes to intimidate his opponents and kept his eyes gazing long enough to make people feel uncomfortable.

William had prepared to face this menace. He looked back at him with a cunning vengeance. William heard about how the minister achieved what his physical dwarf and demeanor could not give him by using his eyes. He used manipulation, control of government resources, and all the instruments of power, force, and harassment. His tactics and conniving mechanism of silencing his opponents in all dealings, whether in business or politics, had made him the President's right-hand man but the most hated and feared. The minister had several mouthpieces in each district. Like clouds discarded over the horizon, his informers or criminal partners spread their influences in all the towns, gathering information about the opponents and those who did not follow in the President's footsteps. The minister's short stature made him look like an overweight teen who enjoyed inflicting misery and pain on others. William had heard many strange stories about this dwarf stub of a man. He wanted to use his height to play the reverse role, but the minister deliberately avoided conversing with him while standing. Otherwise, he had to look at William's giant stature.

John appeared dismayed and lost in his world. His unkempt outlook and hippie-style gestures made him seem like a street hustler. He excused himself and left when the meeting ended.

Later, Mr. Stanley, on behalf of the Dare Seed Company, signed an agreement with the minister of internal affairs representing the government of Kenya. The deal included over 1,500 acres of forest land in the high-potential maize growing in Kenya's Rift Valley. The company could do anything with the land but agreed to help local research stations with the technical equipment they needed to conduct research. There was one clause in the agreement that also pleased Mr. Stanley. The clause gave his company the monopoly over the genetics of the maize grown in the area and the authority to eliminate the local exotic maize.

The deal favored Dare Seed Company with tremendous power and gave the company all rights to decide the country's fate. William smiled with satisfaction. They recommended the gene package to all farmers in the area with all other requirements. Dare Seed Company got everything it asked for. Mr. Stanley also wanted to block all other multinationals from operating alongside Dare Seed Company. The minister had given him the green light, but at the same time, it was difficult to trust the greedy minister. What if other companies paid him more? The highest bidder will always triumph.

William was eager to get the land and willing to go along with the minister on the proposed project. He made sure that the minister left with some tangible things in hand. He could sense the mood and eagerness to participate in what they called here, sharpening the appetite for greed. The release of $850 thousand to help projects of the President's choice was a little more than the minister expected, but Mike, the human resources director, reduced the figure to half the amount. A skillful negotiator, he understood the region's politics and knew how far to push the diplomacy button. The diplomacy nourished and laced with greed, and he was sure to keep other companies out of this lucrative market of East Africa.

The deal with the Kenya government went through as expected, and William, the company's CEO, rectified the agreement. The company would occupy a research field in Kenya in addition to the 750 acres of national forest land leased by the government.

***

Two hours later, John left the hotel, drove down Ngara Road, entered the one-lane street, and parked. From there, he walked across the street to the houses on the opposite side of the road. John paused and approached a gate of a complex building. The watchman allowed him to enter after he told him he had an appointment in room 206. He glanced back, clutching his duffel bag under his armpit, ensuring nobody followed him. John walked towards the door and pressed a button. A voice on the other end responded with a buzz that echoed in the background. A click on the door allowed him to turn a doorknob. He entered the reception area and waited before proceeding to the next door leading to a pawn shop. He approached the pawnshop window and took a queue behind an elderly Asian-looking man. It took a while before his turn to meet with a buyer. John had learned how to bargain and knew the market price and how much he could sell. The Indian trader knew how much he could go up. After inspecting the precious commodity, he offered him a deal.

"Twenty-five thousand dollars a kilo. I am giving you the highest price in today's market."

John knew how much he had paid for the commodity and hesitated. Although he could triple his profit, this price did not meet his expectations. With the current gold market on the rise, John would like to get the best price. The five kilograms he carried could easily fetch him $150,000.

"Okay, I will take it in US dollars, cash." The pawnshop trader ushered him into another room, where he would wait until he cleared. He will provide John with a security escort from the building to his car. The pawnshop had a few guards for hire if needed.

John had been a frequent customer of this place wherever he came to Nairobi.

He exited the building and looked around as if many eyes were following him. He turned and looked left and right. He remembered parking his Range Rover in front of the building on the opposite side of the road. He saw some cars on the same side of the road. There was also a police car not far from where he left his Range Rover when he parked the car. He entered his vehicle and, with shaky hands, rubbed the keys. The car tilted, and he avoided falling into the passenger seat. He pulled himself back to a sitting position and got out quickly. Transfixed at the space, he looked to the other side of the car. What used to be a wheel was no longer attached to the vehicle. His Range Rover was standing on a mounted frame propped with only rims. He checked the radio cassette. John popped his hands into a hollow space that used to hold the cassette compartment and found space engulfing his hand. He pulled out quickly. Everything in there was gone, together with all the audio CD music. Mesmerized by the wicked ingenuity of the display, he looked at the skeleton of his Range Rover. John saw some young boys looking at him from a distance, and they dispersed when he turned his face toward them. People passed by unconcerned. The guards who escorted him looked at each other. He smiled and told them to wait until his taxi arrived. He then dialed a towing company number and waited.

Chapter 24

John had just ended a telephone call when Michael Smith pushed the door open and entered without knocking.

"Did you file any report with the police?"

The look on John's face said it all. "It is a formality; we must report the theft, which is necessary for insurance. If needed, you will get another rental Land Rover, but we must document the events." He added.

John held his face with a disagreeable look. "What do you expect? I suspect the police themselves were involved. They were right there when I parked and still there when I returned to the car." He fumed.

"What exactly happened?" Michael said sarcastically.

"I have already explained. What else do you expect?" John snapped.

"How do you know the place where the vandalism occurred?" John fumed when Michael called the police and reported the matter.

"Well, John, as a Human Resource Director of the company, I consider this part of my job to let the police know about the incident. You didn't bother reporting it. I would not have cared if it were your car. Our company rented the Range Rover, " Michael added. "Besides, you should have a little respect for the laws of this country."

John knew he should have reported, but the circumstances under which the incident occurred required a different approach. He intended to report it later "Mike, those cops knew what happened, and I was troubled by them. I believe they were responsible and knew what happened to the car."

"How do you know?" Michael shot back."

I took down the number plates of the police car parked close to where I left the car, and when I returned, they were inside the vehicle looking at me." John retorted. Michael laughed. "You should know better, John. If you gave them what they call "chai" tips to keep an eye on your car, especially when you decided to park in a questionable area, you could have saved it." He said with a sarcastic smile and added. "What took you to that place anyway?"

John disregarded his remark and shortly afterward said. "I suppose you condone bribery. Did you forget it is illegal, or do you now have to operate under different rules?"

Michael ignored John's moody attitude and beamed with a broad smile. "Great!" He sprinted across the room. "It's time to celebrate. We got the deal." John snapped his gaze back, masking any sign that he knew what the deal truly entailed.

"Yeah, you're right. Phony deal? What a joke! What makes you think that they will commit to this binding?" John twisted his facial expression.

Michael halted. "Well," He raised both his hands up. "We got the better deal. We have locked everything and can control the entire county's maize industry and the food system." Still in the jubilant gesture, he added. "We will recoup all our expenses and even double the soft money we gave for projects and quadruple our profits within a year." He smiled. "Chill out! A corrupt government needs a little support. We can lift them with the elbow as they hang to power. Just enough to allow them to survive from year to year." Michael kept talking and continued but turned his attention to John's rude comment.

"Enough of this trash. Do you think we're better? Look at our corrupt ways of life! We're good at hiding from the eyes of people. Our century-old deceptive tactics at work, blood-sucking parasitic greed. We have perfected and camouflaged under the banner of a free- market economy."

Michael shot a glance with a disapproving swing of his hand. John didn't want to slow down and continued with his barrage of moral lectures. "You won't say anything about this colossal magnitude under which we operated. We used illusionary loans or aid to mesmerize the needy world. We undermined the developing world leaders and got what we wanted to do without any regard for human decency, even to the point of abandoning our treasured values and ways of life. A debacle of the highest order."

He wiped the strings of sweat from his forehead. "Like a castrated bull who had desired but can't perform, our minds had been numbed and weakened with illusions of wealth and addiction to power, and yet we pretended to help them, feed them with hopes, long enough to hold them at bay. They can't do anything to resist." He threw up his hands. "Do you think they don't know our inner motives? Unlike Monge, this country has highly educated professionals who know what they are doing. They don't need any technical help from us. Maybe we need to learn from them." He took a breath.

"The deal! It's laughable. Do you think we can block the rest of the other foreign companies? They are not stupid. Their main problem is limited to ineffective, corrupt leaders in crucial government sectors. Wait and see what would happen when their staggering loan falls behind in payment. China will take over. The greedy, crabby diminutive who negotiated the deal should have insisted on retaining the rights of ownership to keep their maize. Only a fool would agree to that kind of trap. How can he forget the long-term impact of this deal? They will remain dependent forever."

John reached for the glass of water he hadn't touched, then drained it in a single gulp. Michael wrinkled his face.

"It's amazing how much venom you have spilled out. The deal has a mutual benefit for both. I cannot believe what I am hearing from you. Where do you stand? Whose interests do you serve?" Michael confronted him.

"I stand by the truth. Let's face it and get real. We depleted African resources, sucked them, screwed them over, and infected them with our perverted mentality we cherish as beautiful life." John glanced at Michael Smith and continued with his heated argument. "How did our company become so damn rich? We worked very hard. Yes, for sure, I do not doubt it." He wiped his perspiring forehead. "The government bailed us outright! At the taxpayers' expense." John refilled the glass of water.

Michael had never seen this side of John before. He had never argued with him about anything other than a minor disagreement. John's extreme views puzzled him. The side that he failed to recognize. A flicker of memory from the discussion with William made sense to him now after this episode. William instructed Michael to compile a dossier of activities on all scientists.

He authorized the company to use Cold War-era spying strategies and gather everything in detail, including the keeping of filthy records of secret activities on all scientists.

The company initially lured scientists like John with generous bonuses and vacation packages.

Michael did not mind open, honest discussions and disagreements but detested the force with which John spoke against some international companies' activities. John's elusive tactics, secretive attitude, and unpredictable behavior sometimes caused friction among some of his colleagues. Still, Michael did not assess the damage of what his detective work came up with on John's recent activities and the dark chapter in his Peace Corps years. He did not want to confront him on this today because it was so embarrassing for him to ask. How can he ask what he did privately, which places John visited, and his associates?

In this country, it is legal to visit places where people of objectionable behavior congregate, and all forms of illicit actions exist and thrive.

High school girls brawl in bars and nightclubs; some have participated in illegal behaviors. His recent activities could make him a suspect. A new addition to his bulging personal file, with transactions of diamonds and gold.

The rumor that he purchased a home in Nairobi and Mombasa raised eyebrows. Michael's informers were not able to detect John's contacts. They were impressed with how he evaded them in the streets of Nairobi. He was always one step ahead of them. John could park his car and take a taxi. He never used the same route to return to his hotel.

They noticed that John used two or three taxis, even if going to a specific place. He was also good at disguising himself with elaborate make-up with different appearances.

At one time, they spotted him wearing a typical Indian wear- Sherwani, with a long-sleeved outer coat fitted and buttoned down the front. He occasionally added a Sikh's turban head cover, an elaborate disguise.

John was so engrossed in intensive discussions with Michael that he did not notice William entering the room.

"You're forgetting that we brought our capital to invest in developing countries, making them rich." Michael shot back.

"We took everything out," John responded in a sarcastic voice.

"As you can see, we live a life of royalties, amid the sea of misery. We have gardeners, cooks, chauffeurs, and various services and privileges." He sipped a glass of water and continued.

"As if that was not enough, we demand hardship allowances, getting everything we need. A paradise on earth, but where do we attain that? Only here in Africa."

Michael kept looking, wondering whether he will ever get a chance to speak.

"We don't pay tax, no bloody sucking Uncle Sam to watch over us! I love that and won't trade for anything less." John kept on rambling.

He paused as if he was recollecting some vital information he had forgotten.

Michael raised his hands to slow him down.

He would never have his turn to speak with John on any issue. A nauseating feeling of anger crept over him, and Michael attempted to suppress his irritable mood.

He felt like beating a crab out of him. Everybody knew he never liked him anyway. Michael can reprobate John's uncouth behavior in public according to his views or put up with it. At this point, he was not sure which way he would take.

It just seemed the right time had not come. Michael tried to interrupt.

"I have not finished." John interjected, and with his back to the door, he didn't see William enter.

"We paid them miserable wages, which we would never pay our workers in the States—taking advantage of their poverty and inability to oppose our ways of life. We impose our ways of culture and life on them."

"Enough, John. Cut it out!"

"I have not done." John protested.

"We think everything that we do is superior. What do you call what we have just done? A bilateral business deal or another free opportunity to siphon or drain undisclosed wealth from world-poor countries." He wiggled his index finger.

"Remember, we have been buying the peasants' land without them knowing."

He wiped his face again. "What a tragedy! The buffoon we dealt with today was a sucker and greedy manipulator who had no respect for his colleagues in the parliament. I heard his colleagues clamor around him with praises and adoration wherever he arrived at the parliament building. He would think they like him, but I don't think so. They feared and loathed him." He took another sip of water.

"He enjoys putting them down and cannot hide his insidious habit of betrayal and a decade of deception. Like his master, the president. They eat from the same plate of greed."

John noticed a chilly silence and turned around.

He saw William and the look on his face.

John feigned excitement at seeing Stanley and showed him a fake smile.

"We are having fun." John winked. It had been a terrible day for him; to say the least, he did not want to admit his loss. He had at least vented his anger.

John looked at his watch and knew he had to meet with William for another briefing.

In light of bad publicity about the news coverage regarding the seeds produced, William had been eager to find an alternative approach. Until recently, he focused on ensuring and conducting most seed multiplication outside the United States, preferably in developing countries. His strategy was to make a quick turnover and diversify the products. The company was involved in transportation, cargo, and supply of equipment for road constructions, medical supplies, seeds, agricultural chemicals, fertilizer, and pharmaceuticals.

William encouraged diversification and worked collaboratively with prominent businesspeople and the ruling class. He believed that Dare Seed Company could hide its assets and masquerade as the sole supplier of everything the developing world needs.

While the short-term gain in wealth was enormous, it was the long-term impact that William Stanley was concerned about.

When he talked with John over the phone, he also got information from his sources about some activities that John did with the farming community. The news bothered him. In particular, John's sudden change of attitude and sympathetic role he played with the local farmers.

William questioned his motives as a reckless move and doubted whether John's admission that the gene escaped to the wild was a deliberate sabotage attempt.

He had yet to uncover what John kept hiding.

Chapter 25

William reviewed his notes and ensured he covered everything he had wanted to discuss since arriving in Africa.

"Let's get to the point, John?" He broke the silence.

"First of all, we have agreed that it is not in the best interest of our company to announce the little mistake that happened. We have pulled out the seed lot from circulation. We will have people in place to ensure that mistakes like the previous one do not happen." William wrote down some questions on the yellow pad. John also took some notes and wrote something in his notebook.

"Please give me the full update of what was going on with your project. Where are we now?" He glanced at John. "I guess our secret coding is no longer a secret anymore, right?"

"I won't say that for sure. Not everyone knew what color coding represented. Tongo might have known the attributes of those color-coded varieties, but the rest of the people didn't know."

"Did you accomplish the isolation process?"

"One would never be guaranteed isolation within this environment. However, the gene had stabilized unless contaminated."

William rolled his eyes."

"As I told Michael, which I am sure he shared with you. We were not the only ones producing these seeds." William cut him short.

"We talked about this earlier. Our goal had to shift to a long term, and we can achieve that by working with Monge Seed and Fertilizer Company."

William looked at his notes again. "Tell me about the progress of experiments on rats, chicken feed, and what else you've been doing outside our agreement."

"Well, what can I say? People were curious about those cute rats. You will be amazed by the prolific doubling rate of production. I could not cope with the number, and with the help of Tongo, we discovered a beneficial alternative channel to use. I think you would like to hear this. It may be on the menu one day. You will never know."

William tilted his head as if he did not hear what he said. John sensed the distorted expression on his face. "Tongo and his village natives are ripping the benefit and have turned it into a lucrative meat business," John added. "These are special rats bigger than normal with enough meat on their bodies. They said it was delicious." William wrinkled his eyebrows.

"John, are you out of your mind? It is absurd, and I cannot believe you went down this route. What happened to your inquisitive scientist's mind?"

John smiled. "I think we have to rethink how we do our business in this part of the world. The old ways are no longer working. We must invest in the people and uplift them from this pitiful state of life. Since we have full access to their resources, we should at least do something for them."

"Interesting. Is that why you experimented with rats? We are not in the humanitarian business. How do you plan to continue and sustain them?"

"No, Tongo and his village farmers will initiate a restaurant business plan, and I will not get involved. They will be fine if we don't interfere in their daily lives. They don't even need us. We created the need in their eyes."

"You should have got rid of those rats."

John did not want to tell him more about the rats. "If you're worried about the publicity and connection to the company, that has already been taken care of, and they will not link it to our company."

"Are you forgetting that you're an employee of Dare Seed Company? The products that came out of these experiments belong to our company. You didn't file for a patent? I hope you made that clear."

"I understand that." he paused. "I had to stop the explosion by reversing the gene, and I am still working on it. The results seemed astonishing. Within a month, we reduced the population and ended up with a sterile male and female population with zero production. This result worries me more. The same experimental result is happening with egg-producing chickens, where we had an explosion of chicks within a couple of weeks with a miracle gene.

William beamed with joy. He leaned forward with his mouth open. "Oh gosh! What do you mean? Can you reverse?"

William leaped off his seat again and sat quickly with a smile.

"Are you sure about this?" With an elevated voice of confidence and curiosity, he waited.

"I have strong evidence to show that it is possible, and the preliminary results of rats and chicken feeding experiments proved them." He noticed William's excitement and wanted to continue, but his passion had shifted to a humanitarian cause. "This would uplift low- income families, and the discovery of fertility traits gave us an answer." John glanced at his notes. "They can improve their lives if we provide this variety."

William stared and waited with a catatonic expression on his face.

John continued with excitement. "The gene in the variety that we created contributed to this. The outcome will always be the same if the rats, chickens, animals or even humans consume the grain. Either gain or loss of fertility." John concluded.

"Great, we have the power now. Do the people in the area know about this gene?"

"Not in the way you and I expected. They don't know what happened. They could guess and believe our company is creating products that boost fertility, but they had no clue about the gene and never expected it. The people in the village remembered a terrible loss in the area, and it still lingered. However, they blamed the chemicals for everything. You know very well that these people believed in weird superstitions about unseen phenomena that they thought had played a hand in their fates." He paused. "I am not sure how my research field assistant felt.

He handled the varieties for a while and may have suspected something beyond the chemical fiasco."

"Are you sure nobody else knew about the other gene?" He stood up again and paced the room.

"I don't think so. Tongo may have sensed something was wrong with chickens and rats when fed on some grains. I used code numbers, and there was no way he could identify the gene. Besides, I frequently changed the codes and kept the information hidden."

"What's out there now? There was so much noise in the air. Do you have the two varieties out at the same time?"

John gritted his teeth. "No, Monge Seed and Fertilizer Company had the other variety. It had devastated the village beyond the valley. They claimed we were the source of the problem."

"Here are my suggestions. In the meantime, please continue with the miracle gene, multiply the seed, and let the people have the impression that the gene we promoted could benefit the world. We will market it in the West and prepare it for further multiplication in the US for breakfast as a virility-boosting drug. We have to take this off the ground. After a year, we will initiate the other gene to help curb the world population. Somebody has already offered to sponsor this venture; we must move with this option cautiously. We don't want to be labeled negatively. One little mistake could bring us down to the bottom if we deliberately experimented on unsuspecting people in the villages." William waited and, when John did not respond, continued. "I am unsure about the business venture you mentioned earlier with rat meat. Who will supply them? Don't go that route."

"I understand, but we must do more experiments and market the variety in different forms, including the delicious sweetcorn that everybody loves. We could get the results we desire by feeding directly. I want to determine whether it will impact their reproductive and genetic makeup. It looks scientifically impossible, but we could look at something like the taste." John did not know that William knew all the details of his actions. He suspected they monitored and learned everything he did a long time ago. The feelings emanated from the unspoken gestures, the probing questions that would never go away, and the snooping and whispering exchanges in the hallways. He understood what it meant. The hidden eyes are watching. You would see it in the people's looks. How their eyes would dissect and discern, with each expression ingrained in everything around. John knew it from the beginning and took it with a stride of confidence. In the back of his mind, he knew the survival of the fittest law of the jungle played more so in human habitation than to the actual animals they attributed to. His original plan of keeping things secret got blown off when he discovered the role Monge Seed and Fertilizer Company played. Now, his coveted secret of infertility gene no longer mattered. Unfortunately, as he mapped all that into his mind, John knew the reality of his job situation.

The company could easily replace him when they had enough of him. Other scientists could do the same thing he did for them. He could only survive if they needed him and were getting more out of him. The sign of impatience with him is gathering momentum. As the demand for results intensified, he learned to feed them with small doses of information instead of a big bang. The whole thing was easy for him because the company wanted to operate under the cover. A secret behind the secret would make a rewarding diversion. He devised his ways under the pretext of scientific endeavors. At the moment, John didn't care how much of what he knew was known or remained a mystery.

William turned to face John. "Tell me about this weird mix-up you mentioned. How do you explain that fifty percent of genes have fertility traits, and the other fifty percent have sterility genes?"

John took a while before he answered. "As I told you during our telephone conversations, this result puzzled me, and I don't have a definitive answer and can only make a scientific guess."

"About what?"

"I don't know for sure, and I will need time to investigate first." He sat back with a dismal gaze.

"Common, John, is this hocus-pocus game? We cannot have this guesswork. Clear this mess up? Was there an accident? Which gene do you think has played a double role?"

"I am working on it with experiments in a farmer's field with chickens. The results are still preliminary, and we will have solid results by next year." John paused. The sterility gene could cause havoc if we introduced it. The reproduction of any living thing that consumes it will cease, and that will be a disaster, and I don't think we want that to happen. We must think seriously about this or shift our focus and find a different way."

"We don't have much time left," William said, his voice steady but urgent. "Those concerned with population growth have explored all options and know the solutions. Some companies are working on vaccines and will find their methods, but we need to achieve our goal through the food supply. It's the most convenient way. We have promising genes that could deliver what we need. Stay focused on this task—I need results within one season."

William nodded silently.

John hadn't anticipated this turn of events. "I've seen what this gene can do," he said cautiously. "It will surely reduce the population to the level we desire. But once we release it, we might not be able to control it. The gene tends to wander and shift its mode of operation."

"What do you mean, John?"

"I fear its perpetual replication. The gene's DNA sequence keeps copying itself uncontrollably, and we can't stop the transcription."

"How do you know this?"

"I don't have a definitive answer. What I can tell you is that there's more to this gene than we currently understand. The farmers have started noticing unusual things."

"How did they find out? Is there something you're not telling me?"

"I mentioned the experiment on Tongo's farm," John said, his voice lowering. "The analysis of the seed revealed anomalies, something different."

"We'll get to the bottom of this at the Headquarters," William said with finality. "We have the expertise to validate or debunk your hypothesis. But regardless, we will proceed with the gene."

His tone left no room for argument, sealing the conversation and the troubling path ahead.

A long silence engulfed the room.

William continued. "As I said, we don't have much time left. Uncertainty is creeping up in the area; I am sure you know it. We don't want to get caught up and entangled in African tribal wars. Right now, we have time and resources at our disposal. If you are thinking about ethics, forget it. Nobody follows it these days. Get the result we need and get it fast." Another silence endured the atmosphere.

John met his gaze head-on, his stare unwavering.

"John, we gave you the monopoly and exclusive decisions, leeway to plan, explore, decide, and execute without restrictions. Only a handful knew the details of your projects in Monge. It was wrong for you to take it to the farmer's field. We have plenty of land and space in our experimental fields at the station to conduct all experiments. You haven't discontinued the experiments in the on-farm trials?"

"Stan, as I told you, things are more than what we think. I am baffled and amazed at how the same variety behaves in different fields. We cannot predict the outcome anymore, and it's as if the gene has a mind of its own."

"Wait a minute. At what stage are you developing this variety, and when did the mix-up occur? Be specific; which one are you talking about?"

"We are at the final stage, and the variety has merged and become one. The genetic makeup in both is the same. You can call it fertility or sterility gene; the name no longer matters. When you plant one, you will get the effect of both."

William shook his head. It was unclear whether he was surprised or angry, but looking at his facial expression, one can only conclude one thing. John will be in trouble, and this project might end his career with Dare Seed Company. After what appeared to be a serious thought, he concluded. "Do not carry out any further experiments. Destroy all the seeds you planned for on-farm trials. Concentrate on the original seeds, plant them at the station in seclusion, and investigate what happened. I will send Raja from the Headquarters to work with you. Sort out this mix-up first."

"What if," John tried to respond. William interrupted him. "No further discussions about this until you hear from me." He rolled the idea of planting a decoy to keep a close eye on John, and Samuel could be a perfect match for the job.

"Stan, I cannot quit at this stage. Besides, we are dealing with something different. We have to come clean. Everyone knew and associated our varieties with the long-lasting allergy season. They recorded more pollen than at any other time in the village's history, and these extreme occurrences of pollen in the air had caused panic and congestion at the clinics. The clinics no longer accommodate patients with allergies. The pollen could remain viable and stay in the environment for a couple of days, fertilizing anything in its way, including grass. These phenomena puzzled doctors and agriculture specialists.

The doctors could only prescribe the available remedies which failed to work. Patients did everything they could. They took oral antihistamines, decongestants, nasal sprays, and all combinations of medications, including various traditional herbal remedies. Nothing seemed to relieve the allergies." He looked at him. "They blamed us for all these incidents.

"You messed up and violated the company protocol. Clean up the mess by destroying everything you have planted, and don't do anything else until the scientists from the headquarters arrive. In the meantime, write a full report about what happened. There is no need for further discussions on the history and what led to this fiasco." He pointed his hands at him in a gesture of dismissal. "One more thing. I assume the original fertility gene line is secure?"

John nodded.

"Good. We will start all over with the pure line. Take a break, don't do anything."

John turned. "We have to solve these problems".

"Yeah, you have a lot of cleaning to do. Find ways of bringing back the genes and then destroy them. That's the only option left before we reintroduce the gene."

"What about Monge Seed and Fertilizer Company's seed?"

"They will do the same. It's a done deal." He stopped. "One more thing. Your transfer to Kenya is on hold for now." William watched for signs of reaction from John and didn't find it. He then stood up to leave and turned.

"We must remove all the traces of these varieties before we embark on our next project. Monge government is with us."

John also stood up and, with a sober glance, stated. "I am not saying this is an impossible task. Technically, it's possible but unrealistic. You're talking about massive and extensive monitoring, capturing wild plants carrying the gene and then breeding them back in controlled lab conditions to isolate and study the gene again. Where do we have time and resources to deal with that task?"

William wrinkled his face.

John remained defiant and continued "We are plunging Monge into food crisis. This approach will create dependency, and they will never be self-reliant."

"Don't worry about that now. Do your part." With that, he left.

Chapter 26

ongo left the meeting and headed to his house. In about an hour, he would receive a guest. He got a signal to expect a visitor at an appointed time. He had never seen this visitor, and the only way to identify was to remember and memorize the code word instructed to use. Like in the Cold War spy era, the rebel network had recruited a few individuals to their cause. It took a while to build trust, which may be Tongo's biggest test. He was not to trust anybody. His recruitment happened by accident, and it was through a business transaction he had with his long-time childhood friend, who happened to be his brother-in-law. He got introduced to a farmer in the village through him. The last time he went there, he met with his brother-in-law and a friend.

They discussed a restaurant business and buying farmland in the village. Tongo has the know-how and business acumen to make it big in this new venture. His friend in the town sent him a visitor in the evening. Tongo recalled the incidents vividly, such as when he delivered a grain of sack through the window to a dispatcher in the wee hours of the morning. He never saw the person who took the package. At first, he found it difficult to accept his friend's request and only agreed out of curiosity. At the appointed time, he withdrew the curtain, lowered the sack, and didn't know who picked it up. This incident crossed his mind several times, but he shelved it and kept to himself, as the instruction was not to talk about it to anyone. From there on, Tongo received a series of assignments, and when his friend in the village told him to expect a visitor, he took extra precautions and wondered what he had to deliver each time he received the message. Tongo would get the packages delivered to him by another person before the visitor arrived. His friend would give him a hint at first and emphasize the importance and the secrecy of the content of the package. As the visitor's arrival got closer, Tongo started pacing his room and tried to formulate words in his head about what to say and expect. At one point, he doubted whether he could trust his friend in the village. The rule of the game stated that he had to trust him, mainly because his friend was his brother-in-law's cousin.

Tongo had memorized the code word and repeated it in his mind.

The visitor will knock three times, tapping the door, one tap at a time, count three times, and tap again until the third time. Tongo will then look through the peephole. The visitor will show him a fist. Tongo will ask, "Who are you.?" The visitor will respond with the word babysitter. Tongo will then ask, "Where are you going?" The visitor will answer, "I am going to the dacha- a Russian country house. He had all the steps in his head when the appropriate time came. When he gets all the correct responses, he will open the door, welcome the visitor, and give him the cardboard box in a gunny bag, where a sealed glass container and instructions to operate it are enclosed.

At exactly 9:00 pm, he heard a knock and waited as expected, and after the final response, with a shaky hand and unsure whether something would happen to him, he grabbed the doorknob and held it without turning. Several thoughts ran through his mind. What if this is another person working against him, a mole planted to play the inside job, or it could even be part of a secret government spy?

Beads of sweat flooded his forehead. With his other hand on the revolver, he hid under his jacket and a knife nearby, just in case, he released the door handle.

"Comrade, it's me." The visitor broke the silence. "I am here to pick up the package." Tongo nodded and went straight to the fridge and brought a packet. He showed him a sealed glass container. He put the parcel inside and gave him another container packed with ice to keep cool between 32- and 41-degrees Fahrenheit. "This will keep the seeds dry and cool. You must watch the temperature, follow this procedure, and store it within this temperature range. Otherwise, you'll lose it." Tongo repeated his instructions. The visitor did not speak. "Do you need anything else?" Tongo asked.

"No, " the visitor mumbled. He wore a face mask and hand gloves, and Tongo had received the message earlier that he should do the same.

Tongo looked through the window. Outside, it was clear, and the chilly night had gotten darker, with a cool breeze. "You can go now. Take a left and walk along the fence, and I will walk with you until you leave the gate. Don't worry about the watchman."

Tongo understood the nature of this task and his assignment of covert and risky business. He took notes of the events in his head and committed to memory and also wrote in a code word to jolt his memory. As he looked back during his first task, he realized the disaster that devastated the village beyond the valley. No matter how much effort he made to divert the attention, the fingers of blame still pointed in his direction. Tongo knew how to deal with the villagers. He had softened them with his charitable activities. The wrath and spiteful vengeance they harbored dissipated, and he gained the trust of the village elders. Regardless, he knew some whispers and disgruntled individuals who wanted to settle a score with him and stood in his path.

Tongo brushed off the intensive thoughts that crept into his mind. The other side of him that they feared. He struck his opponents with vengeance and malice, and whoever had crossed his path met with unexplained accidents. Tongo's indifferent attitude made him appear neutral and avoided meddling in local politics. It may be why he earned his friend's trust and got entrusted with this delicate task. At the same time, the job required him to operate under strict secrecy. His primary concern was the uncertainty of not knowing how he was perceived. In an environment where you have to watch your back and filter what you say and do. There will always be some risks.

Of the two packets he delivered, Tongo could only talk about the seed with some confidence. He hoped it would be the right one, but after the incident in the village, his trust began to fade away. Tongo initially wanted to avoid the task related to the seed because of uncertainty and what happened in the area.

When John revised the situation, he planted the variety with hidden code. Tongo took time to study the outcome of each of the three-color-coded seeds. He wrote detailed notes of what he observed in the fields and confirmed what the farmers told him. The news about the green color-coded seed that brought abundance reached far in the villages and beyond. The story of the miracle seed circulated widely in the area and increased the desire for everyone to try this seed. There was a rumor that even the rebel group leader showed keen interest.

Tongo shrugged the thoughts off and remained unsettled. He wondered whether he had done the right thing regarding the clandestine activities. It was his second task. It consumed his mental energy with such profound responsibility. The event shook his confidence. He knew if the government discovered this event, it would be the end of his life.

***

Tongo had managed to persuade the villagers to believe his version of the story about the miracle seed. At the same time, he secretly took the blame, although not openly, for the chemicals that affected that season's outcome. He knew the problem was more extensive than they thought and suspected. Tongo always believed that it was something in the seed and remained suspicious.

He had already confirmed his suspicion when he tried secretly on his farm in a small plot and concluded that some seeds that John introduced caused the loss of fertility.

It appeared life returned to normal after introducing the miracle seed. People forgot about the previous season and moved on. Tongo had these mixed feelings and started investigating what John was not telling him. John was precise and did everything carefully, entering misleading data to divert attention.

He never discussed variety with anybody, including even his colleagues. Word soon got out, and everyone knew something had happened due to these seeds. John did not shy away from telling them about the miracle seed, as they called it. It was the other secret John held that Tongo wanted to know when, after four seasons, he noticed strange things happening in his fields. The reports from several farmers with whom he shared seeds had confirmed similar observations. Some chickens fed on these seeds had reduced fertility, while some had enhanced traits. When he saw this anomaly, Tongo kept to himself and didn't want anyone to know it. At first, he thought he had made a mistake and might have mixed the seeds that resulted in the outcome. He replanted the same season one after another for four seasons and got the same results.

Tongo had to play it safe only to the level that would benefit him because he could not trust anybody. With this extra burden on his mind, Tongo thought over his recent packages sent with the stranger. He was unsure what was in the tightly sealed container, but he heard rumors about the smuggled minerals, ammunition, and AK rifles being dismantled and made accessible for transport.

***

Sleep did not come into his head that night as he reclined on his favorite sofa, tracing the steps through his wandering mind. The packet of seeds he sent came from his farm, and he was unsure how the seeds would turn out. Tongo felt confident that the miracle seed came from the color-coded green package.

He had unwavering misgivings that nagged him. The unanswered questions about the different traits of the outcome of the seed. Tongo had accessed John's experimental seeds without his consent, and there was no way that he could approach and let John know what happened. However, what bothered him most was the warning he received.

A demand that he had to comply with, and it came from the rebel leader. Tongo weighed several possible options, and none of them appeared palatable. Whichever way he looked at his situation, it smelled like a danger. As his mind put the puzzle maze together, a flicker of hope began to emerge. He had to contact his brother-in- law, who introduced him to the night visitor from the rebel leader. Tongo heard some rumors in the villages and marketplaces. People shunned away from talking about politics. The image in his mind of the rebel leader was positive and negative, depending on the news he read. Tongo had seen the signs, understood the environment's mood, and had to blend in. The demand for the seed by the rebellious group's leader did not make sense to him. The farming activity contradicts their way of life, and Tongo wanted to find out why they needed seed in the first place.

He was about to go to bed when his phone rang. "Delivered," he heard the voice. Before the caller hung up, he requested a meeting with him, and the phone went dead. The call was to determine whether he did his part, and his brother-in-law made it like a regular family call before he ended. "Your sister sends you regards."

"Tell her I will stop by tomorrow evening." Tongo bade him good night.

Chapter 27

After dinner at his sister's house, Tongo and his brother-in-law, Alfred Balozi, stepped out onto the balcony. The sun had gone down, and the evening wind had seeped through with a slight chilly breeze.

"Do you mind?" Alfred flipped the Marlboro packet and pulled out a single cigarette. He massaged the stick and rolled it between his fingers, a ritual-like habit he had acquired as if in anticipation of divine communication. He started smoking while in high school twenty-five years ago. At forty-four, Alfred still had the stamina of youth and agility, albeit the heavy use of tobacco and other intoxicants.

"I thought you had quit."

"I tried and was not successful." He took a puff until he got a buzz of pleasure and energy. "The package was delivered, and I wanted you to plant it. We don't want the same thing to happen again."

"They did not follow the instructions. I laid everything down step by step. The temperature of the soil and timing was critical." I don't think it is a good idea for me to get exposed. How many people knew my role?"

"Two of us" and "the big man." Technically, it's me and you. We do not call out his name in public, you know. Instead, we use names from other past world leaders, such as Mao, Nikita, Nixon, Nyerere, Caesar, or Kwame. "I will arrange for you to meet with him soon."

"Which name shall we use?"

"Right now, his real name is fine. General Amos Jaja." Alfred inhaled and exhaled the fumes of burning cigarettes and made a popping sound with his lips. "In the presence of other people, use the names of those leaders."

Tongo looked on. "He wanted to get hold of the miracle gene, and you're the link. He must have it." Tongo gaped in astonishment. His facial expression, with raised eyebrows, looked like a trapped animal. His voice, barely a squeaky croak, he attempted to protest. "Why me?"

"Your role is critical for the success of this mission, and your specific task is personal for the big man. There were some speculations about why he wanted the miracle seeds, but it remains speculation."

There is a plan to withdraw miracle seeds from the market. You also know Dare Seed Company's role and Monge seed industry in the future." Tongo interjected.

"We know the plan and the plan behind the scenes. The big man should have his seed supply urgently no matter what because we know the plan to withdraw it."

"My source is not guaranteed, though," Tongo said.

"Don't worry, we will take care of that." Alfred then continued. "The big man had a secret network of people in the village, government, and other private sectors. He had an active network, and some got involved in humanitarian work. They helped people during the fateful incident with the villagers beyond the valley last year. Some people believed your team with Dr. Blake wanted to bury the tragedy." Alfred stopped and, with the tone of a whisper, added. "He got wind, and the remnant of seeds reached him, and the person who sold him the wrong seeds got punished. There was no room for careless mistakes." With a severe facial expression, Alfred looked agitated and, as if summoning an ultimatum appeal request, said, "he wants miracle seeds and nothing else. Do you know the fate of the greedy farmer who got the information and wanted to rip the benefit by supplying the fake seeds?" He again whispered. "You don't want to know." He shook his head. "He cut his left ear, left pinky finger on the hand and leg, and worst of all, branded him with a tattoo on his forehead. As a lesson for defectors." Alfred kept quiet, and Tongo remained mute for a minute or two.

Alfred continued. "They found out it was not the right seed. He had a team of people who verified the seeds. They would first test to verify that it was the right seed and feed the chickens and goats. They would then wait until they produced young ones, and if they failed to produce, he would carry his orders."

"What would happen?" Tongo asked.

"That's the cruel part I disagreed with, but unfortunately, in the current circumstance, strict discipline with swift action could send a clear message. Believe it or not, there is tranquility and peace in the area the rebel leader controls. People are held accountable and punished for the crimes they committed. They will have justice in the court of jungle and guarantee fairness. You can't bribe your way out."

"It's too good to be true," Tongo said.

"There's more. The rebel leader vowed to ban all foreign companies." He believes we don't need them because they would create dependence.

"What about the miracle seed? I don't get it."

"We better get inside the room. The chilly breeze is picking up. People had all kinds of rumors about this seed, which generated excitement, and everyone wanted a piece of it. Even the magicians had their side of the slanting stories to share. They have added the seed as a remedy for the component of their fertility concoction." He kept silent and then continued. Alfred knew Tongo was not convinced. "Everyone wanted to try it, including the big man."

"Does he want to turn it into a lucrative business? How can he even manage from the jungle?"

"I don't know the motives behind his drive. What I heard secretly rumored could be true." He lowered his voice. "They messed him up in prison, and the constant beating from the prison guards affected his nerves and probably dried up his juice. Those cruel, sadist correctional officers should not have hit him in that part of the body. A sacred treasure to protect."

"Do you mean that they damaged it?"

"Sh sh," Alfred looked around. "I don't know; it's just a rumor right now. It would be best if you didn't spread it or hear from me. Right?"

Tongo nodded.

"Most likely damaged and no longer functioning," Alfred whispered.

"I don't know how the seed would help."

"We heard the story about women giving birth to twins after eating food containing grains from the miracle seeds with green vegetables. It was a bizarre twist of tale with flavor, but there must be something in the seed."

"Alfred, this is still a rumor, and there is no proof."

"Yeah, you also spread the success stories about chickens and believed this remedy could revive the dead cells." Alfred continued.

"The big man wants to try. We have to facilitate it, and we need your help." Tongo kept quiet. "If everything went through, he would compensate, which may be the door to bigger things. Remember, there is a whisper about General Bukasa's decline in health and reputation. This group is the only formidable force that can take over the country, and if you help. Who knows, you might be the future minister of agriculture."

"Let's get to the point. What are you up to?"

"I am looking at a date that we can block so that I can arrange a meeting, but it would be nice if you reserved at least three days."

"Why do we need three days while in the same country? Can we do it in one day?"

"It's not as easy as you are inclined to think. There are some vetting procedures, and you must go through some processes. You can't just show up and see the big man. There are steps to go through; sometimes, we may not see him face to face. Security is tight, and we have to follow their protocol."

"Oh, I didn't know getting to him would take this much of a hassle."

"Yep, he's well protected. They said one had to go through five guarded and screened forest gates. They strip you naked to check. They said that an attempt on his life occurred several times in the past, and that's why they took these strict measures."

"What's the point of going there with all these headaches of restrictions?"

"The blockade is to protect him at all levels."

"I also heard terrible things about him and the number of people he killed."

"Some stories we hear are fabrications and lies put out by his enemies. Some actions are justified when you're at war, and it's in the eyes of the beholder."

"Which parts of the stories about him are true?" Alfred waited before he answered. He could see Tongo's face showing wrinkles of worry.

"People have created stories; if they didn't like you, they would find something in you. The truth was that he survived the worst torture in prison, and they beat him, squeezed his bowls, and wanted to deprive him of his manhood. No worse thing could happen to a man than that heinous act of terror." He shook his head.

"Are there internal conflicts within the group? Why was it difficult to reach him?"

"Just like most of the leaders. He's entitled to receive protection. He has enemies everywhere, especially when the whole country knows what he's doing."

"I wanted to be clear about my role. You said that nobody else knew about my clandestine activities other than you. How do I know?"

"Trust me. I won't put you in danger. We are partners in this venture." He leaned closer to Tongo. "No one knows our family relationship through marriage, and I wanted to keep it that way. The less they know, the better." He lit another cigarette, waited, puffed, and then asked." Feel free to ask if you have something on your mind now."

Tongo edged closer. "I bet they knew our relationship. "By the way." He whispered. "I was curious about those packages. You warned me about not getting temptations and the severe consequences if they got lost, but you didn't tell me what the packages contained."

"You passed the test. The items in the packages were worth millions of dollars. If everything goes according to the plan, we will never need to work for anybody. We will have our own company, and I have established business contacts in Kenya and Southern Sudan." Tongo shook his head.

"What! You don't want to get rich? We have to diversify. I'm not too fond of the direction our country is going. If things worsen, there must be an alternative route."

"We have all sacrificed for a cause we strongly believed in to improve this country. Are we not risking our lives right now? If that is the case, we should stick to the end."

"Sure, my brother-in-law. Yes, we can do everything within our capacity and make it happen. If things don't go our way? We can always think of an alternative approach. We have much ahead of us; I will expand my business empire regardless. I learned the hard way and regretted it when the opportunity slid by me many times, and I did not grab it."

"Anyway, it's getting late, and I had to go." Tongo prepared to leave, and turned to look at him.

"What kind of business do you and Fakir operate in the neighboring countries?"

"All kinds. We are the sole supplier of seeds and fertilizers in some countries."

Tongo smiled.

"We support faith-based organizations. We helped orphans and missionary work in some remote parts of Africa as well. You know." He waved and added.

"I will let you know when the time is ready. Bye for now."

Tongo wrestled with questions he had no answer to for the next few days.

Chapter 28

ongo and his brother-in-law boarded a Land Rover early in the morning when it was still dark to a village near the forest farming settlement of about 200 family units. They drove for five hours through the unpaved rough road. The morning sun had just settled on the horizon when they arrived. The early fruit vendors have occupied their regular spots. A woman with a bunch of bananas on her head turned around to pitch her first sale. Another one rushed to the scene with palm fruits and oranges. Tongo's brother-in-law held his hand with a gesture she understood and stopped coming closer.

They walked to a thatched hut not far from the small grocery store. There were very few activities, and the vegetable market vendors had just begun to trickle in. "We can wait here until our guide arrives. It will be a long walk, and we will leave when the sun reaches midday. Take a short nap. We may or may not be in the same group, but we will see each other at the end. Remember, we don't know each other; our connection is only through business. I have a business in South Africa and a seed and fertilizer dealer. That's the only bare minimum you should know about me if asked. The less you talk about yourself, the better. Oh, don't forget, your code name is Choma."

Later, a man joined them, a guide who would take them to their destination.

After grueling hours of walking, they came to a ravine with a small stream of water and rested. They then had a late lunch, Tongo and his brother-in-law ate smoked fish. Tongo conversed in a low tone.

"From here, we will take another detour, go through some shrubs with low bushes, and keep closer to the dense forest trees. We will walk in a single file, a few steps at a time. Watch for my instructions, but I can't promise when we will reach the proper destination." The guide announced and frequently stopped as if listening to a hidden message in the jungle.

"There will be another detour, and we might spend a night in the jungle."

Tongo only spoke for a short duration of their long-distance walk. He was trying to decide whether to trust the guide or not. He cleared his throat. "I don't understand. Is there a change of plan?"

"What plan?" The guide asked, and Tongo did not like how he looked at him.

"Let me," Tongo's brother-in-law stepped closer. "No problem, comrade, he's in orientation." Tongo got the subtle message.

"We have to do all these for security reasons. There were numerous attempts on the rebel leader's life in the past, and they wanted to take all the necessary precautions." His brother-in-law continued. "As you can see, this was needed, and there will be more deviations. It will be a while before we get to the camp."

"You never told me about all this hassle," Tongo commented. His brother-in-law wrinkled his forehead.

"To filter the trash from the real. Only those with a true bone can take it."

"You don't trust me?"

Alfred glanced with a smile. *If the child learns about the snake's trail, he will also learn the snake's wandering.*

"What do you mean?" Tongo retorted.

"It's just an African proverb. There is wisdom in the statement."

They passed through a narrow path winding through the weeds. The ground was a bit moist and soft from the early morning drizzle. Tongo's brother-in-law stopped again, checked the surroundings, and cautioned Tongo to remember the code word he had used earlier. And suddenly, from the right side of the road, they heard a command to stop on their track and move a step ahead.

"Exactly, do what they asked and remember the code."

"I don't remember."

"I told you to commit it to memory. I will help you now, but in the future, keep it in your head."

Tongo didn't expect all this and wanted to respond but held his tongue to avoid suspicion.

They embarked on a tortuous journey without clear direction. On the left side of the road, Tongo noticed some movement in the shrubs, a moving tree. A rebel soldier camouflaged beneath the green canopy of the tree. Tongo looked from left to right and back and forth. Before he knew it, two armed men concealed with forest-colored army wear emerged from both sides and pointed a gun at them. One of them grabbed him. His brother-in-law said something, but Tongo had no time to hear. He reminded him of the code word, but there was no time to display it correctly. The rebel soldiers tied their hands behind their back and blindfolded them. They took them as prisoners to another detour while still blindfolded. They appeared unconvincing, considered them unwelcome, and gave them harsh treatment. However, the rebel soldiers became softer when Tongo's brother-in-law mentioned the leader's secret code name. Tongo glanced toward his brother-in- law and wondered what had happened. They handed them over to another group. They stopped for a rest. Two more rebel soldiers appeared without warning, and the previous ones who brought them there disappeared without a word. They did not know where they had taken them.

The group walked for hours and hours until they reached a creek, where they stopped and switched guards. They untied their blindfold for Tongo and his brother-in-law to see. These rebel groups appeared friendly and initiated the conversation with them. They chatted and called each other comrades. Tongo felt a little relieved after they untied his hands. They then walked together; the rebel soldiers went ahead of them. They got deeper into the dense forest with trees that all looked the same and thicker. The branches at the bottom are compacted and darker. Tongo's brother-in- law appeared relaxed as they meandered through the shrubs; the path narrowed to one line, and they had to walk in a file.

The rebel soldiers spread apart; some left the group and remained behind. It was the only time Tongo could talk with his brother-in- law. He didn't expect all these unnecessary, unwanted setbacks to respond but held his tongue to minimize confusion and misunderstanding. Alfred had deliberately kept his relationship with Tongo, his brother-in-law, a secret. No one else seemed to know other than two top cadres in the rebel ranks. Past midday, the air remained unhinged when the sun's rays stood directly over the center of the head. The forest vegetation thickened as they further penetrated the dense shrubs. The shift in the topography added a level of anxiety in anticipation of the unknown. Tongo fidgeted and waited until his brother-in-law tapped him on the back.

"You looked tense. It's normal for the first time, and there will be more checks and scrutiny."

More than what we went through already?" "You

never know their plans until you see them."

The guide led the way through another narrow path that took zigzag turns in different directions. There was no actual path. They had to make their way through the footpath of uncharted forest territory. The guide occasionally used a machete to clear the way. As they trudged along, Tongo showed signs of a weary look. He surveyed the soil and knew that the tropical rainforest, with its poor soil devoid of nutrients, would need a lot of work to retain the loss. He could see the thick layer of decaying plants loaded with enough nutrients to support a life of abundance, but they had gone and swept away, and heavy rains washed nutrients with none entering the soil. Tongo thought of all these obstacles in the light of his immediate task and wondered where they intended to grow the seed from the exceptional variety. Things were coming together in his mind. The village on the edge of the forest they passed through could be the answer.

They spent two days in the forests and had to change directions several times, so Tongo could hardly remember how to find his way back. They finally came to a remote jungle of a settlement. A camp with about 50 rebel soldiers: Tongo, his brother-in-law, and the guide shared a small tent. Another disappointment for Tongo, after all the trouble he took through the arduous journey on foot, his brother-in-law surprised him with news from the rebel leader. He called him aside. "I know you don't expect this, but I must tell you. We will not meet comrade, Major General Amos Jaja this time." He could see a flash of anger on Tongo's face. "Let me finish. He sent us a recorded message, reassuring us that he would do his best to secure the country, and asked for our support and thankful for our trust in him. He acknowledges the risky roles we took and the sacrifice you made." Brother, trust me, he valued your role as the most critical and told me that he will personally thank you and talk with you." He came closer and whispered. "His gift will make you rich beyond what you can imagine."

At first, Tongo was furious that they had to go this far without seeing what he came for with all his physical exhaustion. The news about the recorded message and promise of bounty softened him.

They settled for the evening meal, which consisted of plantain and potatoes with wild meat. After the dinner, topped with freshly squeezed orange juice, they summoned them to another tent to meet with a camp leader with a rank of major. The camp leader introduced himself as Major Andre Bumba. He apologized for all the inconvenience that they went through. He added. "On behalf of our great leader, Major General His Excellency Amos Jaja, I would take this opportunity to welcome you to our humble unit.

I am sure Alfred has communicated to you the nature of our work and the secrecy surrounding this project. We had to protect ourselves and our leader. He asked me to convey his greetings to you again with utmost gratitude for your valuable role. He would have liked to meet with you, appreciated your contributions, and asked you to continue supporting the project. He emphasized that this project is essential to him and the country."

The next day, Tongo woke up early. He looked around and realized that he was alone in the tent. He sat up and peeped through the tiny hole to get his bearings. He squeezed his eyelid to adjust his focus. A pitch-dark forest canopy dazzled his gaze. He felt the left side of the body, checking to see if he was okay. He slowly turned around. Everywhere he turned, it was dark.

His brother-in-law left him a note, reassuring him that everything would be fine, the guide would return him home safely, and he should follow their instructions. It was just a security precaution.

Tongo and three men returned and took a different route.

Chapter 29

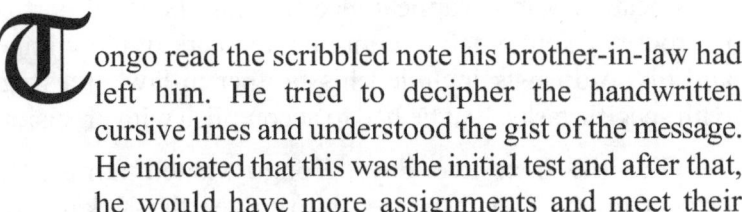

ongo read the scribbled note his brother-in-law had left him. He tried to decipher the handwritten cursive lines and understood the gist of the message. He indicated that this was the initial test and after that, he would have more assignments and meet their expectations.

The tortuous maze they went through was part of the drill to weed out the real men from boys. Tongo knew he had to wrestle with his task and face the uncertainty of the seed puzzle. Even his brother-in-law had shown a sign of doubt about this topic. In this speculative scenario, Tongo realized an opportunity that he could seize. It became clear as he reflected that his recent involvement would diminish his neutrality and expose him.

His brother-in-law downplayed this secretive role and brushed it off when Tongo voiced his concerns. Among the villagers, Tongo was more than just a respected community member. He was one of them. To them, he was both a brother and a valued employee of a foreign company that had done more for their region than any local politician ever did.

Tongo was also known for his honesty and kindness, virtues deeply respected in this community.

After four days in the jungle and not even sure what happened or why he was there in the first place, Tongo assessed the explanation given by his brother-in-law regarding the nature of the job he asked him to help with. His answer elucidated his recent behavior of the sudden disappearance and reappearance that had become part of his routine. Tongo had to continue his work in the village, and his to-do lists included his brother-in-law's message with specific tasks. that he had to accomplish with precision.

For the next two days, Tongo visited farms. His brother-in-law had instructed him to see the Kakai farm enterprise, which he had earlier arranged to connect him with the owner. Kakai farm enterprise owned thirty percent of the Monge Seed and Fertilizer Company and vast acres of land in the country.

Tongo stopped at a small shopping center where they sold various items. He knew one of the farmers who traded with multiple crops, fruits, and vegetables. The woman leased land from the Kakai family company. She supplied fruits and vegetables for most of the restaurants in the area. She grew all the major crops in the area: cassava, maize, beans, and various fruits and vegetables. The woman often proudly announced that she was among the first farmers to try the high-iron bean they introduced. The bean is high yielding, matures early, tastes excellent, and is nutritious. She had boosted her income since she invested in this crop. In addition, Tongo had rented about two acres of land from her for experiments. As soon as she knew about the sweet corn Tongo was growing, she seized the opportunity and got a huge contract to supply it to the neighboring regions. The rumor of her venture spread across the neighboring countries.

Tongo checked the name on the note his brother-in-law gave him and realized that many people operated under this family name, and it looked as if the whole region belonged to this family. He met an older man on the road who directed him to the Kakai family home. Tongo approached a spacious land with buildings, trees, fruits, and gardens. He noticed two men walked up to him and asked what he wanted. Tongo gave his name and requested to see Mama Kakai. After about 10 minutes, the servant ushered him into a luxurious house modeled on French property types. He was not sure what kind of a house. He thought it was a Chateau or Villa. He stood mesmerized to see a massive building with multiple rooms, decorative interior design, and scenic views. He could see numerous gardens, trees, and stone-made walls around. While waiting, he was offered a coffee and told to wait for Madam.

"Madam is ready for you, sir. Can you come with me?" A servant announced and led him into the next room.

Tongo's first impression showed a woman of admirable beauty, confidence, and charm. Although she appeared youthful, he thought she was older after a closer look.

"Alfred talked about your work, and I am considering investing in GMO crops. He wanted to partner with me. He mentioned that you have the expertise we need." She spoke firmly with conviction and knew what she wanted. "My company will invest heavily in agriculture, and we are ready to set aside about 500 acres for this venture. I want to offer you a managerial position. Many things are in the air, but we will get through this. When I was growing up, we had similar crises, and many people were displaced. I believe peace will prevail in this part of the world, and we would like to start the project next year during the rainy season. You can start anytime if you are ready to come on board." She sipped a glass of lemonade and continued. "We're thinking big and don't limit ourselves to Monge alone. Our company has branches in Kenya, Uganda, and South Sudan. You probably know my brother, Fakir. He's also into the farming business, particularly fertilizer and seeds. My brother is a character of his own, involved in many things, and has business ties worldwide." Tongo was not surprised. He had heard rumors about this family before. "Think about this proposal and reply as soon as possible. Here is my direct contact:" She gave him her contact telephone number and an email. Tongo cleared his voice." I will think about the offer and get back to you. Thank you for trusting in me." The meeting ended, and Tongo prepared to leave. She asked him a general question.

"What do you think about the future of this project?"

"I could be biased, but the trend is tilting towards GMO crops, and while we are still lagging in acceptance in Africa, the rest of the world has already embraced them. GMO products are everywhere on the market. We must wake up, understand, and monitor what is happening. Above all, we have to protect our natural resources. We have farmers with small acres who depend on their farms for their livelihood, and I am afraid large conglomerate farms will displace them. We have not reached that level yet, but we are gullible and quick to take things in without question, especially the products from the West. We have abandoned our ways of life and indigenous knowledge that has guided us through the ages. I have to be clear that I am not against GMOs, and I am on the side of caution, and we need to understand the local environment and situation before we accept things at face value." Mama Kakai's facial expression changed.

"I get your point. If we compete with the rest of the world, we must be capable and on equal footing. I am surprised you had some reservations, and I can detect them in your tone of voice."

"No, no," Tongo shook his head. "You're right. For us to compete, we must be at par." Mama Kakai smiled.

"Tell me about your boss. I heard a lot about him."

"He taught me valuable life lessons. I now appreciate my heritage and culture better. Our education system made us hate ourselves and our ways of life. They believed our ways were primitive and encouraged us to abandon them, and what Dr. Blake said to me once stuck with me. He advised. "Don't expect other people to promote your values for you. You have to do it yourselves and protect them. Once you let others decide for you, you will lose control of your lives and become dependent forever." Mama Kakai appeared confused. "Once we fully accept this change, we are at their mercy. Our ways of life will change forever. Our small farmers will never save seeds as they used to. They will have to buy new seeds yearly, which they can't afford."

"Didn't you say that we have to compete? How can we do that with our mediocrity? We have to be better or equal, and I am sorry that our small farmers will have no place in the future. They have to go. We have to merge all these small farms. We can do better and farm efficiently."

Tongo flinched, trying to hold up his courage, and with his confidence tested, he had to find another way to convince Mama Kakai to understand his point of view. He knew he was dealing with a shrewd, intelligent businesswoman ahead of her time. A giant in her ways. The woman he had heard so much about and underestimated her potential. There was no exaggeration in what he heard about her; Mama Kakai can have her ways, and he wondered how she would fit in with the upcoming upheavals. She glanced at her Omega Prestige Quartz; the Roman numeral hour index stood at 11:00. "I had to go." Tongo's eyes fixed on the luxurious watch and missed what she said.

"Pardon, madam, what did you say?"

"I want the miracle seed. If you can deliver it and prove it will work, I will pay you well, but I must have a monopoly. It will just be a matter of time. All the farms around in the valley will be mine."

She tapped her ring on the middle finger and rolled with her left thumb as if scratching. The glittering diamond sparkled, adding pride in comfort and confidence that exuded power, balance, and stability.

"I will need the variety two months before the planting season."

"Madam, the variety has not been released yet. There is a talk about withdrawing. We don't have seeds to plant."

"I heard that, but..." she winked.

"We will have the seed ready by then. We have enough land to multiply the seeds and prepare them for next year's market. Is what I heard true?"

"What's that, Madam?"

"Does the variety boost virility? They claimed it increased production in the chickens that fed on the seeds."

"Yes, to some extent. We noticed some anomalies with the same variety as well."

"What? Why? God forbid. How could this happen?"

"We don't know yet."

"What are you doing about it?

Tongo hesitated. "Madam, it's not as easy as you think, and I don't have full access to the source."

"If you work closely with the person who has access to the source as indicated, you can get access. We can work it out, you know. Name your price. We are aware of the country's plan for seed production."

Tongo had come across people of different personalities and managed to handle them. What he faced with Mama Kakai evoked an emotional reaction he had never experienced. He understood what she wanted him to do. It's the way things are when you have the means. He could sense the intensity in her eyes, and she could do anything to acquire it, and his brother-in-law also wanted the same thing. Mama Kakai adds elegance to the request with confidence that you cannot say no. She's charming and irresistible. Tongo now understands why his brother- in-law sent him to Mama Kakai.

"I think there is a misunderstanding about my role in this variety. Dr. Blake was the only person who could surely confirm the components of the genes that made this variety." Mama Kakai laughed.

"We know everything they do; we have insiders. All this mambo jumbo you're talking about is a delaying tactic. They had ulterior motives. Why did they need to research in Africa when they could do it in their own countries with all the facilities at their disposal? They are interested in our natural resources, or this miracle variety is a quick fix they want to do outside, away from the prying eyes of the scientific world. They are barely known here in Monge. A place where they could do their dubious hidden research without interference."

"I will have to talk with Alfred to clarify some of these things you mentioned." He turned around, "I know that we have not yet released the variety to the market, and my estimate would be within a year after the evaluation in the farmer's field. Again, Dr. Blake is in charge and might do something different based on the analysis and the information he gathered."

"I am interested in the future market prospects. If some of the things I heard about are true, I would like to have a separate discussion with you and Alfred?" Tongo knew how rumors worked in this community and waited to hear what else she would ask. "Alfred will get in touch with you.?"

Tongo gave her his business card and prepared to leave.

"One more thing." She held her hand up for Tongo to pause. "Can you arrange a meeting with Dr. Blake?"

Tongo hesitated, "about what?"

"Never mind." Mama Kakai looked on, sending him her victory smile. When the visitor left, she tapped a number on her watch. "We need to meet tomorrow at dinner."

"That would work," Alfred answered. She knew she had won the battle.

Chapter 30

Tongo received an invitation from his sister the following week. His brother-in-law was back from his trip and had requested a meeting with him after lunch. It has been over two weeks since he last met with him. Tongo had a lot of questions to ask. The saga of the jungle trip still lingered in his head. A traumatic incident that he would like to forget.

After lunch, Alfred motioned Tongo to follow him down to the basement. It was a spacious self-contained room with a tennis table in one corner, a Ping-Pong table in the center, and a coffee maker and a mini bar. Tongo was mesmerized by all these luxurious displays. He followed him slowly. "I didn't know you had all this, and the room looked different." Alfred smiled.

"You haven't been here before; you probably saw the other side of the basement. This site is exclusively for a few guests. Let me show you something." He pushed a small knob, like a button attached to his key holder, and then a tiny opening with downward spiral stairs appeared. They went down the ladder and came to another large room with tables. Still in a state of confusion, Tongo followed him without a word.

"Relax. You can sit down, feel at home, and help yourself. Nobody will come to a private place like this and disturb us. We have all that we need, enough for three months here. Let's get to business. Let me assure you that the discussions we will have here and everything you see should remain confidential." He allowed Tongo to settle down. "I know you will have some questions for me. Let me give you an update on the situation. The good news first." He took a deep breath. "The government is losing, and it's just a matter of time before it falls. Our biggest challenge would be restoring order and governing with all these factions fighting in all parts of the country. There are discussions secretly going on about what to do after the fall. These rebels have to come together and identify one leader to unite the country. After numerous meetings, they did not come to any conclusions. Each wants to rule, and I can see their tendency and greed for power that will lead them to the same path we have taken all these years. I am afraid history will repeat itself. We have a history of bad, corrupt, and greedy leaders who enriched themselves and forgot the cause they fought for."

"What's my role in this, and what should I do?"

"I will come to that later. First, we all have code names and don't know each other. The organization's setup is such that the people who support it can only be known when the group takes over the country. A team is in place to mobilize the cadre and spring to action immediately after the green light order." In the meantime, they will remain anonymous; even at your workplace, we have about five people. You're not alone. Right now, nobody should know your associations. When we went to the jungle, no one knew or noticed. Our relationship was nonexistent. We had to continue this way, and it was for the safety of our families."

"Does my sister know about your role?

"No, but she knows my business role. I trade with gold, diamonds, and other minerals. I told her to keep her mouth shut, maintain our store, and run the building businesses. I am sure she's concerned with my erratic travel back and forth. I have other businesses in neighboring countries, such as Uganda, Southern Sudan, and Kenya. Also, a shareholder and interest in South Africa and Angola." He sipped a soda and continued.

"Here are my updates from the field." The medicine worked very well for the first two weeks, and there was great rejoicing, and then suddenly, the reverse happened and set a panic mood. The big man was upset." Alfred sensed some confusion on Tongo's face. "Let me. I would have to disclose this if you promised not to share it with any soul. The big man needed this medicine. As I alluded to earlier, something terrible happened to him back in the days of his incarceration in the Kenyan prison. The guards tortured him and squeezed the juice out of him. They did a cruel thing and thrashed him severely in that part of the body until he collapsed. They said he spent several days in the hospital. The doctor declared that he would never function and should consider himself a eunuch forever. The big man never accepted this fact of his life and tried several things, including witchcraft. He was known to eliminate anyone who promised and did not fulfill the promise. The charlatans got scared. During the first two weeks, there was some sign of progress. That was the supply of the miracle seed you provided, and he felt it. The supply did not last, and the replacement sample was a disaster. The last two weeks were miserable, and they said that he ordered the execution of a trader who sold some stuff that did not work." Another sip of soda. It looked like Tongo needed a break. He went to the bathroom. "Do you need more time?"

"No, I am fine," Tongo replied.

"I was summoned and had to explain why the medicine failed to work. I had no clue. I smuggled it through my contacts, but the main researcher might know what the medicine contained. I should have disclosed what you told me about the 50% success, and I also kept your name out and had a challenging task. To get pure medicine by any means necessary, even if it means bringing Dr. Blake to him."

"Are you out of your mind? How do you go about doing that?"

"I don't know. That's why I need your help."

"My brother-in-law, I was already torn apart and wanted to step out. I cannot do more than I have already done. Or what I can't possibly do. I don't know whether Dr. Blake had discovered my surreptitious activities.

"How often does he visit the on-farm experiments in the village? Let me know when and on which days. Nothing will happen to him. I can convince the big man somewhat, and I hope the medicine would work for him."

"I don't want the direction this is going. What options do I have?"

"I have built a solid relationship with him, and the least I could do is to mention your name as Dr. Blake's inside contact and close associate. He will understand, and you will not be in danger."

"I must disclose the ultimate source, and that's why we need your help. We have to save our families." Beads of sweat poured down Tongo's forehead. Alfred noticed the fear. "I have also built trust with the second-in- command person. As you know, this is a dangerous territory, and he dealt with people swiftly, with no mercy. There was a rumor that he would include the whole family if he targeted someone for extermination. I am worried about this, but I don't think we can reach this level. They used fear tactics frequently, and it worked."

"What if we supply the seeds and leave him to his men?"

"You knew that wouldn't work. The pure sample of the miracle seed is the solution. We need somebody with expertise." Another beard of sweat trickled from Tongo's face.

"They are pulling out the miracle seed," Tongo murmured.

After a moment of silence, Alfred responded.

"We are family; as I said, we are in this together. Yes, you have the expertise." Another long silence engulfed the room. Alfred sensed the awkwardness of the situation. "We can discuss what's in there for you first with your participation. For your part, hold on." He went to the next room and brought a package. "This is your share for this portion of your help, and there will be more. Open it." A mixture of minerals that Tongo had never seen caught his attention. "Let me show you." He held up coltan, gold, and diamond." He separated each and put them aside. One kilogram of coltan can fetch up to $500. This mineral is highly sought-after. It produces tantalum capacitors in many electronic devices. He held the two remaining glittering minerals. "You know gold and diamond. These are precious minerals that are extremely priced; I don't know how much all of these are worth. By my conservative estimate, the content of this package will not be less than $75 to $100 thousand in a black market."

Tongo kept quiet for what seemed to be a long time. He had to recover from his conflicting thoughts and the temptations of a large amount of bounty that complicated his decisions. "I have buyers who can transfer these into ready cash for you, and those options are also available in Rand, Shillings, US Dollars, or British Pounds. Just let me know." With that, Alfred concluded.

"You know I have not been in this trade, and I know nothing about the value of all these items."

"Okay, let me convert and get back to you. What currency do you prefer?"

"American dollars."

"No problem. We can arrange it." He sensed Tongo's mood brightened up and then suddenly changed. "Is something wrong? You had the largest share." He waited.

"Not about that, Alfred, and this was more than I ever imagined I could get. It's not about money." He paused. "I overheard the fate of our program, and they might dissolve it. When the company's executive director visited Africa, he found Dr. Blake had violated the agreement. Planting the miracle seed in the farmer's field was not part of the plan."

"How did all this happen?"

"Dr. Blake had simultaneous experiments, one for miracle seeds and the other for something else he did not disclose. I sneaked out his experimental seeds, tried them in the field and probably mixed them up. He trusted me and allowed me to use the materials. I planted them and sold some to the farmers. Those were the seeds he wanted to dispose of initially. That probably was what spread and caused the mixed up. Dr. Blake wanted to see how the seeds performed in the fields." Tongo thought he had revealed too much and decided to pause. He didn't disclose another rumor that Dr. Blake might be transferred soon or fired. It was because of this rumor that Tongo did what he did. He considered the action unethical and later regretted it. Tongo multiplied the seeds on his farm without Dr. Blake's permission.

"Can you arrange a meeting with Dr. Blake at Mama Kakai's farm for me? I have a share in their business."

Tongo looked at him straight with a piercing eye and locked it.

"Trust me, brother, nothing will happen to him. I'll give you, my word." Alfred dogged the piercing gaze.

"He had already planned to visit the village farms, and I will find out whether he's interested in visiting the Kakai farms and let you know," Alfred nodded and responded to the door buzz.

"I asked you once but didn't get a clear answer. When I was at Mama Kakai's farm, I was impressed at the level of development and progress." She mentioned her brother Fakir to me, but she appeared to be in charge. What do I need to know? She offered me a job managing her farm. What's all this about?"

Let's take a tea break first. We'll get back to this shortly."

***

"You didn't talk much about Mama Kakai's farm." Tongo initiated the discussion.

"Yes, I worked closely with her brother Fakir on the seed and fertilizer side of the investment, and I am more interested in the seed and fertilizer business." Tongo was unsure whether this was the right moment and hesitated but decided to ask whether what he had heard about the rumor of seed pirating by Fakir was true.

Alfred laughed, "My brother, why do you talk like European people? Who are the pirates?"

"We all know about the Somali pirates, you know. There is a movie about them."

"The media sensitized and manipulated and played on our emotions. For sure, the Somali pirates are bad dudes, and we should not support them." He paused. "Do you remember how the world stood on edge about the news? They made movies about it, yet we knew nothing about what the multinational companies did in Somalia.

The tragedy started a long time ago, in the 80s. European companies have been dumping toxic waste such as lead, cadmium, uranium, and other industrial toxins in the Indian Ocean along the coast of Somalia. In Northern Somalia, a severe report about medical problems led to mouth bleeding, abdominal hemorrhages, unusual skin disorders, and breathing difficulties. Believe it or not, the pirates championed this as their motives for punishing the multinational companies they extorted funds from."

Tongo busted laughing. "Give me a break. They were gangs of hooligans greedy for money and disrupting the peaceful trade. Like most things happening in Africa, their government colluded with multinational companies and participated in the pollution. We must clean our house before we start complaining about our neighbors."

"Let's take it case by case, my brother. In the '80s, during the reign of the General, I forgot his name. The ship that carried the toxic waste from Europe belonged to the government of Somalia. At least one report implicated the partnership. One tiny piece among the gigantic dumping ground and the crime those multinational companies committed had left a genocidal legacy. They were children with no limbs and with cancer. Think about it for a society that has never had this perpetual disease. Beautiful people, proud nomadic society with their free-roaming camels. Did you even know this news about multinational companies dumping toxic nuclear waste in Somalia?"

"No, I never heard about this, but let's get to the point. We have drifted away from the question. Are you aware that your company is pirating seeds?"

"Isn't it ironic, my brother. Our seed company is trying to prevent the pirating of our farmers' seeds by a company like Dare, and you work there and know what they did. When we tried to expose their wicked intentions, they turned around and accused us of pirating. We believe that when the big seed companies collect diverse local seeds and breed different lines for vigor, disease, or any other motives, they should return the profit to the farmers, at least some percentages. We oppose the idea that our farmers must buy seeds from them under conditions that enslave them and rob them of their freedom. These farmers have been farming for generations, saving their grains; our company will allow that to some extent. Dr. Blake, your boss, collected all the exotic local farmers' seeds and used them for breeding to improve his crop. What did our farmers get?"

"I think Dr. Blake was different. We all tended to blame the Western world for most of Africa's problems, but he was ready to point fingers where it was due. Dr. Blake was critical of his company and Western European activities.

Alfred stood up and stretched. "If Mrs. Kakai offered you a managerial position on the farm in the region with good pay, maybe you can consider it." He sipped a glass of water and continued.

"The country's situation is getting worse; the violence is getting out of hand. We need stability. Look at what's happening. The rebels are not united, and even if our man takes over, what kind of a country will he rule? Where over half of the population lived in miserable poverty and fought each other, yet we have plenty of resources to make this country one of the richest. I will send my family out of the country until things cool down. Don't forget to set up the meeting with Dr. Blake."

Chapter 31

The phone kept ringing, and Tongo hesitated to pick it up. It was a number not on his contact list. He looked at it and ignored it. He had a more significant issue in his head to deal with. He paced the room, trying to understand how it could have happened. All gone! He couldn't believe it.

As he gathered the information from the farmers around the area, he discovered that the watchman he hired to guard the seed store had disappeared. Tongo tried to trace back how he got introduced to the watchman. It was the suggestion of his uncle. The man did some handy work for him on the farm and was also introduced to him by a customer. Tongo learned later that the watchman played different roles in the area; some people even suspected he was an informer for the government and rebel groups.

The seed theft from the seed storage remained a mystery, and someone from within probably did it. Tongo had a long list of suspects, including his uncle, but he quickly ruled him out because he had been away for over two weeks and returned the day after the theft. The farm manager had reported the theft, but the police didn't take it further. They scoffed at the idea and appeared not interested in pursuing it. Tongo's secret investigation came to a dead end. Everyone seemed afraid of the watchman and did not want to discuss about him.

"Tongo picked up his phone to answer an incoming call.

"What happened? I called several times and couldn't get hold of you."

"I didn't see your number," Tongo replied.

"That was my other number," Alfred confirmed. "Listen, I heard you made the villagers uncomfortable with your questions. I think you need to stay cool and minimize your exposure."

"I don't get it. Somebody stole all my seeds in the store, and I should just let it go? You don't know how I got those seeds?" Tongo's voice level rose to its peak. The phone line on the other end vibrated.

"Chill out, bro. You probably stole it too," Alfred said with a burst of arrogant laughter. On the other side, the line went dead. "I was joking, bro." He looked at the phone and realized Tongo had hung up. Alfred attempted to call back, but Tongo had turned off his phone.

Tongo continued with his investigations, which led nowhere. There was an aura of silence, and the people in the village seemed to know the culprit. The silent rumor implicated a cover-up plan and pointed fingers at the rebel group. They said the rebel leader would pay any price in gold to get the miracle seed.

That evening, Tongo got a call from his sister: "I am worried about you. What happened to your phone?" He could sense agitation in her voice.

"You don't have to cry. I am okay." He could still hear her sobbing.

"Wait," she instructed, and then Alfred came online. "I will be there tomorrow morning. I said something I should not have said, but you knew I didn't mean it. He tried to cheer him up. Hey, your little sister is devastated. You will always get another seed."

"Okay, you know nothing about this, right? This is not any kind of seed. Are you behind this?"

"No, of course not. How can you even entertain your thoughts? See you tomorrow, and we will talk more." Alfred hung up the phone.

Tongo spent the night at his uncle's farm, as he usually did when he stayed over after the farm visits. Uncle Francisco did not talk much about the theft that happened. As a retired Army Sergeant, he followed rigid rules for himself and his family. The night the robbery occurred, Uncle Francisco was returning from a business trip to Uganda, and it didn't take him much time to identify the suspected guard as the main person behind the theft. However, the guard had a strong alibi that night. He did not spend time in the village; he attended his sister's wedding and was away for three days. He also left the day before the incident. Tongo was convinced and concluded that the guard "Matata" couldn't be in the village during this incident. Matata had a reputation, though; people believed he could orchestrate and maneuver things behind the scenes.

Tongo and his uncle exchanged ideas about what happened with the seed. Uncle Francisco cleared his throat. "This incident upset you, and you clashed with some people. The silent nod from the villagers was understandable, but Matata had an alibi, although we will never know. There is still a chance that he could have done it from anywhere with his accomplices. I do not recommend you confront him, though."

"I don't understand why everybody is chickening out and afraid of him. We can't let him ruin all our efforts." His uncle smiled.

"I can see your courage; it runs in the family. The situation we're in right now warrants a different approach. There is chaos all around us, and it can get worse. I don't care what the rest of the world thinks, but those crazy people in the forest are not better than this senile moron general in power. He had to go. I don't support any of them. None of the current crops of so-called leaders are ready to govern. They have bled the country dry." Uncle Francisco appeared shaken. "I want to retire in peace for my remaining years on earth, and I am terrified for the future with all these unknown variables. We have no country with this imbecile at the top. We will keep going down the drain. All the natural resources and abundant wealth in this country will soon be a thing of the past."

"Uncle Francisco."

"Oh, I got carried away. Anyway, tell me about this strange phenomenon. I heard whispers about the rebirth of new life. People are talking about your miracle seed and probably suspected you stored them here."

"I didn't share with anybody that I had the seed stored on the farm. We are conducting some experiments with the miracle seed and others, all of which were among the stolen ones."

"Is what I heard about this seed true? That it rejuvenates the juices in the reproductive cells and even revives the vigor in the older person?"

"Yes and No, Uncle Francisco, that was a twisted version of the stretched truth, and it depends on the gene. True for the miracle seed, but not for the rest. As with the alternative seed, there is one problem: the seed's genetic makeup is unstable, which is what they wanted to promote."

"What do you mean?"

"It's unpredictable; the gene wanders, it can attach itself to the cells, sap the juice dry, and possibly render it infertile." Tongo had said more than what he wanted to say under the circumstances. He thought of changing the topic and having his uncle Francisco share more about his life experiences. He had lived under a cloud of secrecy throughout his military life, where some people thought he worked for the Secret Service. "Uncle Francisco, what do you know about the rebel leader General Amos Jaja." He quickly switched the topic.

It took him a while to respond. "Do you know the African proverb, "Even the night has ears?"

"Yes, I have heard about it," Tongo replied.

"There are things you cannot discuss in the open, especially at night. I have to say this, though. Whoever stole your seed might have secured himself a lucrative market."

"What do you mean, uncle?"

"Did you hear the rumor about the rebel leader needing the help of the seed? I will probably leave it to you to figure it out." He smiled and continued. "You were sitting on a gold mine. They are people eager to get their hands on the seed you produce. Your brother-in-law might give you more information." He lit his smoking pipe and puffed a stream of smoke slowly. Tongo wondered how long he had been smoking.

"Uncle Francisco, when did you start smoking?"

"A long time ago, in the '60s, I was 18 when we joined the revolutionary group in Tanzania. At that young age, we were inspired and ready for revolutionary action. We had one goal: to liberate the African continent from the yoke of colonialism. I even met briefly with Che Guevara, the legendary Argentine revolutionary leader. We had a desire to make a difference. It's in here." He pointed to his chest. "Real men are gone, no longer available. In those days, we were not afraid to try new things. We smoked all kinds of things but never succumbed to them. Oh, Cuban Cigars were my favorite." He stared into space with a lonesome gaze, reminiscing of the bygone days. "We did the best we could, and there was even a talk about uniting the whole of Africa at that time. Look what's happening now: countries breaking down into tribal sectors, slaughtering each other. We used to condemn the colonial powers for the despicable spilling of innocent bloodshed. Who do we blame now?" He lit his smoking pipe again and turned to face him. "I still didn't get what you said about the seed. What was the purpose of this seed that triggered controversy and endless rumors?"

"That was Dr. Blake's work, and I understand it plays a vital role in restoring reproductive cells. All you need is a cob of sweet corn for breakfast. Unfortunately, there was a hidden agenda intended for local consumption."

"I don't get it."

"Uncle Francisco, the decision at the top was to replace the miracle seed with the seed with an opposite trait. The cursed one."

"You knew this and kept quiet?"

"There was nothing I could do."

Tongo stood up. "Good night, Uncle Francisco, He entered his room. Before sleep entered his head, Tongo made a checklist of to-do items he needed for the next day. From the time of his jungle trip, some odd things kept happening. His mind was not at ease, and he wondered why everyone pretended that nothing happened as if no theft occurred. As he turned on his side, a sense of guilt seized him for not getting to the bottom of the incident.

***

The next day, Tongo and his brother-in-law Alfred had a lunch of roasted goat meat with tofu and soup at Kakai farm. There were many people there that Tongo did not know. They toured the farm, where they saw experimental plots.

"What do you think?"

"Impressed, I didn't expect to see all these interesting developments. I wanted to know more about their experimental seeds, but no one could tell what variety they used. They didn't want to disclose what they were doing."

In the evening, Alfred and Tongo discussed the upcoming plans.

Alfred began the discussions with an apology for his earlier comments. He looked at Tongo and smiled. "Let me explain the whole episode. I will give you the main point and fill in the rest as we move forward. "First, you have successfully passed the test and confirmed your commitment to the cause. You did your part. Congratulations." He waited for a while and added. "The last seed lot's harvest yielded a disaster. After the initial try, the big man gained confidence and was delighted that his long-awaited miracle had finally materialized. Then something happened with the last lot. The outcome was a catastrophe. He wanted to see the person who created this seed. We couldn't reveal your name, but we made it look like you secretly acquired it from Dr. Blake's experiments. He couldn't understand why the results were different, so he demanded to see Dr. Blake"

"How can we do that? It's impossible to convince him to come." Alfred looked around as if expecting somebody. In a low whisper, he announced. "By the way, there is a serious ongoing discussion about how to govern the country after Monge falls. His expertise is valuable and needed, and he must meet with him."

It was Tongo's turn to look around, wondering if he had heard him right. "How will we do that? I can't speak to him about this; I don't think anybody should try. Besides, he's a white man."

"A new government with a diverse leadership team would make it legit. We want the Americans on our side, and there is no better way to bring that closer than having an American as a minister of agriculture in the cabinet. They already owned the country anyway, and we could as well make them believe it." Alfred paused and continued. "I will encourage that to happen, but in the meantime, we must be on the same page. We don't want retaliation. We have families to keep safe." Tongo looked on with eyes and mouth wide open, making the shape of the letter "O." The brothers-in-law exchanged glances without saying a word.

"In any case, let me know when you plan to visit the farms. Someone will speak with Dr. Blake; you don't have to be part of the discussions." Alfred concluded.

Tongo turned to look his brother-in-law in the eye. "Promise me that the meeting will not lead to anything else."

Alfred laughed, "Come on, my brother. Don't burden yourself with regret for what you have no control over. Don't forget. Let me know when Dr. Blake plans to visit the farms. I can arrange the meeting myself. It won't take much of his time. A stop at a village and a few minutes of exchanging words are enough. It could be a casual meeting over lunch in the village with a farmer who wants to invest in the GMO." He realized how Tongo wrinkled his face. "Okay, I understand. We know he can't meet with the rebel leader face to face, and he has his proxies who can represent him."

"Is there any compelling reason why he should see him? He got the seeds he wanted. What else does he want from him? Frankly, I have a reservation."

"I don't know. One thing is for sure. Dr. Blake's life will not be in danger. I will do my best to address that part as I told you. You never know. He can be a serious contender for a cabinet position in the next government." Tongo gazed on as if he didn't believe it.

"I will be back to work this week. Tongo shook hands with him and walked away.

Chapter 32

ongo returned to work after three days. One of his colleagues pulled him aside and whispered. "Did you hear the news? The company is downsizing, and the little people like us would be the first to go." Tongo brushed him off and turned. The colleague continued. "You didn't know about Dr. Blake.?"

"What about him?"

"Someone said they would transfer him to the Kenya office. He lost favor with the general manager after the visit. Someone said that he messed up big time." He lowered his voice. "By the way, your name came up. What is this rumor in the village?"

"I don't know." Tongo walked towards the office wing of the building to see the human resource personnel and then decided to stop by Dr. Blake's office. It took him about five minutes to travel from one end of the spacious building to the other. The spacious building extended to the experimental plots scattered around the premises. Dare Seed Company's experimental site occupied 50 hectares of land, and the edge bordered the forest.

When Tongo arrived, Dr. Blake was on the phone, and the secretary asked him to wait in the lobby. The waiting took longer than he expected. In the meantime, Tongo tried to reconnect the incidents that happened. The discussions with his brother-in-law, the problem in the village with the seed, and the theft at his uncle's seed storage. Can this be a coincidence? He thought.

Dr. Blake could sense when Tongo had something on his mind or an important message to pass on. Not sure what to expect, he waited.

"Someone broke into my uncle Francisco's barn and took all the seeds stored in his storage." He announced with a somber expression on his face. He had learned not to go around the topic anymore. John waited; he knew Tongo had some more to tell. "I stored some of our seeds from the previous season at his barn."

"I thought you collected all the seeds after the harvest and brought them back to the company store."

"Yes, we did, but I left some at my uncle's barn."

John's piercing gaze didn't allow Tongo to avoid giving a direct answer. He typically resists yes-or-no questions. A tactic he uses to dodge the truth.

"Which color-coded seeds were stored in the barn?"

"The green, The miracle seed."

John held his hands behind his back in a reclining position and rocked back and forth. "So, the thief knew what to look for? Interesting." He puckered his lips.

"Tell me more about this mad frenzy commotion with the miracle seed in the village. What was the point of a hype-up?"

The miracle seed is no longer available. The gene has undergone some changes. The results of all the complaints we are getting about weedy plants. Our survey last month gave us a preliminary result, indicating the major shift and genetic reshuffling. The result could be a combination of traits that could differ from those found in either parent. Are people ready for this unexpected outcome? It's already happening."

"Do you still have the original?"

"Of course we do,"

"Do you plan to investigate the chemical pollution we discussed earlier?"

"Tongo, the genetic makeup issue, has a more devastating impact than the chemical pollution."

"What do we do?"

John attempted to show a sympathetic approach. "Maybe it's my turn to ask. What do you do when all your maize crops turn into a weed?"

"You can replace them, I guess."

"Yeah, with what? Not as easy as we think. If we consider the long-term." John then realized he had to respond to the question of chemical pollution and the local collection of seeds. "We already talked about conducting soil samples in the area affected. As for the local seeds, it might be too late to preserve them. We collected the local seeds in the past, but I wanted one more round of collection this week." John shrugged his shoulders. "When your government is ready to destroy the local seeds, there is nothing one can do. I will do my best to store what I can."

Tongo lightened upon hearing that Dr. Blake considered an alternative option: He would analyze the genetic component of all the local seeds he encountered. The best way for him to do that was to visit farms and organize the seed collections, as he did the first year he came when he collected many local seeds.

"Do you think we could find the remnant of the previous season's seeds?"

"There will be plenty. Many farmers saved the seeds from the previous season. The government campaign did not convince some of them to adopt the hybrid. They complained about the high expenses and the additional requirement of fertilizers and herbicides that they had to buy."

John stole a glance at Tongo and immediately sensed something was wrong. Something was eating at him. But he chose to stay silent. For now. Doubt gnawed at John, creeping into the edges of his thoughts. Was he in over his head? The pressure to prove himself was mounting. He had set out to make a difference, to arm farmers with the knowledge they needed to survive. To serve, to provide, to do no harm, but somehow, things had gone astray. His misunderstanding with his colleague had only widened the rift, making his mission feel less like progress and more like an unraveling mess. And worst of all? He had allowed himself to be distracted from the real problem. The village beyond the valley had slipped from his grasp.

Then came the visit with the general manager. Something shifted. The conversation haunted him, twisting in his mind like a shadow he couldn't shake. What if he had been wrong all along? His experiment, once a beacon of hope, now loomed as a potential disaster. A catastrophe waiting to unfold. If he was right, the long-term effects could spiral beyond anything he had imagined. *Could it lead to extinction?*

The realization hit him. It was as if the earth had been ripped out from under his feet. This was his doing. His responsibility. The variety had grown beyond his control, and now, he was running out of time.

The company's latest directive was clear: employees were to take extra precautions and remain within the company premises. John had never been one to blindly follow orders. His defiance had already caused friction with his colleagues. Now, it might cost him everything.

The subtle warning was clear. The memo from William, restricting field operations across the regions, shut all his hopes. The heavy-handed directive only deepened his frustration. They were tightening their grip.

Unaware of the escalating company's internal conflicts and restrictions, Tongo was on a mission of its own. His secret work in the field, his search for the pure line of the miracle seed continued undeterred. He knew John's conviction and his relentless drive to help the local people, but something about this entire situation bothered him. Tongo clenched his jaw. His mind raced, a storm of doubt and self-recrimination brewing inside him. The stolen seeds. The words echoed in his head as he shook it slowly. How could he have been so blind? A series of questions flooded his thoughts.

Had he misjudged the people around him? Some of his friends suspected an inside job. Tongo couldn't dismiss the possibility. Too many things won't add up. He went over his checklist, scrutinizing every detail. Then his thoughts locked onto the night watchman. His story didn't sit right. The guard admitted he had fallen asleep and didn't hear anything. Tongo narrowed his eyes. It was too convenient. Too clean.

He suspected that something was not right.
The night dog was silent. Why?

The question lingered in Tongo's mind, demanding an answer. The seed storage had been stacked with gunny bags full of seeds of different varieties. Why had only the miracle seeds gone missing? The more he pressed for answers, the more people brushed him off. No one seemed to care. Even uncle Francisco had dismissed his concerns with a casual remark: *"Those seeds must be valuable."*

That was it, no follow-up. No urgency, and that was when it hit him. He was on his own.

Tongo couldn't share his suspicions and details with John, either. The risk was too high. If John knew everything, he would get into the bottom of it and Tongo couldn't afford disclosure. With careful steps, he slipped into the office, where he found John hunched over his work, lost in thought. Tongo hesitated for a moment before speaking.

"I think it's not a good idea for you to visit the farms now."

John lifted his head slowly, his expression unreadable. He waited, sensing something was wrong.

Tongo's voice dropped. "The rebel groups have intensified their activities."

"I had to get some samples."
"I can get them for you," Tongo replied.

John smiled faintly, but as he met Tongo's gaze, his expression hardened. He sensed fear in Tongo's eyes.

"I have to do this, Tongo." His voice was steady, but the weight of his words pressed heavily on him. "The whole village issue is bearing down on me. I keep asking myself, are we doing the right thing, or are we chasing the wrong path?"

He exhaled, his resolve firm. "I need someone to show me where the problem started. Which farms received supplies from Monge seed and fertilizer company and which farms you supplied with our seeds. What went wrong and the extent of the damage." John looked at his notes. He raised his head and about to dismiss Tongo. "Thanks for your help. Anything else?"

John turned back to his work, expecting Tongo to leave. But he didn't.

Tongo stood frozen and silent. John glanced up again. Tongo's face had stiffened, his lips slightly parted, his brows furrowed. He wasn't just hesitant. He looked like he had seen a cobra slithering toward him.

Tongo remembered Alfred's other news about the toppling of the Monge regime and the possible takeover. He couldn't say a word about this and tried to find a better approach to discourage him from going to the village. Tongo cleared his voice to speak.

John raised his head and looked directly at him.

"I heard you're starting another branch in Kenya. Is it true?"

"Kenya is more stable than Monge, and we need that stability to thrive. The site in Monge will remain, but we have an alternative option. The outlook of the current situation does not look promising." He turned.

"Tell me about this crazy rebel leader. I heard a lot about him. What do the local people think? Do you think he can succeed?"

"He's encouraged by his success and has the upper hand. The government soldiers had targeted him and his rebel activities for a long time. They had infiltrated all sectors. People don't trust each other anymore. I think you may need a bodyguard." Tongo advised. John laughed.

"Tongo, I didn't mean to ignore your warning. From what I heard, it's not all that bad. We never had any problem in this part of Africa, like in the Horn of Africa with Somali pirates. Anyway, I don't need a bodyguard. Remember, the sooner you arrange my visit to the farm, the better. I need to collect the seed samples, which will be my major task for the next two to three weeks. Also, if you can get hold of the new seeds Fakir company is releasing, I would like to get some samples for my analysis." He looked at Tongo with a worrisome glance.

"After this year, Monge will have no more seeds. Dare Seed Company will become the sole supplier of GMO seeds." John shook his head. Tongo waited.

"I cannot imagine the magnitude of destruction this will cause. The country's entire food supply will be under the grip of a single corporation. A chilling reality. It's a dangerous situation when a private company controls an entire nation's ability to eat. Dare Seed Company isn't just expanding; they're orchestrating submission, forcing the government into economic servitude with no way out.

***

The news from the jungle is in the minds of everyone in the area.

General Amos Jaja got an early morning briefing from his immediate advisers as he prepared to inspect the readiness of his soldiers. He's known for his intensive concentration on the task, but in the past few months, he focused on his personal needs. His advisers were concerned about his safety and took extra measures to tighten the arrangements. Words from his inner circle hardly come out, but one recurring item appeared on his mind as he conversed with his internal advisers. The underground network his rebel teams established worked closely with Monge's government and infiltrated all sectors, even the military. The rebel soldiers had high spirits and were united. They focused on their target as they approached the army military barracks. They attributed their success to their discipline and focus. Their hit-and- run tactics and working secretly with the local people boosted their success.

They had captured several cities and planned to take over some strategic places, including the capital, Sanga, and topple the general and his government. Word had gone out secretly to recruit and enter an agreement with some companies to invest in the country and open up the vast natural resources plundered by a few.

The rebel leader had a plan and knew what Monge could offer. He returned to his tent with his three bodyguards. All sharp shooters were well-trained. The rest of his inner circle commanders will join him shortly to provide updates and discuss action plans. General Jaja will review the briefings with his commanders and issue directives. As part of their strict ethical rules, he had to stay in the tent with his three bodyguards at each corner of the tent.

General Jaja paced in the tent as he always does wherever he had something on his mind. His military advisers will soon join him to assess the weekly progress, update him about upcoming events, and plan for the next move.

The five-member team sat on a semi-circular table, facing a full-sized map of the country and the region. It stretched along the wall of the tent. General Jaja listened carefully as each of the team members provided updates. His deputy commander began with the overall situation of Monge and the status of General Bukasa's condition. The team reached a point of contention and argued about reevaluating their purpose and how it would fit their current situation. "Are we ready to destroy the current society and replace all the institutions with a new structure?" General Jaja reacted when the team members listed the deaths of several people during the previous weeks of ambush and incursions. Several schoolchildren were the victims as well. "We must focus our attacks on the vulnerable military and police outposts and facilities, and don't forget our goal. We must secure arms, ammunition, essential military materials, medical supplies, and communication equipment." He turned and asked. "How are we doing with the indoctrination of the villagers? Everyone in the village should be on our side, and if I may ask again, how far is our influence?"

The member in charge of the operation and clandestine activities prepared to respond. "We have reliable information that the inner circle of the decaying General is crumbling. The army morale is down, their secret agents no longer trust each other, and everyone is in a state of fear."

He glanced at the General. "No one trusts each other, and there is a plan to bring you to the negotiating table."

General Jaja laughed loudly. "Good. I like this part. We can now wear them down, frustrate them, and speed up our harassing tactics. In the meantime, we must have full command or awareness of what the enemy is planning. For instance, the state of their equipment and how efficient or disciplined their troops are. Are they well trained?" He sipped water from a bottle. Remember, we must carefully choose the conditions and only fight when the chances of victory are clear and in our favor. It's time to step up our activities and attack suddenly and viciously within a short time."

General Jaja asked the leader of the covert activities to remain behind after he dismissed the rest of the team members. "Keep an eye on the movement of the Dare Seed Company. Gather all the information you can, " he said, stepping closer. "I have a major urgent task for you, and I will tell you about it a day before the operation."

"How urgent do you want the job done?"

"Gather the information as quickly as possible and then move on to the target, but we want something other than publicity right now. The world has changed, and we want countries to support our cause,"

"The American media has already started digging for information. They are looking for dirt in the name of atrocities,"

"Don't worry. We're ahead in building the relationship.

The Eastern block had developed a craving appetite for our

natural resources. We produced the world's largest natural resources used in cell phone industries. We can use this to our advantage."

Jaja paced the room in a thinking mood. Wherever he stood up and moved from one corner to another, he would follow it with an announcement.

"We must preserve the buildings and international corporation's assets. As I said, the less bad news they gather from us, the better. We have a lot of work after these years of pillage and senseless destruction. Our first impression of the world is critical. We don't accept mediocrity and handling of diplomacy in an inept manner." He looked around and was satisfied that his team was with him.

Jaja then dismissed the meeting.

Chapter 33

The next day, John responded to William's questions about the miracle seed and was hesitant to send the sample to the USA. He tried to persuade him that he could hold onto the seed until he fully confirmed its stability. William Stanley did not need any more convincing.

The miracle seed had to be put on hold and purged from Monge. The plan had to continue. John got the message that Monge's government had the authority to implement them. A prudent decision the country had to live by.

As soon as he ended his message, John noticed Tongo approaching him.

Tongo tip-toed toward John's office and strained his neck for a better view.

"Good morning."

"Hey, Tongo. Come in. There is a change of plan. The scientist from the headquarters will no longer visit us." John held both of his hands together and locked his fingers. He maintained a discreet silence for a while. Tongo sighed.

"And you're not visiting the on-farm trial?"

"I will let you know." He turned towards the computer screen. Tongo waited a little and then went to the lab.

John continued looking at the data and reviewed his report. He felt satisfied and put all the information needed to justify why he spent so much money on the experiment, which was unexpected. The earlier arguments regarding the miracle seed and its experimental ethics no longer hold. The outcome puzzled him, and he was more determined to try this experiment again in a different environment. He had initiated the local seed collection idea and met opposition from his employer. John found himself at odds with everything his company did in Africa. He didn't hide his opposition towards the exploitative nature of his company and its disregard for human beings. At times, he acted as an advocate for the indigenous communities and often played the role of an environmentalist. This approach put him in a confrontation with his regional director. John had openly discussed his views, and they knew where he stood.

John browsed through William's earlier memo regarding the patent of the trait of the local farmer's variety. He remembered how he argued against it because of the nature of gene mutation. John won't consider a naturally occurring phenomenon as an invention. While he had his suspicions about the cause of the problem, John never ruled that pollen transfer from another location could be the source of the genes in the variety. He used that analogy to oppose the patenting and, for the same reason, did not claim property rights for local seeds in the village. These exotic varieties he collected and used in his experiments were available to them for generations after generation. It was an uphill battle for John to fight his employer to recognize this fact. He recounted his argument with William over the Indigenous people's rights. With an exasperated look, John understood the arm twisting, intensive lobbying, bribing, and all the dirty tricks his company employed. It would just be a matter of time before the big corporations owned every living thing on earth.

The feeling that there is nothing he can do to change the situation irritated him.

Tongo came back again later after lunch. He knocked and waited. John lifted his head and ushered him in.

"Dr. Blake, the other seed companies are aggressively fighting to be recognized, but they don't help farmers like we do. They have infiltrated and got hold of seed, fertilizer, and chemical industries."

"It's the free market of the capitalist world, Tongo."

"I have a question about miracle seeds. I understand that you used the local variety line to enhance strength."

"That's right."

"What will happen to the local variety if you patent this for our company?" John looked up and asked Tongo to sit down.

"I know this trait exists within this local variety. Once the patenting process passes, our company will have exclusive rights to everything about the seed, including breeding, growing, and selling the product." He turned to Tongo with that kind of serious look. "You know what that would mean?" Tongo waited because he was not sure what he wanted to say. "Your local farmers will no longer have access to breeding, sowing, planting, and harvesting. They will need permission to access everything I have just mentioned."

"I can't believe that would happen."

"You don't know about large corporations, Tongo. They can buy your leaders and the whole country and silence everything, and the rest of the world is with them."

"What can we do then? Nothing?"

"At this point, the farmers must unite and demand that the patent of living things they had depended on all these years should stop, be banned, and restricted. However, if their resources are patented, they should receive the benefits. They may need the support of a strong advocacy group, who can advocate for your farmers."

Tongo looked puzzled. "Listen," John continued. "All that I have said was not new. Some proponents of biodiversity would argue for fair and equitable sharing of benefits that could come from utilizing genetic resources."

"I get it, Dr. Blake. Nobody else would do it for us."

"Africa must unite and speak with one voice." Tongo looked at him surprised, as if the phrase had come out of the sky. Indeed, he often heard this as the politicians' favorite word when they wanted to shift blame elsewhere. Tongo prepared to leave.

"When will you visit the farms?" He asked.

"Two weeks from today, let's see." He checked the calendar, and Tongo acknowledged the date and left.

John remained behind and continued working. The discussions with Tongo gave him little consolation.

The local farmers and his colleagues knew him as a scientist who stood up to his company when it came to the interest of the local people, yet he lacked the courage to say no to many other things he noticed. In the world of ethics, this behavior portrayed hypocrisy. He had struggled with all these conflicting issues in Africa. At times, he felt helpless, and the more he thought of doing something, the better he felt.

To overcome his guilt, he tried to educate someone like Tongo and supported him. He provided him with tips and resources if needed. Having lived in Africa for all these years, Dr. Blake felt he belonged here and should protect what he could and preserve this indigenous knowledge. He had no one he could trust to protect and maintain the extensive collections of seeds. One thing John did from the beginning was to keep the seeds in a cool, dry, and airtight dark storage container. He ensured the seeds were thoroughly dried and labeled with detailed information like variety and collection date. He even added silica gel to the container to absorb excess moisture. At one point, Michael and his colleagues teased and joked that John was preparing for a doom's day. John had accumulated a reservoir of a wealth of precious value to the human race and never got discouraged. He would do his job well, but the question that bogged him was the uncertainty of its impact and the detrimental effect it could have on the local people. He had to decide what the next step of his life would look like.

After he visited Africa, William Stanley initiated swift changes in the company policy that reflected the country's political situation. Monge had deteriorated and was on the brink of collapse. John thought over the messages and started rethinking his career role with all the controversial episodes of the seed fiasco. He even considered going into the nonprofit world and helping people in need in developing countries. As John switched his mind back and forth, his inner feelings and desires settled on one thing that kept coming back to him. To preserve the African seed genome.

In the meantime, his dilemma was not knowing where to keep all the seed collections. The facility where he stored them at the lab could not preserve them for a long time, and he was afraid that the company's structural changes at the top and the policy direction could undermine the future trend of the seed industry. He thought and concluded that Monge Seed and Fertilizer Company could take up this task, besides, this is the only local seed industry in the country.

The continuous civil war in the region has exacerbated and drained energy. The loss of lives long forgotten by the whole world continued unabated. John had lived and witnessed war atrocities and documented some unreported stories he had heard. The paradox and intricate daily happenings continued to puzzle him including the guerrilla war activities. He read the biography of General Jaja and was surprised about his early secondary education at his formal school, where he taught during his Peace Corps years in Kenya. John tried to recall and concluded that Jaja was not his biology student because he could have remembered a name like Jaja. What if he changed his name? he pondered.

A flow of adrenaline rushed through his body. John sat back as if watching a horror movie and let his imagination traverse the tropical jungle. He tried to regain a moment of calm. His body remained tense and engulfed with rapid breathing. The news and stories John ignored about the rebel leader began to frighten him. He wondered whether his former student had caused this havoc.

John shook these bizarre thoughts out of his mind. He tried to recreate a picture of each of his former students in his mind. No matter how much he tried, no image formed in his head. His mind opened with a void of emptiness. The blank of vague imaginary visions occupied his mind. Not a single student came to mind. After twenty-five years had passed, it was obvious that most of them were now in their late 30s or early 40s. Unfortunately, he couldn't recall most of them and lost the class photo he had with them and contacts in a college dorm. A few of them stood out after he read them in the Kenya Nation paper. One of his students became a minister, and two were members of Kenya's parliament. He thought Jaja was probably in the same school but not in his class. On the other hand, after all these years, anything can happen, and character can develop. He was unsure whether he could remember a name like Jaja, and with 25 years gone by, it's unlikely he could remember.

John decided to let this off his mind for now. No matter how curious he felt, there was nothing he could do to change the past. After a series of nerve-racking blank stares, John stopped in his thoughts.

If the rebel leader was his former student, he might want to meet with him, an encounter that could lead to either the best or the worst possible outcome.

His mind started picturing the worst-case scenarios, but he reminded himself that he'd been popular with his students. Most of them had wanted to be in his biology class, though a few had complained about his American accent.

John had never encountered issues during his Peace Corps experience, except when he taught human anatomy. The students were curious and asked him many uncomfortable questions. His open, factual responses landed him in the principal's office with a warning: *No sex education allowed.*

As his recollections returned, one incident towards the end his Peace Corps year resurfaced. It involved one of his students, Barnabas. He had buried the memory for years, but now it came back with a jolt. His heartbeat quickened, each pulse heavier than the last.

He vividly recalls reading headlines in *The Nation* newspaper while leaving the airport. A student from his former school had been arrested. The article mentioned an ongoing investigation linked to a botched abortion.

The recent report on Jaja's early life revealed that he had attended the same school, and that the arrest occurred during the same period John was there. Although the details remained sketchy. There was something about drugs and abortion.

John froze. *Was it a coincidence?* His mind reeled, revisiting the encounters he had in the final weeks before leaving Kenya. He couldn't admit it, or even entertain the thought, but the question loomed: *Could he be the father of the aborted child?"*

Chapter 34

ongo arrived early at the office on the day of the farm visit. He checked with the driver and briefed him on the trip's itinerary to the farmers' fields. The driver already knew about the trip and made the vehicle ready. The planned itinerary would cover several farms near the forest.

The farmers expected the visit with jubilation. Some of them had gathered exotic seed varieties, and even those who lived in the neighboring countries sent their seeds when they heard they could get money for sharing. A local businessman from the village took it upon himself to facilitate this process. He organized his group to collect as many seeds as possible and sold them to Tongo for more profit. Tongo then stored them all at his uncle's farm.

John was excited and eager to see the collections of various local seeds and kept propping Tongo with questions.

"How many collections have you made so far this time?"

"Oh, it's overwhelming. We received some exotic seeds from neighboring countries. We saw some of them for the first time."

"Great. When can we bring the seeds to the station?"

"Anytime you want. I have secured everything in my uncle's farm storage. After what happened recently, we may need to transfer them to the station as soon as possible." John kept quiet for a while and switched the topic of the discussions to the current upheavals in the forests caused by the rebel groups.

"What's your take on this movement by the rebel leader, General Jaja?"

Tongo didn't respond right away. Instead, he tried to generalize the answers. "They had advanced and captured part of the country. The report confirmed that the government army had defected in great numbers, and they are predicting Monge to fall." John brushed off the news. He heard the same thing last year, and nothing happened. His attitude towards the upheaval appeared nonchalant. He often joked that he considered himself more at ease in the African environment. Some of his colleagues thought he was an informer for the rebels. John laughed and shrugged. He knew they were joking, and they teased him all the time.

They gathered information and collected enough soil samples as they drove from one farm to another. Then, they stopped for lunch at a roadside eating place. They ate plantain with goat meat stew. After lunch, they took a different route.

On the horizon, the line of forests' topography borderline demarcated the scenery. John enjoyed the ride and was more fascinated by the landscape. The familiar farmland dotted with different kinds of crops, mainly cassava, and plantains, is the favored crop in this area. They stopped at several farms. The guard Tongo employed for this trip knew the area very well and took them around to farmers who grew maize and stored ears of maize from previous years. You can see the excitement on John's face when a farmer brought varieties of maize that John had never seen before, with different sizes, shapes, and colors. This farmer claimed he always saved his seeds and showed some from the last three seasons' harvest.

"This was one of the last farmers who preserved his seeds." The guard confirmed. After side discussions with Tongo, the guard concluded that there may not be any exotic seeds left in the area to explore. Tongo consulted with John and decided to head back to the station. It will take another three hours to reach home.

The driver followed a paved dirt road wide enough for only one car. It curved through thick shrubs and, for a stretch of distance, winding and leading into surrounding savanna woodland towards the forest. The driver slowed and navigated the harsh terrain of the cramped dirt road, littered with dust trails. Nearby, they heard the grunting sound of baboons and the chattering noises of squirrels.

Suddenly, they heard a loud blast, a little further from where they were, and felt the vibrations.

"What in the world was that?" And then a military plane flew above and disappeared.

"Let's follow a shorter route." The guard suggested. They took a rough, bumpy road. The driver slowed down. He knew the car-the Land Rover Defender could do well and often was used as an adventure vehicle. Its large tires with deep, open treads and flexible suspension were ideal for this rough gravel surface. The detour led to a tortoise pace that could have gone better with the patience required. Tongo noticed the look on John's face and apologized for the inconvenience. The various landscape features of the terrain dominated by tropical savanna grassland dwindled to a bushy shrub of taller trees with thick branches. They witnessed a second explosion in the sky towards the edge of the forests. A cloud of black smoke rose from the ground and stood still.

"Are we under a terrorist attack?" John asked.

The driver shook his head and stopped. "We better take shelter. It's unsafe to drive, and I think we should hide the vehicle and walk back to the village."

"It's a bad idea. Are you out of your mind? We can easily be targets, and they will think we are part of the rebel soldiers."

"Tongo is right. We should not go on foot, but we can wait here until it gets dark." John suggested.

***

That evening, the local news reported heavy clashes and casualties between the army and rebel soldiers. The government news version claimed victory, but everyone knew the army lost ground, and the rebels gained.

A memo from the company headquarters had already alerted the company employees to evacuate and arranged to fly them to Nairobi. The CIA had warned of the danger weeks earlier, and all foreigners had started leaving Monge. The local government news tried to downplay the danger and calmed the people that everything would be fine, and that the government was in control.

At the emergency meeting before the end of the day, they took all the employees' headcount. There was no trace of Dr. Blake and Tongo. The log entry to the company office building indicated that the last login and out for both was three days ago. John usually made his work schedule and was known to take off a few days to visit farms, sometimes without informing the office. His colleagues started to get worried. John and Tongo did not respond to numerous phone calls. His colleagues knew John's response to text messages were usually swift and brief, and he did not respond to any of them sent to him in the last three days. It then dawned on many of his colleagues at the company that something might have happened to him. The farm area he visited with Tongo was close to where the army and the rebel groups had skirmishes, and rumors had it that the military used helicopters and dropped some bombs in the forest nearby. They reported many casualties.

Just before the emergency meeting ended, John's servant, escorted by a security guard, busted into the conference room. He steadied himself with his hands on his knees, panting, then stopped.

"They! They! took Dr. Blake."

His words were barely audible, almost hysterical and desperate for breath.

"And Tongo, and the driver too. The rumor confirmed that the army plane hit them."

"What? How? Where were they?"

"We suspected the rebel group had something to do with their disappearance unless something worse happened. There were some casualties. The news from the village indicated that the army attacked the camp, used air raids, and dropped some bombs that killed many people."

The company organized another late meeting of the senior officers to assess the situation. Samuel Barasa was appointed to be in the station if the company had to evacuate. They wondered what steps to take regarding the news about John and his team's disappearance. With more than half of the employees in the evacuation plan, the whole area remained in an emergency. The frequent updates about missing staff members slowly seeped through the bureaucratic government media, and the chance of recovery diminished with time. As the company's representative, Samuel will be the primary contact person. The press had already covered the news of the missing employees of the Dare Seed Company. They reported the disappearance and expected the worst outcome, especially when the heavy attack happened in the area where they saw them last. Survivors and eyewitnesses of the casualties after the attack reported seeing a charred body of a Caucasian male among the corpses. No one had a complete account of how many people died. The matter worsened when, the next day, the rebel group returned to the area of attack, dug a mass grave, buried all the dead bodies they found in a hurry, and left.

While sobbing, John's servant commented, "I heard that some military leaders had fled the country. They predicted the worst would happen. People will slaughter each other, and who will prevent the mass massacre if all foreigners leave us." Michael, the regional manager of the company, consoled him.

"We will be monitoring the situation from our Nairobi office. In any case, we had an agreement with Monge's government. Regardless of who controls the country, Michael believed that some of the clauses in the contract have to be honored. He noted the contract's human rights section and the company property's protection." He projected his voice to address the rest of the team members. "I suggest tonight we all bring our family members to the guest house on the site of the company land, which can accommodate about 50 people. There is also a safe underground bunker with fortified concrete in the basement that we can use if needed."

The company had prepared a cargo flight to Nairobi early the following day. The airport still had heavy security, and some sections were closed to the public. The army took over most surrounding areas to protect the airport's facilities.

Michael approached Lucy and consoled her. "We will do whatever we can and find out what happened to John. We are waiting for words from some local people in the village who can better understand what happened, and until then, we will have to wait. Let me know if there is anything we can do to help." Samuel joined them and talked briefly, reassuring her that he would do his best.

"If you hear anything, let me know. We can follow the lead." Samuel said.

Lucy hesitated, wondering whether to tell him about his last call before she heard the blast and the command of the instructional message telling him to hand over his phone. She wanted to say something, and then her emotions took over. "What?" Samuel asked.

"Nothing. John did not call. There was no text, and I wondered why. Whatever happened, he didn't get a chance, or they probably took his phone away, and he never got time to react." She sobbed.

Samuel consoled her.again "That could be possible." Anyway, we will keep you updated. And from your side, if you hear anything, let me know immediately. We are in touch with the investigation team, who will gather all the information. They might even conduct interviews, so feel free to answer their questions. They are there to help. With the help of the CIA, our team is on the ground assisting the Monge government. Take care." He then walked away and turned to look at her as she was leaving. He could hear a sound coming from her direction, something between a cry, a sniffle, and a faint sob.

Lucy walked to a waiting car; a chauffeur opened a passenger door to let her in.

She saw Fakir in the back seat. He put his hand on her head and consoled her.

"I' m here for you no matter what, I can't imagine what you're going through, but please know I'm here for you. You can stay with us until things are settled. I will see what we can do. We will figure out something." When they reached their destination Fakir gave a quick glance and added. "It's okay to feel scared and sad. We will update you on the progress.

Chapter 35

The clouds of smoke from the destruction had covered the atmosphere, leaving a trail of an ominous layer of dark air on the horizon. "I hope you know your way around," Tongo whispered to the driver.

"Shsh, I can see a roadblock ahead."

"Are you serious? There is no police or military presence around here, and no one drives on this road. How can there be roadblock?"

"Stop and turn around," Tongo suggested.

"Too late. I can't turn around."

"Then make another way. I can see trees moving. The government soldiers probably used tactics to camouflage from the rebel soldiers, and they devised ways to remain hidden."

"Stop and don't move!" A command came from the right direction. The driver braked. A sudden movement from the side of the road brought him a chilling awareness. They were not government soldiers. Another command followed. "Get out of the car with your hands up." Tongo and Dr. Blake looked at each other.

Tongo spoke to his team. "We have to follow their orders. These are ruthless psychopaths, mercenaries, and they can kill and maim, even for fun, and instill terror in the hearts of people they encounter."

"The look of their uniforms suggests that this group is different. They are under General Jaja and don't participate in that terror, " the guard said in a low voice.

"They are coming closer to the car, and we need to get out as requested," Tongo whispered.

"Tie them together two by two and blindfold them." The rebel commander ordered.

"The vehicle is clear. No weapons." The rebel soldier reported to his commander.

"Check them thoroughly and collect everything they have in their possession quickly. Cellphones? Tell them to turn them off immediately, watch for anything electronic, and then take the vehicle and the driver to the camp."

"I need to keep my watch," Dr. Blake requested.

"We must check all electronics before we return them to you."

After an estimated time of what appeared to be an hour, John asked Tongo. "How long do you think we have to walk?"

"Shsh, no talking, you two."

A soldier came closer. "As long as it can take. Maybe a day or even more."

Tongo noticed that the rebels had focused more on John, and two rebel soldiers were guarding him. An indication that he was the target of their operation. Unprepared for this unexpected event, John realized the danger and knew he had to do what they wanted, but at the same time, he set his mind on planning an escape strategy. They trudged through the jagged earth, each step dragging them deeper into what felt like an endless journey. The dry soil heaves under pressure. "Ouch," Tongo exclaimed when John stepped on his left foot.

"Sorry, I hate walking in zigzag directions."

"It's a strategy, and they wanted to disorient us," Tongo whispered.

"I don't even think about disorientation. We are already in the midst of it with this blindfold," and before John finished the word, he felt the muzzle of the barrel of a gun push against his neck. An eerie silence engulfed him, "I can pull the trigger and split your brain. Let me not hear any more sound from you."

He heard the rebel soldiers exchange words. The one in charge appeared conciliatory and told the junior rebel soldier. "Watch out, and don't harm him." They spoke in the pidgin form of French, and John understood some words.

The slow, treacherous journey took a toll. Somebody groaned.

"What's wrong?"

"I need to relieve myself."

"Okay, take a short break." The soldier in charge instructed.

They took their blindfolds off, and Tongo noticed the driver was missing.

"After 15 minutes, we will leave. If you need to relieve yourselves, this is the time," the soldier announced. They offered them food, dried cassava, and bananas.

The sun had gone down when they reached the camp in the forest. They arrived at the time of the evening meal. Night darkness had swallowed the horizon. A creepy-looking, dark-green massive expanse of forest trees stood defiantly, with creaking and rustling branches.

With the rebel soldiers in front and behind them and no longer blindfolded, the prisoners, tied together, marched in a single file. Their visibility is limited to the person ahead or behind. The silence was interrupted by a slight whistling of the wind. The forest habitats came to life, and a disturbed lizard scrambled on the bark of a tree and disappeared. Two squirrels chasing each other chattered through the branches, unaware of the impending ill omen.

Tongo counted the seventh checkpoint they went through in his head. It took a while before they let them proceed. As they approached the concealed tent behind the shrub line, the forest buzzed with a lone tone of voice, and somebody was giving instructions.

The rebel soldier ushered them into a tent. The three prisoners, later joined by the driver, sat in a small tent accommodating six to seven people. The rebel soldier, who spoke English and French fluently, addressed them. "Tonight, you will sleep here. Don't think of escape because you won't make it alive. Our soldiers have orders to kill on sight. We are at war. Today, the government army and our patriotic liberators collided with casualties on both sides. We are confident of success. Rest assured that we will return your property if we decide to release it, but that is up to the General."

John raised his hand.

"Yes," the rebel soldier turned to him.

"Why are we arrested?"

"You were kidnapped and will meet with the General tomorrow." With that, he bade them good night and left the tent. Two soldiers came in and allocated space for them to sleep. The little tent with a raised above-the-ground sleeping bed-like structure seemed spacious and accommodated seven tiny beds.

"Soldier," Tongo called.

"Call me Captain. What do you want?"

"Where do we go for the toilet,"

"Oh," he laughed. Let me know if you need to go, and I will take you there. We have a pit latrine."

A silence descended for a while as the prisoners settled for the night respite.

John felt cold and wanted an extra blanket. He missed his multifunction watch with the campus for directions and temperature sensors, which also measured the air pressure, altitude, and surrounding temperature. Tongo offered him his blanket.

As he lay down, John waited to sleep, but that did not come. He could hear the sounds of the nighttime creatures vibrantly leaping to life. Insects buzzed, probably crickets chirped, frogs yelped, bats clicked, and other unfamiliar sounds of the mammals scuttled. The forest trees vibrated with sound as if they ricocheted off from the sky and bounced back to the ground.

***

The next day they had breakfast, that included sweet corn, yam, and sweet potatoes. The rebel soldiers took John and Tongo to a different camp. They blindfolded them again and walked through the dense forest. After an hour of grueling meandering paths, John faltered in his steps. He complained of dizziness and felt hot. The guard thought the Mzungu (white man) was playing a trick until one of them concluded something was wrong. The supervisor ordered the soldiers to remove the blindfold and have him checked and rested. "I have a high temperature, a fever, and need medicine. I have some in the vehicle."

The rebel soldiers looked at each other and waited for the supervisor to speak. "You will be rested. We can treat malaria and any ailment. Our rich forest, teeming with all kinds of life, can provide you with anything you desire. He instructed a guard to prepare a drink concoction from the bark of the Cinchona tree for him. John pulled back. "It's medicinal and can treat malaria." Tongo nodded. "You can rest now," he added. They brought him a blanket and covered the ground layer with twigs and leaves to prepare a resting place for him. "We will wait until your fever goes down." John lay on his back, closed his eyes, and opened them again. The forest canopy above appeared like a giant umbrella in his mind, with trunks jutting out with outgrowth and creating a sense of bewilderment. In the state of sleep and awake, he drifted. The legends of the diabolical Biloko of the African mythology of the tropical forest came alive in his head. A hairless spirit dressed in leaves with long claws and pig-like snouts reached for his

322

head. He tried to lift his body, which appeared too heavy to move. The stories he heard of the legend of all hideous monsters bent on vengeance and thirsty for blood clamored above his head. He tried to run but tripped, landing hard on his face. The spirit turned him around. He attempted to scream.

"Dr. Blake, Dr. Blake."

"Am I alive?"

"Yes, you're alive. Your fever probably caused delirium, and you had a nightmare. You screamed."

Tongo then gave him soup.

***

"Africa is not new to you. You have an impressive background." General Amos Jaja stared at him in his striking appearance of full military fatigue. His piercing eyes, sunken into their sockets with raised eyebrows and a large bushy beard, created an image of a gorilla ready to strike with vengeance. He waited. "You knew my demand. I know what your company plans to do, and it won't happen. You hang on to the decaying regime in demise. Half of their soldiers have defected to our camp."

John kept listening.

"I found something else too. Do you know that I was your student back in the days of your Peace Corps service in Kenya? You didn't know?"

"It was over 25 years ago, and I lost my former students' names. You can refresh my mind, and if you say so, I will believe it."

"I am sure you'll remember the incident where you sponsored the medical bill, but it didn't help to clear your name."

"I helped many people in need when requested."

A guttural laugh filled the tent, echoing off the canvas walls, as General Jaja stooped forward. "Sure, if you call killing a baby help." He shook his head slowly. "That was no help at all."

"Listen, they asked me to help with medical expenses, and I didn't know what happened. I left the country the following week or the day after. I had no idea what happened."

General Jaja pulled out a page of a newspaper headline that he had saved. The headline read: Backyard abortion fiasco. The girlfriend of a former American Peace Corps volunteer was found dead. The hunt for perpetrators uncovered a ring of shoddy deals that involved drug trafficking and money laundering. The police detained the leader of the gang for questioning.

"That was what happened."

John remained mute.

"I am lost for words. I didn't know the girl, and she was not my girlfriend. My only role was to give money for the medical bills. They asked for money to pay medical bills, and I had no reason to doubt their motives."

"Your name came up in court. Now, you have a different name, and nobody would know you. What a clever way to disguise. I am sure they didn't check your filthy background when you came to Africa. Not at that time and not even when they hired you for this job. The color of your skin gives you a free ride." He spat.

"It's time to get rid of these incompetent narcissistic greedy people in positions." He paced the room, clenching his fist.

"Did you know what happened? I got framed and spent many years in a disgusting rotten jail for a crime I did not commit. Do you think I will ever forget that?" He paused and continued.

"There is an African proverb. *Ashes fly back into the face of the one who throws them.*"

"Sure, I am not taking any revenge, but we all have to be accountable for what we did. They wanted to put me in jail for 20 years. That's a lifetime of our miserable short life span; "I served almost half my term before escaping to freedom. Do you remember Salim, your skinny informer pet? He's in Canada now. His brother Fakir paid the cops to let him off the hook. And who was left to be the scapegoat?" He twisted his lips, leaving the sentence hanging.

John raised his eyebrows.

"How can you forget? The boy whose brother had a missing finger." Jaja paused and looked John in the eyes.

John remained silent.

"And now, the puppet master is at the helm of our food industry, selling Monge to the highest bidder. You know the plans. I wouldn't be surprised if you're giving him leeway. His sister lives with you, after all. You're part of his family now. What a coincidence."

He allowed the words to sink.

"I know a lot about what you did."

He brought his face closer.

"Don't tell me it was just another coincidence, and you had no idea about these connections. His clever, cunning days are over."

"I don't know what to say about all these allegations, General Jaja. What can I do for you now? They asked for help, and I helped. They never said it was for abortion. I still don't understand why you dragged me into this. I was in the same predicament as you were and not even there to defend myself. I am sorry for what happened to you. Let's discuss the current situation and why you kidnapped me and my team?"

"Dr., you know exactly why you're here." His voice was low, measured. and Lethal.

"You've been briefed. So don't insult me by pretending otherwise. Don't dance around the answers.

He leaned in, his gaze unyielding. "Let's cut to the chase. I need the seed. No more fraudulent hybrids. No more genetic sabotage."

His words came like hammer blows.

"You manipulated fertility and sterility genes at the same time and twisted experiment with a single, unmistakable objective. Depopulation."

He pauses with a heavy calculated sigh and then, with quiet finality, continued. "Don't look so amazed, Doctor.

The truth is written in your own research. *The silent yield.* You engineered this catastrophe."

He straightened. His expression was unreadable. "We know exactly what your company is doing under the pretense of humanitarian aid." He looked at him intensively.

"You're not feeding Africa. You're bleeding it dry." He shook his head. "I won't stand by and watch while you and your kind exploit and gut this continent for its resources."

He interlocked his fingers, his voice dropping to an almost menacing whisper.

"You're tampering with the very essence of survival. Playing God with lives you don't value."

He let a slow, deliberate breath, and delivered the final blow. "I know your darkest secret."

Jaja let the silence hang, letting the weight of his words settle like a suffocating fog. "You're not just modifying crops." His eyes gleamed, cold and knowing. "You're harvesting genes."

John narrowed his gaze "If that is all you wanted, I can get it for you. Allow me to get to my lab."

General Jaja laughed.

"Did I leave anything, Dr.? Is my message not sinking.?" He looked at him intensively with a grimace. "You will not leave the camp."

"How can I get it for you, then? I used my laptop to get to my research projects, and I have everything I need there."

"We will send Tongo to get them."

"No one can get my password."

"Don't worry. We have experts who can unlock any password in the world."

"I use fingerprints and facial recognition to unlock my computer."

"Leave that to us, and we will find ways."

A soldier entered the tent and called General Jaja aside. After a few minutes, another soldier entered the tent and announced that the General had another urgent matter to attend to and would schedule another meeting later.

Chapter 36

D r. Blake waited. He didn't know how long he would
wait and wondered why Jaja had taken so long. The
waiting took a heavy toll on his weary, exhausted
demeanor. A soldier entered the tent with a folding
table and two wooden chairs in his
arms. He looked around where to place the table. He
inspected the surroundings, ensured everything was in
order, and told John to expect the meeting with General
Jaja.

"We got interrupted yesterday. You didn't change
much, Dr. What did you do to keep your youthful status?"
General Jaja started with a lighter approach.

"I emptied negative thoughts off my mind every day.
I don't dwell on the past. I do regular exercise, eat right,
and meditate."

"A great principle to live by. I guess no drugs or
alcohol."

"Nope."

A moment of silence permeated the atmosphere. A
soldier brought a thermos of coffee and a biscuit and placed
them on the small table. He then served them and left.
General Jaja pointed to the cup of coffee with his mouth.

"Good coffee from Kenya. Enjoy it."

He then took his cup, sipped, and waited for another long silence before speaking.

"Tell me about the variety you're developing for the market."

"I did all kinds of experiments, some out of curiosity. I developed a variety to benefit the developing countries. The rumor about my involvement in developing sterility genes to reduce the African population was false. People were trying to sabotage and discredit me."

"You got involved finally, so what's the point of denying it?"

"I don't deny anything. I am culpable for my role. However, I was against developing this gene for this purpose and never intended it for mass production. Things happened, and the current variety has traits in the gene carrying 50% of each."

"Can you undo it and leave it pure with only the desired gene.?"

"I can't. Only the original source will work. The collection of local varieties I had with specific genes was all gone. Someone stole them. And it can take a lot of time to gather and identify them. Even with that, I need the original sample."

General Jaja scoffed at the response.

"Your company wanted to destroy all the maize in my country and replace them and turn us into perpetual beggars for food handouts."

John shook his head and looked him in the eye.

"I have contacted the International Maize Center in Mexico. When that happens, we can get the original exotic variety. We have to start all over."

"I don't know whether I can believe you after all you have done. You are right about the stolen seeds. We have them, but you also have variety at your seed lab cold storage and you're trying to hide." He smiled.

"We have over 300-page dossiers on you. We also know that you developed the purest single line from which you can derive the desired variety." He sipped a cup of coffee again.

"You haven't touched your coffee?"

"I am okay,"

"Dr, let me remind you what you already know. Your company does dirty work in Africa: mineral exploration, exploitation, pollution, dirty dealings, and disregard for human lives." He leaned forward. "I don't know how you can work with the people who betray you." John looked at him.

"How,"? He asked.

"You didn't know? They stole the sterility gene you developed and gave it to the local seed company to do a dirty job for them. Guess who possesses them? General Bukasa and his cliques, and your brother-in-law. The four-fingered bootlicker had full authority to distribute the seed to Africa. We know him as Fakir in Monge, a reincarnation of the mighty seed industry."

He paused for John's reaction and continued.

"Fakir, Fakir, Fakir, he did not change. You know the saying: *Old habits die hard.* He was behind the scheme. You saw what they did to Monge. I can't wait for the day I get my bare hands around his neck. Squeeze the last breath out and snap. it." He puckered his lips and clenched his jaw.

"His greed took him all across the Horn of Africa. He set up non-profit organizations, but they were just vessels for smuggling, driven by his demonic hunger."

He stopped and lessened his grip on his knuckles.

"If you don't know, their plan is set for next year. The initial attempt was to distribute free food to Africa through food assistance. After that, as usual, they would sell their products at a higher price than usual. Of course, the multimillionaire financier from your country had already paid everything to make the project successful."

John interlocked his fingers and listened.

"You probably knew the plans of your company. You're too valuable to dispose of easily. They are afraid you might expose what's happening with the sterility gene. It will be a big embarrassment of genocidal status. So, they have a Christmas gift for you. The plan is to wait until you get to Nairobi, and silence you secretly. Make it look like a little accident in the African street. Very easy to do, and no one would know and even miss you. Now, it looks like you have planned to settle in Africa. You even have some lucrative assets in Kenya. Your beautiful lady might be the only one who misses you. After all, you adopted her children and removed her from the jaws of deprivation. I heard you're taking great care of her."

John wrinkled his face, "Why are you telling me all this? What do you want?"

General Jaja smiled. "I like Americans' way of thinking. As your saying goes, "What's in there for me? Right?"

"Yes, I want to know what you want."

The rebel leader paused. He had all his cards aligned and ready to strike. He knew he had the upper hand with the information he held.

"I will have you do what you love to do. Improve the fertility gene, your so-called 'miracle seed," and do away with the sterility gene. Reverse the trend. We will turn it into a pharmaceutical drug for people to use as a pill. You will be under house or forest arrest and 24-hour surveillance."

With that, General Jaja stood up and prepared to leave. "One more thing," He turned. "Fakir's Monge Seed Company had access to your lab, and your ingenious plan of putting them off worked. You're too smart for them and never trusted anyone. Anyway, I would like you to work with us. We are your strongest ally at this time." John held his chin and listened.

"Tell me about the wrong variety mixture. Did you do that on purpose? Or did you have a mole who worked for or against you?"

John did not speak. "I have nothing to say, " he sighed.

"I suspected that was what happened. They rushed to get it to the market, and now we have no control."

"You have collected all exotic seeds and can start over." He stretched his neck.

"There is more than you think," John replied.

"The genie is out of the box, and some villages have become ghosts. The maize plant is turning into a weed. The pandemic of allergies has devastated the area and is spreading fast. The World Health Organization is on alert to declare pandemic."

The rebel leader twisted his mouth with a grimace of pain crossing his face. "Do you have any solution?" He stared.

"The short-term solution is to stop growing all maize in the whole country, which won't happen. There will be panic and chaos."

He gave a long, weary sigh and added:

"There may be no maize variety left in the country after what happened. The gene spread had reached all parts of the farmland with a catastrophic blow to the food supply."

Jaja interjected. "Our local team on the ground is monitoring the release of the recent seed from Mongo Seed Company. We don't trust them. Fakir and his friend, the Monge dictator, have sold the country to your company and the Western world. They don't have many days left." He turned.

"Where is my team? Tongo, the driver, and my vehicle?"

"Don't worry. Everything will be fine. Your colleagues are doing fine."

With that, he left John alone in the tent.

***

Life in the jungle remained on high alert for the next few days, and they frequently shifted camp locations. Armed rebel soldiers moved in pairs and took prisoners to different camps. John had not seen Tongo since the first day of their arrival, and it had been over a week. He noticed he received special treatment, a rare treatment of fresh fruits, chicken, fish, goat, or wildlife meat.

Two rebel soldiers guarded him and followed him wherever John went in the forest. He even started befriending them, but their supervisor kept an eye on them. Once, the guards took him to a clearing ground where they planted crops like plantain, cassava, and maize. The maize plants caught his attention, and he knew why they brought him there. That will be his experimental field. He looked at the plants and liked what he saw. The person who maintained the small farm told him that the maize variety was unique, and the General expected to get his supply from there. "What's special about the variety?" John asked. The gardener looked at the rebel soldiers and didn't like the look on their faces, so he kept quiet.

John surveyed the maize plants and recognized the variety. The unique traits of the shape of the cobs stood out. He smiled as he looked around the small farm and noticed the replica of his handy work.

Around the corner, he saw a greenhouse hidden under the tree. He followed with his eyes the thin rope hanging from the tree and raised his head to the canopy of the trees above. He saw light strings of sisal ropes stretching from one tree canopy to the next, and he followed with his eyes. When he carefully scrutinized it, the line twined around the branches of trees in a circular shape.

As he observed the structure, the ingenious use of the string became clear. A net-like structure was connected to a green shade, and when pulled, it could open up and serve as a cover. Any plane flying over the forests won't notice any activity underground the forest layer. What an ingenious way of tricks, he thought.

John went around the dense, bushy shrubs and got curious when he noticed a dark object. He peeked through the branches and couldn't believe what he was looking at, and before he went further to survey more of the surroundings, a guard pulled him away violently without any warning. He must have left his eyes off the prisoner. John was not supposed to see this object.

"No, this way." He pulled him out of the enclosure.

The guard turned to him and asked. "You didn't see anything. Didn't you?

"I didn't," John lied.

From the guard's reaction, he thought this was the secret the rebels were hiding.

John was not precisely clear, but he thought he saw artillery M107, a self-propelled howitzer. He didn't know this artillery was still in use. He remembered seeing it in the museum. They used it during the Vietnam War. It could fire shells as far as 25 miles away. He wondered what the rebels harbored in the forest.

From that day onwards, John was restricted to the farm and could not move around. He observed that rebel soldiers guarded him daily and didn't engage him. As time went by, John learned the routine and discovered that on Fridays, a shipment of some sort, mainly food supplies and some equipment, would arrive, and they were porters who regularly transported them. He didn't know what they did there. He could only guess the importance they attached to this place from how they guarded it with armed soldiers following them. They usually passed by the farm and went into what looked like a hidden cave in the belly of the earth. It descended beneath the trunk of the forest trees. They took their time, and he never saw them come out. He usually took his break and sat on the wood log at the edge of the farm. One porter attempted to greet him in Swahili when the guards were not looking, and John responded.

One day, the last porter looked at him as the guards talked to each other. He dropped something wrapped in a piece of cloth. The porter looked back at him and winked. John walked around the edge of the farm, stretching as part of his regular exercise.

He approached the spot where the porter dropped a package and stopped. The guards were still talking to each other and didn't notice him.

He pretended to stretch, bent down, and touched the ground in the manner of a warm-up exercise several times before he picked up the small package, the size of a closed fist, and put it in his jacket. Later, when he returned to his tent, he pulled out the item. He unwrapped it and read an inscription note "Be ready. Next Friday at the same place and time." He quickly pulled back, thinking that somebody was watching him. That evening, he requested to see a supervisor.

"I want to know how long you'll keep me here and when I will see my colleagues."

The supervisor, a captain of the rebel soldier, a soft-spoken man, responded. "I don't know how long you will be here; we will try to make your stay comfortable. Unfortunately, your colleagues were in the camp where the army dropped a bomb that caused heavy casualties. Both of them were among the victims, and they did not survive. I am sorry about your loss and for disclosing the news to you in such a manner." John froze.

***

With a solemn look, John asked to be left alone the next day, and he remained in the tent, saddened by the news. He thought over everything that happened, shocked and amazed by the thorough and detailed information that General Jaja shared. The precise details of the information that he thought no one else knew.

The supervisor and another man visited him later that day.

"I will introduce you to our agriculture field officer, Mr. Mumba, who will work with you. We have a big farm where we planted the variety." The supervisor motioned for John to sit.

"There is no way I can verify the variety without my lab."

"If you need anything from your lab, we can arrange it. Just tell me what you need to do to make this work?"

"You can't get access to the lab without my login code, and it would require touching with a finger and works only with my finger. We talked about this already."

"This work is crucial; even if it means parting with your finger, we must do it."

"It's not as easy as you think. The ID sensor will also scan your face and eyes. Just so that you know, the dead finger won't work. If you thought of a cruel way of achieving your goal." John added.

"The General's instructions were clear."

"I don't know how to explain it to you, but I need five steps to use biotechnology to create a new variety. First, you will extract the gene, then copy, modify, put it into a plant, and finally breed a transgenic plant with your line of interest. How can I do any of this without a lab?"

"Listen, Dr. Blake. I am following orders, and we can build a facility for you. In the meantime, you have to do whatever it takes. Name anything you need. We can provide. Mr. Mumba can now take you to the field and show you the data and notes from the other fields."

Chapter 37

The only news source John received was from the rebel soldiers. They told him about several clashes between the rebel soldiers and the Monge government army. The rebel soldiers who took turns guarding his camp shared information freely about the number of casualties and how the army indiscriminately bombed innocent villagers who they believed supported the rebel groups. Some days, they kept him in total darkness.

It was Thursday, and John looked at his note. He tore the scribbled message note before leaving his tent and made sure there was no trace of any of his writing notes. John then hid the notes under his vest and wore a coat over it. He slowly stepped out of his tent. In the first few minutes, they usually allow him to do push-ups, exercise, and activities of his choice.

At the appointed time, he went to the farm. The guards had already gotten used to him and didn't follow him all the time like at the beginning. The warm and humid temperature added layers of sluggish disposition. He looked for any sign of rain and knew the dry December season would soon set in.

"Hey, Doc, how long will you inspect your plants?"

"Maybe about an hour or more. I have a lot to do today."

"Okay, go ahead. If you need anything, you know where you can find us." The guards started playing cards.

As he entered the farm and walked between the rows of plants, he wondered whether the assistant would stop by. John was eager to see how things would turn out. Today is the day. His hair stood on end, and he attempted to focus, but his heart was hammering. He checked the cobs with his shaky hands for any insect damage and pretended that he was inspecting the plant while, at the same time, keeping himself alert for any sign. A chilly silence engulfed the serene atmosphere. John turned around at the sound of the crack of leaves. He looked out for the guards and turned his face towards the bush from where the sounds came. Somebody beckoned, making hasty gestures with his hand to move fast.

"Shsh," the person tapped his mouth to indicate total silence.

"Put this on quickly and follow me."

John hesitated.

"You need the mask for your face to blend in. You can cover your hair to disguise it. Here," he gave him a wig.

"Put on the gloves," he commanded. "You have to be next to me all the time. I will be the spokesperson for the porters. After the checkpoints, everything will be fine. I understand you speak Swahili very well, and that's great. Try not to speak in English, though. A little French is okay. Your accent will give you away."

He gave him piles of sacks of charcoal and some extra empty to carry on the back.

"We normally carry two bags each, and they knew it. Here is your identification card."

He handed him a worn-out old card that belonged to Joseph Mwamba.

"Try to remember the name and live your life through it for now. Get closer to me, and the other two porters will be around you when we reach the checkpoint."

They passed through the first three checkpoints successfully but met with some delays at the final checkpoint. The head porter stepped aside with the guard in charge of the checkpoint. The rest of the porters waited and knew after exchanging things in the hand. They will be free to leave and there is no reason to stop them because they do the same thing daily. Bring products and take charcoal away, and that had been the routine.

***

In the meantime, fighting intensified, people panicked, and confusion and chaos reigned. Another bombing took place in the camp where they held John as a prisoner, and many people died, but nobody was sure about the fate of Dr. Blake. However, some news media announced that the Dare Seed Company scientist who pioneered the fertility-enhancing variety of maize was among the dead.

The various news outlets from Nairobi indicated that Monge was on the verge of collapse, and the rebel leader Amos Jaja had taken over the country. The whereabouts of General Bukasa and his family and some cabinet members were unknown, but the latest news confirmed that he fled to one of the countries in West Africa. Many fled the country in fear for their lives, on foot, on donkeys, and used whatever means to get out of the country.

Among the first group to arrive at the Southern border of South Sudan was a catholic priest with a convoy of five nuns. The travelers trickled and lined up the routes and trekked the long journey. They appeared exhausted and drained of all their energies. The news of the downfall of Monge's government surprised many pundits who predicted that General Bukasa would survive the storm. Some believed that his own army generals betrayed him. They were obsessed with their ambition to worry about the whole country.

The upheaval in the country has widely spread and spilled over to the neighboring countries. The international organizations were concerned that they won't cope with the pressing refugee issues and increasingly desperate people pouring from every corner of the country.

***

The weary travelers, a priest, and two nuns arrived at the border.

"It's a long way, Father."

The immigration officer handed him back a Brazilian passport.

"You're ready to fly."

The weary priest boarded EgyptAir to Cairo, and from there on Turkish Airline to Lisbon-Portugal. He will take his final non-stop flight to Brasilia in Brazil on TAP Air Portugal for his final destination. The passengers made their way out of the plane and went through customs. After a long line, Father John Oliveira got his passport stamped and walked toward the phone booth. He dialed a number and waited. He went to the bathroom with his carry-on luggage in his left hand. His black cassock still wore the sign of exhaustion from the long journey.

He booked the motel for one month. There was no better time to visit Brazil than in December, the peak season with all types of visitors flocking to the country to experience the warm weather and Brazilian Christmas. He will need the warm sunny weather and visit the beaches. He will need an extended vacation and visit Rio to enjoy its seductive samba beat and fantastic panoramic views. He changed to a white cassock, packed his dusty black garment, and retained his Roman Catholic attire. He then stretched the collar and noticed a crooked hand-sewn knot. He untied the knot to reveal four seeds. He recognized and sealed the knot.

On April 1st, John's mother got a postcard from Mexico City with the inscription, *The cat has nine lives*. She flipped the card over, her breath catching in her throat. A tremor ran through her fingers as she traced the words. A sob rose in her chest, but she held it back, closing her eyes as fresh tears welled up.

There was no return address. No phone number.

"It's not April Fool's Day," she whispered.

She pressed the postcard to her heart, allowing the tears of joy to fall freely now.

"He's alive. After all," she mumbled.

www.ingramcontent.com/pod-product-compliance
Lightning Source LLC
Chambersburg PA
CBHW072342020726
47506CB00004B/970